The Cloaked Escort Gestured....

"What's this about?" Seth demanded. "What're you doing?"

He went hesitantly forward because there seemed to be nothing else to do. Seth's heart thudded, his hands clenched and unclenched at his sides, and a sense of inadequacy climbed his constricted throat like an ill-digested meal.

At the base of the stairway stood the Tropiard who had not unhooded. As Seth passed him, he noticed the alien's impersonal stare—an impersonality heightened by the slitted goggles he wore—and his impossibly smooth, coffee-colored flesh. He was tall, taller by a head than Seth, and he seemed as perfect and as unreal as a mannequin.

"The Magistrate expects you," the Tropiard said in Vox. His mouth—a thin, smile-shaped scar—scarcely parted to speak these words.

Seth crossed the threshold and faced a being of prepossessing power and appearance. . . .

"An impressive, fully-realized achievement"
—Norman Spinrad, author of *A World Between*

"Superb! Like all good writers Bishop gets better by going deeper. . . . A stunning achievement"
—Barry N. Malzberg, author of *Beyond Apollo*

"Michael Bishop is a spectacular writer!"
—Vonda McIntyre, author of *Dreamsnake*

Books by Michael Bishop

And Strange at Ecbatan the Trees
Stolen Faces
A Little Knowledge
Catacomb Years
Transfigurations
Eyes of Fire *

* Published by POCKET BOOKS

MICHAEL BISHOP

EYES OF FIRE

PUBLISHED BY POCKET BOOKS NEW YORK

POCKET BOOKS, a Simon & Schuster division of
GULF & WESTERN CORPORATION
1230 Avenue of the Americas, New York, N.Y. 10020

ISBN: 0-671-82835-5

First Pocket Books printing January, 1980

10 9 8 7 6 5 4 3 2 1

Trademarks registered in the United States and other countries.

Printed in the U.S.A.

For my mother

AUTHOR'S NOTE

In February of 1975 I published my first novel, *A Funeral for the Eyes of Fire*. If I had my way, the text of that early book—if not the title itself—would vanish forever from the Earth, and from any other planets to which insane, bankrupt-bound book distributors may have bootlegged it, to be supplanted utterly by the text of *Eyes of Fire,* the novel now in your hands.

Several people are indirectly responsible for the shape this book has taken, although not for its structural or thematic deficiencies: I, of course, am solely accountable for those. Let me mention in particular Ursula K. Le Guin, Betty Ballantine, David Gerrold, Alexei and Cory Panshin, and my editor at Pocket Books, David Hartwell. The original version of this novel had an epigraph from Theodore Roszak's *The Making of a Counter Culture*. My title derives from Chapter VIII of Roszak's book, "Eyes of Flesh, Eyes of Fire," a trenchant essay on the conflict between the world views of the shaman and the technocrat. I do not, however, pretend to have any answers to the questions arising from this conflict, which, if books like Robert Pirsig's *Zen and the Art of Motorcycle Maintenance* and Fritjof Capra's *The Tao of Physics* are valid indices, many thoughtful persons are attempting to resolve.

Finally, I would like to acknowledge the contribution of my cover artist, Gene Szafran.

—Michael Bishop
Pine Mountain, Georgia

September 1, 1979

Characters

Humans

ABEL LATIMER, isoget of Günter Latimer, lately slain
SETH LATIMER, his isohet
K/R CARANICAS, pilot of the *Dharmakaya*, an Ommundi
Trade Company light-tripper

Jauddeb

LADY TURSHEBSEL, Liege Mistress of Kier on Gla Taus
PORCHADDOS PORS, Point Marcher of Feln, Kier's Winter
Capital
NARTHAIMNAR CHAPPOUIB, aisautseb, or patriot-priest,
advisor to Lady Turshebsel
CLEFRABBES DOUIN, advisor to Lady Turshebsel and Kieri
man-of-letters
AN AISAUTSEB (PATRIOT-PRIEST), assigned by Lady
Turshebsel to the *Dharmakaya*
VARIOUS KIERI SHOPKEEPERS, AISAUTSEB (PATRIOT-
PRIESTS), SOLDIERS, PALACE ATTENDANTS, TAUS-
SANAUR (ORBITAL GUARDS), etc.

Gosfi

ULGRAJI VRAI, Sixth Magistrate of Trope, political heir of
the founder of the Tropish state, Seitaba Mwezahbe
EHTE EMAHPRE, his Administrative Deputy
COMMANDER SWODI of the Palija Kadi surveillance force
CAPTAIN YITHUJU, driver of the lead vehicle of the evacu-
ation convoy

THE PLEDGECHILD, sh'gosfi heir of the departed Holy
One, Duagahvi Gaidu
LIJADU, her heir and fleshchild of Ifragsli, recently deceased
HUSPRE, attendant and advisor to the Pledgechild; a midwife
TANTAI, attendant to the Pledgechild
OMWHOL, a child, recently appointed keeper of the gocodre
VARIOUS J'GOSFI GUIDES, ADMINISTRATIVE WORK-
ERS, SURVEILLANCE-FORCE PERSONNEL, etc.; VARI-
OUS SH'GOSFI ELDERS (MIDWIVES), LABORERS,
CHILDREN, etc.

GLA TAUS

Primary: Gla Taunt
Equatorial Circumference:
39,942 Kilometers
Major Continental Mass:
Kier

★ = Capital Cities
● = Major Cities

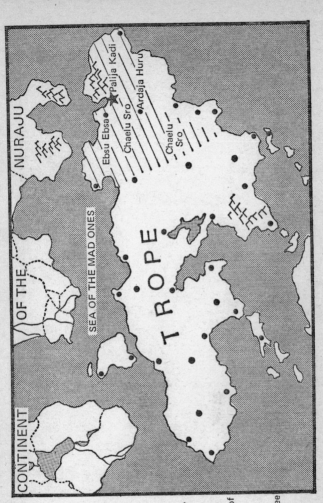

TROPE

Primary: Anja
Equatorial Circumference:
37,412 kilometers
Major Continental Areas:
Trope (southern hemi-
sphere) and the Land of
the Nuraju (northern
hemisphere)

● = One of the Thirty-Three
Cities of Trope, the
nation

★ = Sh'gaidu Basin

Prologue

Long ago there was a jongleur-thief in Kier, before Kier was yet a nation, and the name of the jongleur-thief was Jaud. Gla Taus, The World, was new in those days, only lately formed from the primordial slag, and in every situation in this new world Jaud acted out of the selfish center of himself. This was not unusual, for in the beginning the world was without law and the people had no word for conscience.

Jaud's disposition was merry and cruel at once, and he chose to live by stealing. After each theft he pirouetted before his victim and deftly juggled the items he had stolen: rings, bracelets, coins, seashells, beads, digging tools, and even weapons. Not infrequently his victims applauded these performances. Only rarely did the aggrieved Gla Tausian attempt to recover his belongings, for Jaud was impatient of those who interfered with his juggling, and throughout the land his deadliness with knife and hand ax was well known.

In the infancy of Gla Taus, then, Jaud honored no one but Jaud and a few fellow thieves who had declared themselves his disciples and retainers, having recognized in him a sorcerer of chicanery and bloodthirstiness. For untold years after the world began, the Thieves of Jaud preyed upon the people of Kier before Kier was yet a nation. They made themselves a bastion in the Orpla Mountains, from which they often undertook forays of theft, jugglery, and slaughter.

But as time passed, people drew together against the indifference of Gla Taus and the cruelty of Jaud. From these first feeble bands tribes arose, and from

1

the tribes chiefdoms, and from the chiefdoms primitive states, and from the primitive states a nation that called itself Kier. Kier exercised dominion through the authority of the first Prime Liege, whom everyone knew as Shobbes or Law. Only Jaud and his fellow jongleur-thieves failed to acknowledge the preeminence of Law, for they were free spirits obeying no statutes but those written in the unintelligible runes of their blood. How could they know that the superstitious taboos of the first bands had become the inhibitory customs of the tribes? How could they know that the customs had become ordinances, and that finally Shobbes had had these ordinances codified in writing?

In truth, Jaud and his family of cutpurses, clowns, and cutthroats did not know. Not, at least, until a contingent of Kieri soldiers captured one of their number after the fellow had robbed and slain an innocent citizen of a village on the Mirrimsagset Plain. For instead of ordering the beheading of the outlaw, Shobbes sent him back to the Orpla Mountains with this message:

"Jaud, Shobbes has told me to say that at last the taboos, the customs, the rules, and the ordinances have become the Commandments of Law. And Law declares that no Kieri may steal from another or commit murder. Not even Jaud stands outside the Commandments of Law. Shobbes demands that your thieving, your juggling, and your killing instantly cease." The messenger bowed low before his lord, and Jaud struck off his head.

"It is not in the blood for us to follow Law!" Jaud raged, brandishing his short sword. "Therefore, I ordain—not with my own voice, but with that of our singing marrow—that we shall continue to thieve, to juggle, and to slay! So be it always!"

Shortly after Jaud delivered this impassioned speech to his followers, he journeyed alone out of the Orpla Mountains and down the Tarsebset Morraine to Sket, the summer capital of Kier. Full of bravado and curiosity, he had determined to breach the manifold fortifications of the Summer Palace and behold in person the upstart Prime Liege whose name and word were equally law. By stealth and cunning Jaud got past the outer walls of Sket and into the curiously buttressed chambers of the sovereign's sleeping quarters and throne room. Soon he would meet Shobbes face to face.

A noise halted Jaud in his tracks. He turned to find himself set upon by a host of helmeted guards. Although he struggled like ten Kieri and slew one of his attackers, Jaud was eventually overcome and delivered to Shobbes in halt-chains and wrist-irons.

Shobbes, Law, was an aged gentlewoman wearing starched black skirts and a seamless black overtunic. Her mien was gracious and refined, her voice pedantic and precise. Never before in his life had Jaud seen or heard anyone like her.

"You are banished to the Obsidian Wastes," Shobbes told Jaud in a tone of matter-of-fact authority. "You may not return until you find Aisaut, Conscience, in his dwelling there and bow before him in sincere obeisance as his vassal. Only then may you know again the company of civil and inhibited beings."

Northward along the Kieri coast in High Summer an ice barge carried Jaud into exile. At Ilvaudset Camp he was put ashore and abandoned to his sentence. Facing inland toward the pole, Jaud could see beneath the half-frozen ground cover irregular veins of the extrusive black glass that gave the Obsidian Wastes their name. He despaired of surviving the decree of Law and of finding amid such desolation the hidden dwelling of Conscience. The bigness of his task both appalled and invigorated him, and he departed Ilvaudset Camp and its modest garrison of Kieri soldiers in a strange humor of elation and self-doubt.

For seventy days and seventy nights Jaud trekked into the hardening wilderness of the Wastes. He neither ate nor drank nor slept. At the end of the

seventieth night he came upon the Escarpments of
Aisaut, a labyrinth of towering obsidian walls and
interconnecting canyons of glass which none but the
innocent or the penitential could negotiate with ease.
Jaud was neither, but he entered the daunting maze
and for seven more days and nights wandered through
it in search of Conscience. On the morning of the
seventy-eighth day he found himself approaching a
wall of such dizzying height and perdurable finality
that he knew he could go no farther. Looking back,
Jaud saw not one opening into this compartment of
the labyrinth but seven, and he was unable to single
out the one by which he had come to his destination.
How would he ever return to Kier and the Orpla
Mountains? Jaud gazed again upon the final wall,
thinking that finally, after all the merriment and bloodshed he had known, it would perhaps be sweet to die.

But a voice called out, "Jaud, you may not die until
you have confronted me and sworn your allegiance!"

Although these words possessed the ring and tenor
of authority, the voice conveying them sounded thin
and distant. Jaud, perplexed and vaguely irritated,
looked about for the invisible crier.

"Approach me, Jaud! Come toward me!"

"Where?" Jaud shouted.

"Here in my prison of glass, child!"

Jaud did not care to be called child, but he approached the towering cliff face and peered into it
like one looking for flaws in a jewel. "Who are you?"
he asked the thing moving sluggishly inside the glass.
"What do you want of me?" He pressed his face and
hands against the obsidian, and the piercing light of
three high morning stars revealed that the crier in the
rock was none other than himself, a second Jaud.

But this Jaud was dressed in starched black skirts
and a seamless black overtunic embroidered with
threads of an even darker black, and Jaud was
amazed to see that his double had no hands, only a
pair of stumps which he moved back and forth through
the channels he had worn in the glass.

"I am not your second self," the imprisoned creature said. "I am the half you denied. Shobbes has sent you to reclaim that half by bending before me and asking pardon for your crimes."

"You are Aisaut, then?"

"Yes, I am Conscience, Jaud, and you must let me rule."

"But you are not the half I have denied, Aisaut. I've denied no half at all. I am complete without you and always have been."

"Shobbes decrees you outlaw, and therefore unfulfilled. Both of us were born when Gla Taus took shape from the matter of creation, but the lava flows of that anarchic time captured me in their searing floods and swept me into this great prison of obsidian. You—more fortunate than I—awoke in the Orpla Mountains, faulb blossoms dancing red and orange upon the hillsides and a hymn of self-celebration coursing in your veins.

"All that has prevented the Kieri from destroying themselves during my imprisonment here and your mad profligacy in the world is the fact that I took a precaution. Before the lava flow entrapped me, Jaud, I bit off my hands and summoned a pair of hawks to carry them southward into Kier. These brave birds dropped a bleeding finger at every place where people might have a chance to thrive, and my fingers pushed up through the earth in the shapes of great-boled mirrim trees. By every tree a village also grew, and when the villages merged each with each in the Mirrimsagset Alliance, Shobbes at last had a nation over which she might beneficially rule and she called it Kier. I am therefore cofounder of your country."

"Over the Thieves of Jaud neither Shobbes nor Aisaut has the least dominion," Jaud scoffed. "Law has sent me here, but she rules neither my followers nor my heart."

"That's because my absence is felt," Conscience replied. "The nation of ten villages has grown beyond the ken of Shobbes, and to your own and the Kieri's disadvantage you have ignored her suzerainty from the beginning."

"What would you have me do?"

"Release me from the rock and permit me to lead you home."

Jaud laughed. "Aisaut, you are wrong. I have never felt your absence. And by sacrificing your hands to found the state, you became less complete than I."

"Law demands that you release me."

"Where is Law, Conscience?" said Jaud, turning slowly around. "I do not see her here. Nor any of her vassals, either."

"The Obsidian Wastes are still untamed," the creature in the wall admitted. "But one day the people of Kier will come to subdue them. Already there is a garrison at Ilvaudset Camp. With these soldiers and pioneers will also come the Commandments of Law, in full and magnificent panoply."

"Where, then, is the necessity of my releasing you?"

"You must do me homage if you wish to see Kier again."

"My mind brims with memories of the Orpla Mountains. Perhaps they are enough. Perhaps I no longer desire to return."

The thing in the wall shifted uneasily.

"Further, Conscience, I am far older than you, for the Kieri recall in legends the upheavals that shaped the Obsidian Wastes. Of my birth, however, they have no record at all."

Aisaut protested, "I am as old as you."

"Not so," Jaud told the despairing image of himself. "But lacking hands and trapped in this wall, you are certainly more helpless than I."

"What do you intend to do?"

"Await the arrival of those who come to tame the Obsidian Wastes. As in the old days out of Orpla, I will fall upon them and take their belongings. Any who resist I will murder before your eyes, even as you cry 'Stay!' and look upon my deeds with impotent horror."

"Law prohibits these enormities, Jaud!"

Jaud glanced showily about. "Where is Law, Conscience?"

"She will come! Mind you, she will come!"

But Jaud turned his back on the creature in the wall, and Conscience knew that Jaud's true name was something else altogether. The jongleur-thief had fallen into Shobbes's hands too late to alter his nature, and Aisaut could gain no hold on either his emotions or his intellect. The future, at least in the Obsidian Wastes, would unfold exactly as Jaud had prophesied: Conscience, crying out "Stay!" as he struggled to free himself, would witness both the banditry and the bloodshed.

And would weep because he could not intervene.

—A Cultural Sourcebook: Myths, Legends, and Folk Tales of the Kieri. Retold in Vox by Clefrabbes Douin, Minister-at-Feln, 6209 G.

BOOK ONE

Chapter One

"Why, you callow couchling, you'd think it was the middle of the night! Wake up, Seth! Wake up!"

Seth roused slowly, recasting his brother's idiomatic Kieri first into Vox, the established galactic tongue, and then into their native Langlish, which they had purposely avoided speaking together for several Gla Tausian months. But in Seth's grogginess nearly every word drifted athwart his understanding, suborning the act of translation. Sleep held him like a womb.

A hand closed on Seth's forelock, and tugged. "Damn it, Seth, it's three hours to sunfall! Get up! The Liege Mistress of Kier, and thus of all Gla Taus, wishes to see you!"

To awake is to be reborn. Seth felt like an infant hoisted into the air by its heels and slapped resoundingly on the bum. Such a sensation was impossible of memory, for it lay outside Seth's experience. The little parturitions of ten thousand previous awakenings, however, had given him a vivid, if eventually numbing, analogue of the shock attendant upon live birth, and he knew with a galvanizing dread that it was chaos and uncertainty to which Abel was delivering him.

Seth, bolting upright on his couch, struck aside the elder isohet's too familiar hand.

"Damnation, Seth!" Abel sucked the wounded hand, then histrionically shook it. "What's the matter with you?"

Seth regarded Abel with the same commingling of

fear and grudging admiration that had marked his relationship with Günter Latimer, the slain Ommundi mercantile representative to Gla Taus. Latimer, although two weeks dead, was preserved genetically in the persons of his "sons." Seth and Abel were isohets —as clones of disparate age were called both on the Earth of the Ommundi Trade Company and elsewhere throughout the range of Interstel that Vox was spoken —and Günter Latimer, a man of towering commercial ambition, on-again/off-again charisma, and a convincing humility in the presence of "quasi-humans," had been their common biological template, their *isosire*—if not, in fact, their "father." In any case, Latimer's genetic legacy lived in the persons of his isohet Dopplegängers stranded now in Feln, the winter capital of Kier. Abel had been twenty-eight years the dead man's junior, and Seth, at twenty-one, was fourteen Earth-standard years younger than Abel.

"No one's responsible for what he or she does in the first full minute after awaking," Seth declared. "That's a period of legal insanity." He was disoriented. His head hurt.

Abel, portly at thirty-five, was still trying to shake the smart out of his hand. Seth saw him as a blowzy distortion of their isosire, Günter Latimer. . . .

What a hideous end the old man had come to. A host of angry *aisautseb,* or patriot-priests, had caught Latimer outside Feln's Winter Palace, stripped him naked, and hoisted him by the heel up the southern face of the Kieri Obelisk in Mirrimsagset Square. Palace security had been unwilling or unable to intervene, and by the time the turreted copperclads from Pedgor Garrison arrived to disperse the crowd, Latimer's body was spiculed with hundreds of glinting glass darts from the rioters' ceramic blowguns, weapons they wore like necklaces and whose ancient Kieri name meant "demon killer." But even violated to this unspeakable degree in death, old Latimer had retained an aura of dignity unobtainable by Abel. Abel could not muster a comparable presence even in parade-dress pantaloons and formal mourning cap—the attire, Seth too vividly recalled, that both his isohet and he had worn to the interminable state funeral directed by Master Douin, their host. Jauddeb, like human beings, appreciated ritual. . . .

"While you lie here at midday sleeping," Abel complained, "I'm planning for our future, consulting with Kieri both high and intermediate. And when I come back to report that my good offices have secured us an audience with the Liege Mistress, you give me the greeting of a viper. *Damnation,* Seth!"

Abel glanced at Seth so searingly that the younger isohet forgot Abel's infantile, wheedling tone and realized again that Abel could be a very unpredictable, occasionally even treacherous man. In his lumbering way, before Latimer's death, Abel had proved himself an effective stand-in negotiator with the Kieri. Seth, on the other hand, had remained by his relatives' mutual decree in the background, a grandchild to the one and alternately a little brother and a sexual object to the other. Toddler and concubine, Seth had come to resent the suppression of his innate talents and to despise himself in the person of Abel, that grotesque caricature of his own face and figure. At the same time, Seth was afraid of being cut adrift from the only human being who had ever made, or been forced to make, a long-term commitment to him. Günter Latimer had merely called Seth into existence; Abel had nurtured him like a natural parent.

"The question is whether we'll live as exiles in Kier or as freegoers among the nations of the Ommundi Company on Earth," said Abel, shifting into Langlish for the first time that winter. "Do you want to spend the rest of your life on Gla Taus, shuttling back and forth between Feln and Sket with the monkeys of the Kieri court? Or would you like to see Lausanne again and live among genuine human beings? Those are your options, Seth."

"The Kieri seem as human as you or I;" Seth murmured in his native tongue.

"Because they're born? Monkeys are born. Polecats and ratlings descend through a uterus. Birth is a negligible criterion for the assignment of humanity, Seth. The Kieri are jauddeb, not human. Just because—"

"All right. All right."

Still in Langlish, Abel continued his assault: "Take your pick. Stay on Gla Taus or return to Earth."

"The latter, of course."

"Very well, then. That demands that we cooperate with Lady Turshebsel, the Liege Mistress. Also with her supercilious Point Marcher and our own well-meaning Master Douin. I've bent myself to that end every waking moment since Günter's murder. We have no ship, Seth. We're at the mercy of the quaz."

"Why do you use that shabby epithet?"

"Quaz?" said Abel, lifting an eyebrow. "No one here understands Langlish. No need to worry. And what more suitable term for the assassins of our isosire? The memory of his death still makes me sick."

In truth, it did. Several successive nights since the aisautseb attack, Abel had awakened sweating ice water and trembling uncontrollably. Only after vomiting in the carved stone urinal in the step-down lavalet of Master Douin's rambling Ilsotsa Era home could Abel return to sleep. And, clutching Seth to him atop the sour-smelling quilts of their couch, he slept fitfully. These had been the only occasions in the past year, discounting perfunctory bouts of "love making," that Seth had felt even remotely necessary to his isohet. He was grateful to Abel for his vulnerability—which, however, was hardly a sentiment Seth could voice aloud.

Instead he asked, "Will the Kieri permit us passage home aboard the *Dharmakaya?*"

"That depends on you."

"On me? Nothing depends on me, Abel."

"This does. That's why I've risked a broken hand" —shaking it reprovingly—"to wake you up. We have an audience with Lady Turshebsel in half an hour.

If you give a good accounting of yourself, we may yet get home."

"A good accounting? What am I supposed to do?"

"Answer her questions. And those of Porchaddos Pors, her Point Marcher. And those of Clefrabbes Douin, who's already kindly disposed toward you."

"Questions about what?"

"About the mission we'll soon be undertaking to earn our passage home, even if we must earn it aboard a vessel already rightfully ours. Be yourself Seth. That will bring us through."

The *Dharmakaya*—whose Mahayana Buddist monicker derived from Günter Latimer's first and only wife's fascination with Eastern mysticism—was the ship by which all three men had come to Gla Taus. It was a light-tripper, a modular vessel of more than five hundred Earth-bound metric tons, and it belonged to the Langlish Division of the Ommundi Trade Company. At the moment, it was hovering in synchronous orbit six hundred kilometers directly above Feln, the winter capital. Two days after Latimer's murder, the Liege Mistress, urged on by the increasingly vocal aisautseb, had revoked the formal trade agreement with Ommundi and seized the *Dharmakaya* for the Kieri state. The seizure of the ship, Master Douin had apologetically told Abel and Seth, was in compensation for the violence done Gla Tausian spirituality by the elder Latimer's desire to open up to cultivation and animal husbandry the forbidden territories in the evil southern ocean. That Lady Turshebsel herself had enthusiastically championed this project until the aisautseb uprising merely demonstrated the mutability of Kieri politics.

Seth swung his feet to the floor, knocking to the carpeted flagstones the plastic microfiche viewer with which he had fallen asleep. Abel stooped to pick it up, then examined its casing.

"What were you reading?"

"Myths, Legends, and Folk Tales of the Kieri,"

Seth replied. "Master Douin gave me the first several chapter cards this morning."

"Ah, yes. How did you find these little jauddeb histories?"

"The story of Aisaut's release from the final wall of the Ilvautsettan labyrinths put me to sleep."

Abel laughed. "I can see that it did."

"And the motion of the draperies," Seth hurried to add. "And the comfort of the couch. And my own fatigue and distraction."

"You protest too much. Come on, then. The author of this soporific masterwork awaits us without."

Clefrabbes Douin—advisor, diplomat, man of letters—sat on a stone bench in his ancient house's *laulset*, or pool court, staring thoughtfully into the loosely roiling, reddish water. Most of the power generated for home and industrial use in Kier derived from geothermal sources, and the households of powerful or wealthy citizens were often distinguished by the laulset. The central feature of the pool court was a natural hot spring surrounded by colorful ceramic tiles and equipped with hand rails and submerged stone steps to facilitate bathing.

During the long winter just past, Günter Latimer and his isohets had bathed frequently with the Clefrabbes *geffide*, which consisted of Master Douin, his two wives, an elderly female parent, and five young children. Seth had come to conclude, on anatomical as well as metaphysical and sociological evidence, that the jauddeb were undoubtedly *approximately* human. Moreover, he liked Master Douin's geffide, as a unit and as individuals. How could Abel call them quaz?

Douin rose to greet his guests the moment they entered the echoing laulset, and Abel's first question was about conditions in the streets and whether they could safely venture out again.

"There's been no danger in Feln since Lady Turshebsel claimed your ship," Douin responded in

Kieri. "Did you feel threatened during your earlier outing to the palace, Master Abel?"

"Not in the palace itself, but in the streets—"

"You were perfectly safe, despite your fears. That's another reason we seized the *Dharmakaya:* a sop to the aisautseb, you understand. It's necessary to placate so powerful a force with the people."

Douin turned to Seth. "Good afternoon. If we don't hurry, Master Seth, we'll be late for our audience with the Liege Mistress." He led the isohets toward the door opening on Mirrimsagset Square.

The Clefrabbes geffide—the term implied the physical structure of the house as well as the family within it—stood on the southeast corner of this great square; and from a window in Douin's third-story library Seth and Abel had witnessed the last act of their isosire's martyrdom and the cutting down of the body from the obelisk. Seth had not been outside the geffide since the state funeral, and until this morning Abel had hazarded trips to the Winter Palace only after sunfall or in the dim cold hours before the dawn songs of the patriot-priests. Now Abel was venturing forth for the second time that day, again in brazen sunlight, and Seth was undergoing a kind of baptism of his own. His heart fluttered like a hammer in his breast.

Pedalshaws and motorized carts cruised through the vast, immaculate square, but most of Feln's citizenry were afoot.

Near the obelisk, an aisautseb was selling tinfoil prayer-and-proclamation balloons. These he inflated with lighter-than-air gas from a compressor tank on wheels. He then decorated the balloons in elegant Kieri script with religious or patriotic squibs. The stylus he used looked vaguely like a weapon, and his customers were adults rather than children. Instead of walking merrily off with their purchases, these people found shop railings or bench backs or parked pedalshaws to which to tie their balloons—so that their prayers or proclamations might soar aloft on however much string they had been able to afford. Sunlight ricocheted off the tinfoil balloons, whose alien messages revolved against a backdrop of unceasing mercantile activity.

High above the square, tethered to the Kieri Obelisk itself, drifted a monstrous hot-air balloon whose message was patched against its off-white bulk in velvety black letters as tall as any adult jauddeb.

"What does that one say?" Seth asked Douin. Although Abel and he could speak Kieri, they still couldn't read the fluid characters in which it was written.

Douin replied, "The legend on the big balloon says, *God is the foremost patriot, for the land is holy.*"

"It's a veiled allusion to the presence of offworlders on Gla Taus," Abel told Seth as they strolled northward toward the pool of the Shobbes Geyser and the stone-and-ceramic facade of the Winter Palace.

"Nothing of the kind," said Douin, without rancor. "It's an expression of belief—pure, if not altogether simple."

"But it wasn't there before the murder," Abel said.

"Then let's simply note that the proposals of Ommundi Company have led to a resurgence of religio-patriotic fervor in Feln. Even so, Master Abel, the proclamation on the obelisk's balloon is a traditional one."

"What about those on the smaller balloons?" Seth asked.

"Prayers, market slogans, warnings, even a few secular witticisms. The sale of the balloons is an exclusive aisautseb monopoly, and their customers, by purchasing the balloons, are exercising their legal rights to creative expression and free speech."

"Do the customers make up the slogans, then?"

"Many do, yes. Of course, Master Seth, the aisautseb may veto any message he doesn't care for and refuse to hand over the balloon. It's customary, though, to pay him before announcing the slogan you wish written."

"Ha," said Abel, disgustedly.

"Please translate that one," Seth said, pointing to a balloon jiggling from the awning of a bakery just ahead of them.

Douin halted, cocked his head to one side, and read, *"Beware such demons as would drag us back to Hell."*

"Meaning us?" said Abel.

"This time I would suppose so," admitted Douin. "But let me comfort you by pointing out that this is also a ritual warning of some antiquity. Its pertinence to you, if any, may be accidental."

"I doubt that," Abel declared.

"So do I," said the affable Kieri.

When they began walking again, shouldering their way through a crowd devoid of deference for Douin's ministerial skirts and hard leather cap, Seth noticed that almost everyone in the streets was wearing a "demon killer" about his or her neck. Some of these lethal ceramic flutes hung straight down, while others were strung crosswise like tubular gorgets. *Dairauddes,* the Kieri called them. And the small glass darts that these instruments propelled the people wore on combs in their hair, or as pins in their clothing, or even as ornaments on bracelets and boot tassels. Since everyone was armed, including the patriot-priest near the obelisk, Seth took scant comfort from his knowledge that a single *thet,* or glass dart, was seldom sufficient to kill. Too, Seth had gradually become aware of the attention that Abel and he were attracting: long, contemptuous stares and snatches of angry conversation in bistro and market-stall doorways.

As they edged past one shop, a woman weighing a handful of gnarled tubers in a metal scale shouted at them, "Go back to Hell!"

To show that Abel and Seth were under his protection, Douin passed an arm over the isohets' heads; and the woman, thus rebuked, turned mute and mottle-faced back into the fusty darkness of her produce cove. But she had spoken her mind where others had held their tongues.

Hell, Seth knew, was all of Gla Taus south of Kier, which was country, continent, and world. Hell was especially those equatorial and subequatorial regions— the Evashsteddan—where for ages a terrible volcanism had held sway in the great hemispherical ocean called the Evashsted Sea. The islands scattered throughout this sea the Kieri regarded, quite literally, as stepping stones to damnation. In the mythical pre-historic past of Gla Taus, according to accepted aisautseb lore, God had deserted the Evashsteddan, and anyone who left Kier to explore the southern ocean and its smoldering archipelagoes automatically forfeited his soul.

This belief, Günter Latimer had told his isohets, appeared to stem from a strange complex of causes: an ancient war or natural upheaval that had displaced early Gla Tausian peoples toward the north, the continuing volcanism in the Evashsteddan, the eerie variety of sea- and island-going life forms in the south, and the inability of present-day Kieri to tolerate temperatures very much above 17°C. This last was one crucial respect in which jauddeb differed fundamentally from human beings; and when Lady Turshebsel had allowed word to go out that she and Latimer had concluded a long-in-the-formulation agreement whereby Ommundi representatives would exploit the untapped resources of the Evashsteddan, the patriot-priests had called upon believers to make their outrage known. Few in Kier were not believers, and the principal mistake of the Liege Mistress's advisors— Porchaddos Pors and Clefrabbes Douin among them —lay in their failing to foresee the likely reaction of the Kieri to such a public announcement. The aisautseb, sluggishly complacent through nearly four decades of Lady Turshebsel's rule, had leaped awake, and the citizenry had leaped after. For these reasons, then, Günter Latimer had died. He was a demon, and his spawn were demons, and religious patriotism was the order of the day.

Seth watched a shopkeeper finger his dairauddes.

Uncanny to think that the people of Kier regarded Abel and him as something far worse than quaz, as soulless beings who sullied the holiness of their country. Although Seth half expected Douin to rebuke this ugly jauddeb with either word or gesture, as he had done the woman at the scales, Douin fixed his eyes on the Winter Palace and led Abel and Seth upward from the square as if escorting them to a gallows.

Chapter Two

At the palace's outer gate a pair of sentries from Pedgor Garrison halted the three men and took their names, even though Clefrabbes Douin was far from a nonentity in Feln, even though Abel and Seth were recognizable as living if imperfect mirrors of the dead Latimer.

Seth stared past the guards.

Through the gateway, a pool outlined by tiles and pinched about its circumference with immersion nooks. It was in these nooks that pilgrims could give themselves to the waters of Shobbes. Today, however, the inner court was empty, and the tiled façade of the palace reflected the face of the pool as the pool reflected that of the palace. . . .

"You must wait for Shobbes to pass you," said one of the guards. He and his companion were wearing leather pantaloons and vests. Carrying mech-rifles, they radiated a hostility that seemed to encompass even Douin.

"It was like this morning, too," Abel told Seth. "Before the aisautseb uprising you could walk in whenever you wished, so long as you had an invitation. But now, as in the old days, you have to wait for the blessing of Shobbes."

The geyser in the pool, Seth knew, had a regular interval, but he had forgotten what it was. How long would they have to stand in the shadow of the stone-and-ceramic palace before certification came? The guards blocking their way and the Kieri in the teeming square below them made Seth equally nervous. He was caught, with Abel, between Scylla and Charybdis.

At last Shobbes Geyser blew. The eruption was preceded by a churning movement in the pool and then an audible bubbling—whereupon the surface seemed almost to peel back and a pillar of reddish water shot upward, fanning out like a peacock's tail as it climbed. Although the continuous plashing of the geyser made talk impossible, its eruption lasted scarcely a minute and soon a guard was able to say,

"Now you may pass."

Seth was startled by the *warmth* of the drops that had misted down on him. The eruption had been too well foretokened to surprise him. But as Douin led them through the gate, Seth could still see—in his mind's eye—the central plume dancing eighteen or twenty meters in the air.

It was a long way—over the flooded mosaics surrounding the pool, then across an apron of enormous flagstones—to the palace entrance, and only when they were well beyond the hearing of the guards did Douin speak:

"Master Seth, did you see Aisaut in the geyser?"

"Aisaut?"

"A man of conscience is supposed to be able to see the image of Aisaut projected against the palace through the geyser's dancing. I was wondering if you saw such a thing. I know better than to ask your isohet."

"I'm afraid I saw nothing but water," Seth said. He looked at Abel. The expression on Abel's face was quick with apprehension and disgust. It seemed to say,

*Haven't you the sense to give your host the answer he
wants to hear?*

"Nothing else?"

"No, sir. Only water and sunlight and tiles."

Douin's eyes were cryptically merry. "That's all I
ever see," he said. "In twenty-three years that's all
I've ever seen." He led the isohets up a final set of
steps and into the Winter Palace.

Despite its ancient façade—the building supposedly
dated to the early days of the legendary Inhodlef Era
—the palace was luxuriously appointed within and
almost shamefully comfortable. As in Master Douin's
geffide, the interior flagstone flooring was carpeted
with a synthetic fabric both durable and eye-pleasing.
Here, however, the carpet's nap was iridescent, dyed
cobalt blue and crimson in an immense cartographic
pattern representing the world. Seth, who had stood
in this anteroom once before, waiting for Latimer to
return from an audience with the Liege Mistress, dis-
tinctly remembered that on that occasion the pattern
in the carpet had depicted stylized figures thieving and
juggling.

"Lady Turshebsel has changed the decor," Seth
whispered. For Douin's benefit, he nodded meaning-
fully at the carpet.

Douin was briefly puzzled, then finally comprehend-
ing. "Oh, no," he said. "The same carpet, Master
Seth, but a different alignment of its nap. It has four
separate designs, this carpet, depending on the direction in which its fibers are brushed. Master Günter
was very interested in the process."

Abel said, "I prefer walking across it to talking
about it."

"Very good," Douin replied. He indicated a tilework archway farther on and led them toward it.
There was a sound of gently lapping water from the
higher chamber just ahead.

Seth had never set eyes on Lady Turshebsel, Liege
Mistress of Kier. He knew that her people considered

her the rightful inheritor of the geffide which was their
nation, even though she had won her place not through
descent from any previous ruler but instead from the
happenstance of a lottery conducted by the aisautseb
on the death of her predecessor. She was Liege Mistress, then, not through primogeniture but rather
through the influence of patriotic prayer. Only young
jauddeb females who obtained menarche on the death
day of the last Liege Mistress, and who were residents
of the city in which she had died, were eligible for
selection. To ensure that no geffide sought to feign a
daughter's eligibility by misrepresenting the advent of
her womanhood, the Kieri had long since evolved
joyous first-blood festivities encouraging the geffide
to proclaim a daughter's time and to celebrate it before the world. Kieri girls, therefore, were quick to
tell their parents of their arrival at menarche so that
the news could be spread. A tardy report was almost
unheard of, for girls were considerably more likely to
err on the impulsive side. Further, to prevent the
adults of a geffide from conspiring to place one of
their daughters on the Kieri throne, tradition demanded that the family of the new Liege Mistress suffer the confiscation of all its goods and exile to a
remote and overwarm area of the continent, usually
to Feht Evashsted, a coastal area near the great southern ocean. For many, particularly the aged, this was a
virtual death sentence. That, too, was why the passing
of each Liege Mistress was customarily made public
three full days *after* its occurrence, when an official of
the court could verify, with very little fear of error or
deception, all the first-blood registrations of the regal
lady's death day. After that, the aisautseb selected her
successor from among the available candidates by a
lottery that Seth did not wholly understand. Latimer
had said that it involved the immersion of the bleeding
girls in either the pool of the Shobbes Geyser (if the
Liege Mistress had died in Feln) or in the sulfur baths
of Shobbes in the forbidden morraine territories west
of the Summer Capital (if the Liege Mistress had died

in Sket). Purity and endurance were important crite-
ria, and the characteristic pinkish cast of the waters of
Kier was said to derive not from ferric oxides but from
the pure, enduring tincture of the royal menses.

Although Seth had often heard Abel describe the
Liege Mistress as an unprepossessing woman with a
squat body and a full-moon face, he now began conjuring images of a dragoness or Gorgon—only to step
into her laulset and find Abel vindicated.

Lady Turshebsel was standing beside a small but
exquisitely proportioned bathing pool shaped like the
central cluster of a meadowland flower; each of its
nine semicircular petals was an immersion nook. The
tiles here were a dazzling burgundy, and to keep from
slipping on them, the Liege Mistress wore a pair of
thongs with adhesive soles and carried a rubber-tipped
metal staff. In a row of tilework chairs growing out of
the floor behind her sat Lady Turshebsel's advisors,
attendants, and sycophants: the members of her
palace geffide. Not counting the Kieri over whom she
ruled, Seth reflected, they were all the family the Liege
Mistress would ever have. As an avatar of Shobbes,
she was betrothed forever to the state, virgin to her
death day.

But otherwise, old Latimer had said, she was an
enlightened woman who quite early in her reign had
renounced all but the most trivial ritual authority of
the aisautseb. She had forced them out of the palace
by command, securing their obedience because they
themselves had chosen her and could disobey her only
by openly conceding their own fallibility. Until two
weeks ago Lady Turshebsel had been able to survive
—in fact, to prosper—without the aisautseb, largely
because Gla Taus had remained for so long outside the
range of Interstel's benign meddlesomeness, and because the patriot-priests of Kier had found no cause to
dispute the wisdom of her rule. Then, after sending
an emissary to the court in Sket, Interstel had given
the Ommundi Trade Company permission to seek
mercantile rights on the planet, and the Latimers had

come to Gla Taus to negotiate these rights with the Lady.

Seth could not help noticing that one of those sitting in a tilework chair was a priest. Engulfed in robes, his legs drawn up beneath him on the ceramic seat, his unblinking eyes like silver nail heads, he sat in a chair reserved for a prominent advisor. Two weeks ago that chair had belonged to another, but to appease the aisautseb after their uprising, Lady Turshebsel had not only declared the *Dharmakaya* Kieri property but had reestablished a patriot-priest advisorship. This man was the first to hold that position in thirty-seven Gla Tausian years.

"Welcome, Master Seth," Lady Turshebsel said from across the laulset. "I invite you to join me in the waters."

A woman came forward from another doorway, took the Liege Mistress's staff, and carefully removed her starched skirts and jacket. Then, wearing only her awkward-looking thongs, Lady Turshebsel descended into the pool. Her squat, naked body, like that of other Kieri, was lightly haired across its entire surface (excepting only the face), with the hair deepening in color rather than in thickness at the pubic region. An unremarkable body, really; at least on Gla Taus. Once she had positioned herself in her immersion nook, her smile seemed that of a little girl who has tasted some forbidden confection. If she was indeed past middle-age for a jauddeb, she bore her years well.

"Come," she said. "All others may attend this conference from vantages of their own choosing, but Master Seth must join me in the waters."

Kieri garments were made to don and doff without any lifting of the arms or raising of the feet, and before Seth could protest or demur, an attendant had unstrung his jacket, then split and peeled back the resealable leg seams of his pantaloons. Seth was suddenly standing before the mighty of the land in gooseflesh and breechclout, and that the Empress also wore no clothes was paltry consolation. Half panicked, Seth looked to Abel for aid.

"I suffered through the same thing this morning," Abel said in Langlish. "Off with your breechclout, too. She wishes to take your measure."

But Clefrabbes Douin took Seth's wrist and led him toward the immersion nook opposite Lady Turshebsel's. "Perhaps he'd be more comfortable, Lady, if only those who are immediately concerned with this matter take part in our talks."

Lady Turshebsel looked to right and to left, nodding each time, and in a moment there remained in the laulset only Seth, Abel, Douin, the silver-eyed patriot-priest, and a tall, ugly Kieri dressed in blue pantaloons and a long, rope-hooked coat. This man Seth knew as Porchaddos Pors, Point Marcher of Feln. It was his function to formulate and implement local policy. Although one of the highest-ranking courtiers in the Liege Mistress's service, Pors was legally subordinate to the Point Marcher of Sket, who, possessing his title through a more ancient lineage, exercised a greater authority nationwide. Pors was of the Kieri nobility, whereas Douin was a career civil servant who had won his position and his house through the often uncertain preferment of scholarship and ability.

Seth did not like Porchaddos Pors because of his aggressive temperament and the animalish cast of his features. Although he was grateful to Douin and Lady Turshebsel for emptying the hall of unnecessary onlookers, he still did not like to remove his breechclout in front of this man. The stare of the aisautseb, enveloped in his stiff, white robes, was also disconcerting. Why must he uncover himself in front of strangers?

Abel and Douin flanked him, and Abel, nudging him in the side, muttered in nearly inaudible Langlish, "Remove it and get in. The priests believe that a naked jauddeb speaks the truth. Naked humans, too, perhaps."

Bathing with the Clefrabbes geffide had seemed a natural thing, a strengthening of the social bond be-

tween host and guest—but this, despite the kindness in
Lady Turshebsel's eyes, seemed designed either to
humble him or to test his resolve. Both, maybe. And
because Abel had earlier said that getting back to
Earth depended on how he conducted himself here,
Seth was afraid. What was he being tested on? What
did they want of him?

He unknotted the breechclout and dropped it to
the floor. Immediately his scrotum contracted, and his
legs threatened to give way beneath him. But he kept
his teeth clenched and entered the warm water, set-
tling himself into the immersion nook and relaxing a
little the moment his body was covered. Water moved
around him, and Porchaddos Pors came to the edge of
the pool to stand behind the Liege Mistress. Half
visible in the glare of light behind and to the left of
Pors, the unblinking priest kept watch.

"Your isohet says you wish to return to Earth,
Master Seth," Lady Turshebsel began. "In the
Dharmakaya."

"Yes, Lady."

"You understand that the ship you came in, formerly the property of the Ommundi Company, now
belongs to us. The aisautseb, however, agree that you
may regain the vessel if you and your isohet and the
pilot who now lies aboard it in cold sleep agree to
undertake a mission on behalf of the Kieri state. Master Abel has already agreed. The pilot, he tells us, will
obey him, for Master Abel is now the Ommundi representative on Gla Taus with legal authority. But because you're your isohet's equal in all but age, Master
Seth, we've asked you here to acquire your consent,
too."

"I agree to whatever Abel has agreed," Seth said,
still not understanding what they wanted of him. He
had the uneasy apprehension that he was being played
like a fish with a hook in its gill, and yet . . . and yet
Lady Turshebsel's voice and manner were kindly.
Her pale round face, framed with coarse ringlets of
blue-black hair, bobbed languidly above the waters

flowing between them, and he could see no deception in her.

Pors, accompanied by the sucking of his thongs, approached Seth by stalking around the pool. "Have you no questions about what we require of you? No curiosity about the task? No doubt that you may be able to accomplish what we wish you to accomplish?" He halted halfway around and stared impatiently at Seth, towering against the backdrop of a farther portal.

"If Abel believes we can do what you want—"

"Not Master Abel and you together," Douin broke in, "but you alone, with Lord Pors and myself as minor accomplices."

"You're at the very center of our plan," said Pors.

"But why?"

"Because of your innocence," Lady Turshebsel responded. "A quality that everyone else in this laulset has long since forfeited. Your innocence, Master Seth, is your principal asset and an essential factor in our calculations. Let me be frank: We wish to use you. You lack many of the preconceptions and biases that are likely to thwart Lord Pors, Master Douin, and your own capable isohet. You are clean and unspoiled."

Seth wasn't altogether flattered. *We wish to use you.* In his association with Günter Latimer, dating from his sixteenth year, he had visited four solar systems, mastering Scansh and Kieri (in addition to Vox, Langlish, and two other human tongues), and he had heard of or actually witnessed cruelties that many human beings far older than he would never have credited. His brief experience of the universe had appraised him quite early, in fact, of the ubiquity and multiformity of Evil. To be termed an innocent, he felt, was to contradict the entire thrust of this experience. *We wish to use you.* He could still see his isosire's body hanging like a butchered carcass from the Kieri Obelisk. . . .

"You don't care for my candor?" Lady Turshebsel asked.

Seth had no answer.

"All right, then. Let me pose a question. You have lived among us better than a year. Do you regard the people of Gla Taus, us jauddeb, as"—the Liege Mistress shaped the alien word with humorous distaste—"what your isohet sometimes disdainfully calls . . . *quaz?*"

"Oh, no," Seth blurted, reddening. At his back he could hear Abel shifting from one foot to another in sudden, acute embarrassment.

"This word implies a lower order of development and intelligence, does it not?" said the Lady, pressing her advantage. But Seth's reply was apparent in his flustered silence, and she continued: "We have unpleasant epithets of our own for foreigners and offworlders, Master Seth. But I believe you when you say that *you* don't regard us as . . . quaz. Your isohet's true feelings I'm unable to determine, however. The word first fell from his lips, you see."

"Lady Turshebsel—" Abel began.

"Be quiet," Porchaddos Pors reprimanded him.

"My question now," the Liege Mistress resumed, "is if your openness to the humanity of other intelligent alien species is broad enough to include the inhabitants of Trope?"

"Trope, Lady?"

"The world that circles Anja, seven lights from our own star, Gal Taunt. Do you know that world, Master Seth?"

"It's a technologically advanced planet that holds itself aloof from Interstel, I believe. It has lighttrippers, it communicates with passing vessels by means of Vox—but it refuses either consular contact or trade. Interstel is biding its time, as it did with Gla Taus until granting Ommundi permission to attempt a mercantile alliance."

Pors said defensively, "We wished to develop certain aspects of our technology without aping the methods and paraphernalia of Interstel. Now we have orbiters of our own, if not light-trippers, and we did it by techniques and designs of Kieri origin."

Lady Turshebsel ignored the Point Marcher's chauvinistic outburst. "But what do you know about the gosfi themselves, the people of Trope?" she asked Seth.

"Their eyes—"

"Yes?"

"Their eyes are strange. I can't remember how. Otherwise, they're shaped in their bodies as . . . as you and I are shaped."

"That's what we suppose," Lady Turshebsel conceded. "Master Günter had told me, however, that Interstel had recently induced the most populous Tropish nation to become a provisional signatory of its charter. By your own official classification system, then, the Tropiards are *jauddebseb.*"

Seth realized that by this word Lady Turshebsel meant to say "humanlike" or "humanoid"—but the silver-eyed priest made disapproving wheezing noises at her mentions of both Latimer and the Tropiards, and it was clear that in his view only Kieri were without question jauddebseb.

Lady Turshebsel continued her argument: "Knowing these things to be true, and knowing that we on Gla Taus have been in contact for some months with the Magistrate of Trope by means of the communication system aboard the *Dharmakaya,* would you regard the Tropiards as quaz if you had to deal with them?"

"No, Lady."

"You would deal with them"—the Liege Mistress surprised Seth by saying her final three words in Langlish—*"human to human?"*

"Yes, Lady," he responded, disguising his astonishment. Latimer must have taught her a great deal before his murder. . . .

"Good. Because at this very moment, Master Seth, I'm appointing you my personal envoy to the Magistrate of Trope. His name is Ulgraji Vrai, and his nation is called by the name of his world."

"But what am I to do?" Seth craned his neck about

to look at Abel. Rising within him was the panic occasioned by his own inadequacy.

"As you're told," Abel said unsympathetically.

"Lord Pors," said Lady Turshebsel, "while Master Seth is relaxing in the bath, please recite for him the details of his mission to Trope. Leave out nothing, but make the explanation brief."

Pors stalked about the laulset's pool, his thongs making their distracting sucking noises, and in fifteen minutes he had outlined both the economic basis of the Kieri plan and the nature of the protracted cultural conflict on Trope that appeared to make this strategy feasible. Nothing but benefits for all concerned. But as Pors spoke, Seth glanced frequently into the ceramic glare nimbusing the white-robed priest.

It was plain to Seth that Lady Turshebsel's plan had grown out of priestly resistance to her trade agreement with Ommundi Company. The aisautseb wanted no one to exploit the very real resources of the Evashsteddan, even though in order to acquire the basics of an interstellar technology Kieri scientists and industrialists were even now venturing into the Obsidian Wastes from Old Ilvaudset, the first explorers into this region in several centuries. They were looking for rare ores, insulating materials, natural conductors, and any other serendipitous loot the Wastes might contain. The aisautseb had no objection to this expansion because it was northward, but because the Wastes could support neither crops nor livestock, the Liege Mistress had been counting on Ommundi Company to establish food-producing strongholds among the islands of the Evashsteddan and a reliable supply line to both Kier and the pioneers pushing poleward in the Ilvaudsettan. That hope had died with Günter Latimer. This plan involving Trope—which Pors was now explaining—was a contingency operation, and its chief virtue seemed to be that it was acceptable, if only barely, to the aisautseb.

"What do you think?" Lady Turshebsel asked when Pors had finished.

"I don't like it very much, Lady," Seth replied.

"Why?"

"It works hardships on everyone, even if Gla Taus and Trope both stand to benefit ultimately."

"The Latimer isohets are also beneficiaries," Lady Turshebsel pointed out. "If you succeed, Master Seth, you return to your home world. If you decline my appointment, the *Dharmakaya* stays in orbit and you and Master Abel remain our guests. Narthaimnar Chappouib and his fellow priests have approved this expedition as well as the reward attendant upon your coming home to Gla Taus." She made a motion of the head indicating that Narthaimnar Chappouib was her silver-eyed advisor, and Seth's suspicions about the man's influence were confirmed.

"Gla Taus isn't our home," he said, "and the *Dharmakaya* is already ours."

"He agrees," Abel said quickly. "He accepts your appointment as envoy to the nation and world called Trope."

"He accepted before he'd heard the whole of our proposal," Lady Turshebsel quietly rejoined. "I'd like to hear his opinion now."

Seth hesitated, frightened. He had no certainty whatever that he could accomplish the task they had set him.

"Tell her," Abel urged him in a whisper.

"I accept your appointment," Seth heard himself say.

"Then all that's left is for you and the others to receive the blessing of Aisaut Chappouib. Go to him now, please. You'll depart Gla Taus tomorrow— whereupon my court will remove to Sket until your return." She raised her arms above her head and clapped her hands. A woman entered the laulset with Lady Turshebsel's cloak, helped her from the water, and draped the cloak about her shoulders. Wet, the fine black hair covering the Liege Mistress's body lay along her limbs and flanks like a delicate fur.

When the two women were gone, Clefrabbes Douin
assisted Seth from the pool and pointed him toward
the unblinking priest.

"My clothes?"

"Not yet," Douin said. "Go to the aisautseb."

Seth obeyed, walking naked past Lord Pors and
halting before the ceramic throne of the priest.

"Kneel," said Narthaimnar Chappouib.

Seth lowered himself to the cold tiles, his knee caps
aching with the hardness under them, his flesh crawling with too many different kinds of chill to name.
He was kneeling before one of those instrumental in
bringing about his isosire's death. Naked. As Latimer
had been naked going up the side of the tower in
Mirrimsagset Square. . . .

"You must carry a gift to the ruler to whom Lady
Turshebsel is sending you as envoy," the priest said
tonelessly. "This gift will be my blessing, for you have
no belief in aisautseb prayers. In any case, your nature
is such that they would have no meaning." Chappouib
looked about for someone to command. "Master
Douin, would you assist me?"

Douin came forward and freed from the inside of
the aisautseb's collar a chain on which was strung a
dairauddes. This tube was black ceramic, as long as
Seth's hand from wrist to middle fingertip.

"Give it to me," Chappouib said.

Douin extended the dairauddes toward the priest;
and Seth was taken aback to discover that when
Chappouib reached to receive it, lifting his great
sleeves so that they fell to his elbows, he accepted the
dairauddes between a pair of raw-looking stumps.

This aisautseb, like the mythical namesake of all
Kieri priests, had no hands.

The dairauddes dangled precariously between his
stumps, threatening to slip away and shatter on the
floor. Nevertheless, Chappouib was going to attempt
to put it around Seth's neck, and Seth, despite not
wanting the thing to touch him, inclined his head to
make the transfer easier. He felt instinctively that the

ritual had sexual overtones, and he was confused and frightened by them. Was he being honored by the aisautseb's gift, or was the transfer a contemptuous mockery of his manhood?

At last Clefrabbes Douin took the dairauddes from Chappouib and bestowed it on Seth. Now he was wearing a "demon killer," and to many Kieri—this thought chilled—Seth was himself a demon.

"Your dairauddes," Chappouib said, shaking out his sleeves and covering his stumps again, "once belonged to Lady Turshebsel. She forfeited it when she drove the aisautseb from her service. I brought it back. Now she bids me give it to you to bestow on Magistrate Vrai of Trope."

Seth waited, wondering what was to come next.

"You may depart his presence," Douin told Seth, and Seth hurried to do so, retreating toward a young Kieri attendant who had come back into the laulset with his clothes.

Dressing, he watched as Abel, Douin, and Pors went forward to receive Chappouib's blessing—even Abel, who supposedly could not benefit from the recitation of an aisautseb prayer. Afterward, the silver-eyed priest spoke in low tones to Pors and Douin, excluding Abel and punctuating his advice with vigorous nods and shakings of the head.

At last, quite audibly, he cried, "You are my hawks, the hawks of Aisaut, and I ask you to go forth with truth and courage.

"Aye, my hawks, go forth!"

"He had no hands," Seth said as Douin led Abel and him back down the steps of the palace toward the teeming square. Sunfall was imminent, and Gla Taunt —perversely, it still seemed to Seth—was dropping down the eastern sky like an egg yolk sliding through its white.

"A traditional aisautseb practice," Douin explained. "The holy one who keeps a place at Kieri court sacrifices his hands for the honor. He becomes the con-

science of the nation. His handlessness signifies that
he neither gives nor takes, for his domain is spiritual
rather than worldly."

"He gave me the dairauddes."

"A spiritual gift, Master Seth, itself to be passed on
to another."

"When did Chappouib lose his hands?" Abel asked.

"On the very day Lady Turshebsel decreed that she
was restoring the aisautseb advisorship abolished
thirty-seven years ago. Chappouib was chosen by his
fellows, and gladly relinquished his hands to the
sword."

"Barbaric," Abel said. "Barbaric superstition."

Douin halted at the entrance to the square, his dark
eyes flashing. "I agree," he said, in a tone suggesting
that a degree of doubt still plagued him. "It's the sort
of thing Lady Turshebsel fought successfully until the
arrival of Interstel, Ommundi, and your isosire."

This veiled accusation was as close to rudeness as
Clefrabbes Douin had ever come in his dealings with
the Latimer isohets, but Seth was strangely sympathetic to their host's point of view. Their presence
on the planet had been an irritant and a provocation,
and now they were preparing to go somewhere else, on
a mission for which Seth could summon little enthusiasm.

"Barbaric," Abel repeated.

Now Douin said nothing, and Seth, looking toward
their host's stately geffide, saw a marketplace filled
with bobbing tinfoil balloons. The dagger shaft on
which Latimer had died, the Kieri Obelisk, pierced
him to the heart even in the gathering twilight. As for
the dairauddes about his neck, it mocked him—Seth
was sure of it.

Chapter Three

The cabin's blackness was riven by a scream. Although Seth had been having a nightmare (a succession of blurred images underlain by an impalpable distress), the cry was not his.

"Dear God!" Abel was pleading. "Dear God, *don't let them put their hands on me!*" The plea soared into a bloodcurdling falsetto that seemed incisive enough to split the hull of their light-tripper and let the void spill in.

Seth pressed a button. Their cabin was filled with a soft, Earthlike twilight. His isohet, clad only in a pair of nylon sleep trousers, had scooted across his bunk so that his naked back met the bulkhead and pressed insistently against it. His pupils were fat, black suns.

"I'm here," Seth said, lowering himself onto the foot of Abel's bunk. "I'm here. We're aboard the *Dharmakaya,* five days out from Gla Taus on our way to the Anja system."

Abel's pupils collapsed spectacularly, drinking in the reality of the cabin. Seth reached out and gripped his isohet's ankle. He saw that Abel was finally focusing on him—but his flaccid torso ran with sweat, and his hair was plastered to his face as if he had just returned from a shower.

"Again?" Seth asked.

"They were preparing me for the obelisk," Abel responded. "A rope hung down from its highest grate, and the aisautseb were moving in, moving in to . . . to disrobe me."

"They didn't get you tonight, then?"

Abel fixed Seth with an outraged, uncomprehending stare. "He was our isosire, Seth, and I'm your *brother*. How do you remain immune to what happened to him, immune to my suffering of what he suffered?"

Seth removed his hand from his isohet's ankle.

"It happened to you, too!" Abel informed him for the umpteenth time. "You and I went up that tower with Günter Latimer, but the truth of that still escapes you. For you, Seth, it was an external rather than an inward occurrence. That's not the way it's supposed to be!"

"I'm supposed to have nightmares in living, bloody color?"

"Yes!"

"And wake up screaming?"

"Yes!"

"And go stumbling into the lavalet to heave up my panic and my compassion?" This was a hit, Seth knew, because now that Abel had recovered from the psychic pummeling of his nightmare, his body would begin to react. His face had already blanched, and his breathing was quickening again. Fresh diamonds of sweat were popping out on his already sweat-lacquered jowls and forehead.

Abel controlled his temper with difficulty. "My *self*-compassion, you're trying to imply, aren't you? Well, that's all right, that's fine. The word of Interstel is that we're all imperfect isohets of the same perfect progenitor."

"You don't even pretend to believe that, Abel."

"Compassion begins at home."

Seth winced at both the hypocrisy and the banality of this bromide. "That, perhaps, you believe."

"You don't *feel* anything!" Abel countered. But the trauma of the nightmare was belatedly catching up with him, and he swung his feet to the floor and headed for the lavalet, replete with the sanctity of his suffering and so close to being caught short that the argument was effectively over. Having no desire either to confront or comfort Abel on his return, Seth pulled on a pair of coveralls and let himself into the corridor outside their cabin.

The *Dharmakaya* was immense. Its living, sleeping, and study quarters occupied a pair of windowless nacelles positioned below and aft of the triangular conning module. Up there, the pilot—K/R Caranicas, an indentured Ommundi triune—was installed in cybernetic linkage with the astrogational and life-support capacities of the vessel. Caranicas, who possessed a single left cerebral hemisphere interwired with twin right cerebral hemispheres, had remained in cold sleep during the Latimers' entire stay on Gla Taus, the equivalent of nearly ten Earth-standard months, and so had known nothing of the murder of Seth and Abel's isosire or of the coopting of shipboard communication systems by the Kieri. Not until revived by Seth had the triune understood that its (the ship's) body had been violated by forcible entry and its voice commandeered by agents of Lady Turshebsel's *taussanaur*, or orbital guard. Now, seemingly indifferent to the master it (the triune) served, Caranicas was transporting five of the *Dharmakaya*'s captors—Clefrabbes Douin, Porchaddos Pors, two officers of the *taussanaur*, and a minion of Narthaimnar Chappouib—through subdimensional reality toward the world called Trope.

Caranicas was neither male nor female, neither isohet nor natural child, and Seth mentally referred to the triune as "it" because no other pronoun seemed to work. What gender did you consider a being whose body lacked sexual differentiation and whose fundamental *raison d'être* was conning five hundred tons of vanadium and vitricite through a nonexistent medium that Interstel wags had long ago dubbed The Sublime? Moreover, except through the computer in the conning module, Caranicas couldn't speak.

An inability to speak struck Seth as the perfect recommendation for a companion. After composing himself against the shock of being on his feet again, he set off through the corridor toward the step-shaft leading to the command unit. On the way he passed the ad-

jacent cabins which Douin and Pors were occupying,
and recollected that one of these jauddeb was probably already aloft. Their sleep cycles aboard the
Dharmakaya were unpredictable and seldom over-
lapping, and he hoped that if one of the Kieri had
chosen to visit their pilot, Douin would be the one.

Seth's argument with Abel still rankled inside him.
Isohets—just as the members of a contemporaneous
clone—were supposed to share a heightened em-
pathic sense, a bond of profound dimensionality. No
such bond existed between Abel and Seth. Although
Abel had raised him—except for Seth's first eight
years at the Ommundi Paedoschol in Lausanne—he
had never felt a genuine psychic communion with his
isohet. Gratitude for Abel's love Seth had often
known, and a deep affection, and a terrible fear that
without Abel he would never be able to achieve a
viable identity. But Abel and he had never shared
any of those telepathic insights, swift and accurate,
that isohets were supposed to experience. He could
read Abel's feelings only in the usual ways, by direct
observation and a merely human sensitivity to nuance
and mood; Abel's mind he couldn't read at all.

Never, Seth reflected angrily as he climbed, had he
ever known anyone so prone to vomiting as Abel.
Günter Latimer had never quelled his anxiety attacks
—if, indeed, he had ever had anxiety attacks—by
retching up his guts. And Seth himself got that shamefully sick only when he had eaten or drunk too much.
Most people, he had learned, were not so susceptible
to nausea and vomiting; and yet if anyone should
share Abel's unenviable combination of body chemis-
try and hypersensitive mind, why not he? He was a
duplicate of Abel, for Abel was a duplicate of Günter,
and Günter Latimer was the die from which they had
both been struck:

$$\text{If } A=G, \text{ and if } S=G, \text{ then } S=A.$$

In which case, of course, it was probably surprising
that their minds so seldom strained along the same

cable toward a common anxiety, and that Seth was not likewise a vomiting fool. Must he feel guilty for having escaped the harsh confessional of the lavalet?

"No," Seth said aloud, climbing through the step-shaft.

But speaking the denial aloud didn't alter the fact that his guilt was even now pursuing him through the corridors of the *Dharmakaya*. His guilt was Abel's revenge for his own unfeeling innocence.

Pors rather than Douin had preceded him to the conning module. It seemed to Seth that every card dealt him bore a black spot.

At the auxiliary astrogational console, he eased himself into a lounger next to the one occupied by Pors, then studied the Kieri's oddly concave profile. The man's nose, eyes, and mouth all seemed to be set inside a dish of bone—but, in spite of that somewhat apish facial arrangement, he was recognizably alert and cunning.

We are all imperfect isohets of the same perfect progenitor, Abel had said. A ludicrous declaration. Abel's belief in deity ascended little higher than had Günter Latimer. . . .

"Good morning, Master Seth," Pors said without taking his eyes from the astrogational display screen. He spoke in Vox, which all the Kieri but the aisautseb had agreed would be their official tongue for the duration of their mission.

"Is it morning?" Seth asked, amused.

"For me it is. Master Douin awakened me only a brief while ago."

Douin and Pors took turns babysitting the *Dharmakaya*'s pilot in order to ensure that Caranicas didn't craftily maneuver the vessel off true toward some reasonably obtainable Interstel world. Considering that the triune's programmed mission kept it course-correcting for the whole of any subdimensional voyage, this was an altogether unlikely possibility. An override required either Abel's own conspicuous feed-in or an apprehension of disaster on the part of the triune itself. A passenger would quickly notice any major alteration of course because of subfield resistance and the resultant shipboard discomfort: heat, oscillation, and noise. A wholesale shift from The Sublime to the more predictable ridiculousness of normal Space/Time would be even more wrenching. But the two Kieri took their self-assigned work seriously and monitored the astrogation consoles round the clock. Seth had taught Douin the basics of this monitoring, and Abel had taught Pors.

Both were already well versed in the operation of the ship's communication system: Shortly after the Latimers' arrival on Gla Taus, Günter had conducted a tour of the *Dharmakaya* for several high government officials and a contingent of Lady Turshebsel's taussanaur (literally, "world circlers"). One of the highpoints of this tour, at least for the Kieri, had been Latimer's demonstration of the sublimission radio/receiver, with which he had rather showily contacted Ommundi Station on Sabik II and an Interstel facility on a colony world circling Acamar. These brief exchanges with jauddebseb beings hundreds of lights away, along with the vivid sublimission images hovering like ghosts in the radio's receptor well, had immensely impressed one of the taussanaur—who had asked permission to put through a call to Trope, picking that world because of its relative proximity to Gla Taus.

Latimer had graciously instructed the jauddeb in the use of the unit, and even though the Tropiards were not full-fledged signatories of the Interstel Charter, the guard had easily raised a response from a tracking outpost in the Tropish hinterland called Chaelu Sro. Latimer had translated the guard's Kieri into Vox, and the Vox of the anonymous Tropiard back into Kieri; and then, in order not to lose face before the delighted taussanaur, Porchaddos Pors and Master Douin had each politely demanded a turn at the console, speaking Vox to impress the others with

their erudition. That this entire exchange had proceeded without any visual input from Trope had dulled
the excitement of the touring Kieri scarcely a whit.

In fact, the episode had seemed such a triumph of
public relations that Seth had inwardly approved his
isosire's spontaneous suggestion to Pors that a pair of
orbital guards remain aboard the *Dharmakaya* to
monitor the radio and study first-hand the electronic
and mechanical intricacies of a bonafide light-tripper.
Trust was the order of the day, and no one had then
suspected the possibility of an aisautseb uprising, the
seizure of the ship, or the need to negotiate with the
Tropiards an alternative to the doomed Ommundi
trade proposal. Who could have foreseen that the
taussanaur aboard at Latimer's personal invitation
would turn pirate because of the archaic belief system
of a priestly order that had exerted little real political
influence for almost four Gla Tausian decades?
Neither Abel nor Seth had advised Latimer of the
foolishness of his trust, and K/R Caranicas, who
might have had an idiosyncratic opinion in the matter,
had been deep in cold sleep. . . .

"How much longer must we share our subdimensional nonexistence with that . . . that creature who
pilots us?" Pors suddenly asked, nodding forward.

Seth glanced at the gyroscopically mounted chair
in which Caranicas, blinkered and belted, could move
either vertically or horizontally past the various astrogational computers and both in and out of the cystlike
conning turrets positioned about the nose of the module. The triune itself was scarcely visible in this chair.
Its arms and legs were wired, and at the back of its
head was the cranial prosthetic housing the additional
right lobe cloned from an embryonic extraction of
brain tissue before Caranicas's "birth." The housing
was pure platinum, and the appearance of this artificial
cap always put Seth in mind of an enormous silver
goiter that had rotated unaccountably around to the
nape. Caranicas was not pretty, not by any means,

and Seth could easily understand how Pors could call the triune a "creature."

"Can't you tell from the display on the console screen?" he asked the impatient noble.

"The figures beside the miniature vessel say"—Pors shut his eyes, working to deduce the Kieri equivalent of the Arabic numerals he had so painstakingly learned months ago—"twenty-three, I think. Twenty-three more days."

"If the texture and consistency of the subdimensional field we're generating doesn't change in the meanwhile. Then, yes, twenty-three days."

"Earth reckoning," Pors stipulated.

"That's nearly thirty of your own," Seth replied.

"If conditions in The Sublime don't alter and so delay us from our destination."

"They're just as likely to alter in our favor, Lord Pors. The Sublime is highly mutable. That's why a light-tripper must have a pilot who reads the subdimensional fields quickly and expertly, and who's able to compensate almost intuitively for the changes. Interstel and most of the trade companies develop their pilots from birth. In truth, the selection is prenatal, and one such as Caranicas is destined for no other occupation. This triune has spent almost sixty years in the service of Ommundi, although much of that has been in cold sleep."

"Of what . . . species . . . is your pilot?" Pors asked.

"Caranicas is human." The fact that in Vox the pronoun "it" had three forms—one for animals and plants, one for inanimate objects, and one for abstract concepts—momentarily stymied Seth. After sifting among his choices, he settled almost at sheer random upon the feminine pronoun. "Despite her appearance, she's human—of the basic stock from which Latimer, Abel, and I derived. The differences are genetic, surgical, and cybernetic.

"The platinum lobe on the back of her neck augments her ability to create a cognitive map of The Sublime. It gives her a heightened awareness of spatial relationships. She has good depth perception, good orientation in nonlinear environments. She's capable of rapidly synthesizing all this simultaneous intake for navigational purposes. The third lobe was cloned and developed especially for subdimensional flight, Lord Pors, and Caranicas uses it almost exclusively when she's jockeying back and forth among the conning turrets. The computers handle many of the analytical functions involved in piloting, but she feeds the information gleaned from her observations to the machines by way of the keyboard at her left hand. Her own right hemisphere—the one she was born with—processes a musical code through the keyboard in order to file the information."

"She?" Pors asked.

"Or he," Seth admitted. "Caranicas is without sex, although a chromosome study would probably reveal her original *in vitro* gender."

"She doesn't speak?"

"Only through the keyboard, to both her consoles and to us—when, that is, she has anything to say to us. We talk to her through the computer, which converts our speech to her musical code. It's an eerie, triple-layered twelve-tone system, if you amplify it, with some difficult phonetic correspondences."

The triune emerged from an overhead turret, whirled in its chair, and spun along its gyroscopic tightrope to a bank of equipment directly in front of the two men. In many ways, Seth suddenly realized, Caranicas seemed even more alien than the Kieri lord whose manner and appearance he had grown to dislike so. Pors was at least a personality, whereas their pilot seemed merely an inarticulate complex of tropisms and linkages that defied anthropomorphic cataloging. Did anything but spatial calculations and solid geometry happen inside Caranicas's head? Of what value was his/her/its humanity? Latimer had never said, and Seth had never inquired.

We are all imperfect isohets of the same perfect progenitor.

Pors looked at Seth with an expression full of loathing, whether for him or for Caranicas Seth wasn't sure. "I wouldn't be your triune for all the wealth of Ommundi," Pors said.

Seth attempted to change the subject. "Have you been in contact with Magistrate Vrai's people?"

"You've cut away her spirit," Pors persisted.

"No," said Seth. "This is all Caranicas has ever known. Her existence is piloting. Piloting is therefore her happiness." He was amazed to find himself on the defensive, particularly since it was the brutish and insensitive Pors who had put him there.

As Seth understood it, Pors, like the male children of all Kieri nobles, had been raised in a camp in the Orpla Mountains northwest of Sket and trained to a life of aggressive self-reliance. The products of this system were seldom well attuned to the feelings of others, although they did emerge competent and independent. You recognized a courtier on Gla Taus by his swagger and his latent hostility toward the lowborn rather than by his mastery of the social graces, which latter were largely the province of appointed officials like Clefrabbes Douin. But here was Pors expressing an angry sympathy for Caranicas and holding Seth responsible for the triune's denatured spiritual state.

"I want to talk to her," Pors declared.

"But what for? Talk is a small distraction from her piloting. She can handle it, of course, but it imposes a low-level strain she'd probably be better off without."

"Doesn't she eat, eliminate, sleep?"

"She slept while we were on Gla Taus. She feeds and eliminates through the hookups on her chair. It's also possible for her to rest by switching back and forth between her original right hemisphere and the cloned one. She shuts completely down, though, only in cold sleep."

"Does she pray?" Pors asked.

Seth's exasperation mounted. First, the argument with Abel; now, this inane discussion about Caranicas. "I don't imagine she has the time," he said, carefully concealing his impatience. "Nor would I imagine she's ever had the opportunity to think about it."

"Ask her."

"Ask Caranicas if she prays?"

Pors irritably gestured his assent, and Seth removed the microphone from the astrogation console, switched it on, and said, "K/R Caranicas, a visitor aboard the *Dharmakaya* wishes to know if you pray." Nothing more. He felt infinitely silly framing the statement.

Even before he had finished speaking, the computer had begun coding his words into the three-layered dodecaphonic language by which the triune communicated with its shipboard colleagues. The weird music of the translation ran through the pilot-house like a bevy of electronic mice.

"I may have to define that term for her," Seth told Pors, averting the microphone. "I hope you have a definition ready to hand."

But when the triune's chair whirled away from the equipment bank in front of them, threaded noseward, and dropped into an underslung turret at the module's apex, Seth began to fear that—in spite of the eerie music from the computer—his message had not coded through at all. He was about to repeat the message when a second series of indecipherable notes began toodling in cryptic response to the first. An instant later the translation sounded from a console speaker:

"My piloting is a prayer."

Seth felt vindicated. He had not expected this answer, but because it seemed to turn the tables on Pors, he inwardly congratulated the triune on its cleverness. If the life of the *Dharmakaya*'s pilot was a prayer, how could Caranicas be spiritually bereft? As for Pors, skeptically watching the triune scoot and spin along its gyroscopic tracks, he made no more demands on Seth to have it speak. Its first response had killed rather than piqued Pors's interest.

"Have you been in touch with Trope?" Seth asked him again.

"Master Douin informs me that the Tropiards prefer to wait until our arrival to begin full-blown discussion. They keep their radio contacts brief and send no visuals."

Seth had hoped to see a Tropiard by way of a sublimission image. Here on the *Dharmakaya* he had reviewed all the library tapes devoted to the Anja system and its one inhabited planet. The available information was scant and often self-contradictory. Interstel had never established a secure foothold on Trope, and because its level of technology rivaled or surpassed that of the most advanced members of Interstel, no one could pretend that coercing Trope's full partnership would lift that world out of the dark ages. Therefore, only an ambiguous partnership—if any— obtained. The result was ignorance about both the planet and its people. That the Tropiards had long ago adopted Vox for their dealings with Interstel ships and agents seemed highly promising of a comprehensive accord, but no one could guess when that accord might come. Seth realized that it would be a rather humbling irony if Porchaddos Pors, Point Marcher of Feln, proved instrumental in bringing Trope into full alliance with Interstel. Gla Taus, after all, was a somewhat backward newcomer to the partnership.

For now, though, the principal thing Seth knew about the Tropiards was that their eyes were hard and gemlike. The text accompanying a solitary photograph in the library tapes described their eyes as "an organic variety of crystal"; the photograph itself, meticulously enlarged, revealed a more or less human face studded with a pair of water-green jewels where its organs of sight should have been. Seth had a good deal of trouble crediting legitimacy of the photograph.

We are all imperfect isohets of the same perfect progenitor.

Maybe that was true, each humanoid species either a small or a grotesque distortion of some hidden Platonic Norm of Ideal Humanity. One theory held that aeons ago a common ancestor had seeded as many of the galaxy's inhabitable planets as it possibly could, before succumbing to extinction on its own dying world. Another hypothesis assumed, against countless subtly or grossly dissimilar planetary backdrops, parallel evolution. A third pointed to the instrumentality of God. The first theory, Seth knew, ran headlong into the unsupportive archaeological records of Earth and other Interstel worlds; the second was statistically unlikely; and the third seemed to ascribe to God a shabby paucity of imagination. You didn't win with any of them. Nor, apparently, were you supposed to.

"Where's the dairauddes Chappouib gave you?" Pors suddenly asked.

"In my cabin," Seth said, surprised.

"You should be wearing it."

"Even when I sleep?"

"It's your gift to the Magistrate, which once belonged to Lady Turshebsel. You should have it about you until you've actually presented it."

"A demon killer?"

Pors studied the display screen, feigning or perhaps actually experiencing a profound interest in the movement of the *Dharmakaya* through The Sublime.

"I didn't believe you a follower of the aisautseb," Seth challenged Pors. "I thought you a courtier and a progressive."

The Point Marcher turned on him angrily. "You should have it on your person," he said. "When awake, have it on your person!"

In the corridor outside his own cabin, Seth encountered the priest whom Chappouib, with Lady Turshebsel's grudging executive consent, had assigned to them for their voyage. This man was young but dutiful. He seemed to sleep only for brief periods. Now he was wearing garrison pantaloons rather than robes, and his head was uncovered. He was obviously on his way to the conning module, either to relieve Pors or to engage him in conversation. A true aisautseb, he spoke no Vox, and made no attempt to learn.

"Good morning," he said in Kieri. Regardless of the hour, this was his standard greeting.

"Our triune's piloting is a prayer," Seth told him in Vox.

"Sir?" the priest said.

Seth repeated his words, knowing them to be unintelligible to the aisautseb but taking a perverse delight in the fact.

The priest's expression darkened, and he brushed past Seth with cold dignity, lengthening his stride at every step. Seth suffered a pang of remorse for his pettiness, but couldn't bring himself to call politely after the jauddeb in Kieri.

Instead, he went in to Abel, who lay on his bunk again, somewhat recovered from his bout of nausea but still pasty-faced and glassy-eyed in the cabin's artificial twilight.

"You're a bastard to leave me in this shape, Seth. You're a bastard to escape my nightmares."

"Neither one of us quite qualifies as a bastard." Seth smiled to show his isohet that he was joking, but it didn't take.

Abel pulled himself to a sitting position to renew the attack: "They were going to hoist me up that tower! They were—!"

"If it'll make you feel any better, Abel, I was on the verge of a nightmare of my own when you woke me up."

"But you couldn't quite get tuned in, could you?"

Seth gestured at the cabin's door. "This nacelle has nineteen other cabins. Why don't I take another one?" He proposed this as means of making peace, not as a threat—but, again, his intended meaning failed to register.

"No," Abel said, frankly conciliatory. "I'd appreciate it if you stayed. Give me a moment, just a moment, and I'll be out of this again." He pointed to the foot of his bunk. "Sit down, please. Please sit down."

Seth lowered himself to Abel's bunk and stared across its linen into a face that was a bloated and admonitory likeness of his own. That—not Abel's nightmares—was what he couldn't escape. . . .

BOOK TWO

Chapter Four

Twenty-three days later, the hangar doors of the *Dharmakaya* parted like the lids of a great eye, revealing the green-gold mists of Trope's atmosphere. A transcraft floated free of the hangar bay, dropped languidly toward those mists, then turned to align itself with its programmed path of entry.

Seth Latimer was piloting. His passengers were Clefrabbes Douin and Porchaddos Pors, neither of whom said a word as he maneuvered the transcraft out of the cold shadow of the mother ship. Looking up, Seth saw the fanciful bulk of the *Dharmakaya* retreating against a backdrop of unfamiliar stars and wondered if he'd made a mistake allowing himself to be isolated in this way with the two Gla Tausians. His gut ached, and his hands—even within a pair of lightweight, vented gloves—were clammy with sweat. On the afternoon of his visit to the Winter Palace, Seth remembered distractedly, Abel had said, *"Monkeys are born. Polecats and ratlings descend through a uterus."* Now, falling away from his isohet's companionship and guidance, he felt that he was being expelled from the great Ommundi light-tripper with a pair of decidedly inhuman litter mates.

The transcraft plunged, its heat shields already incandescent.

As Seth monitored the controls and watched the horizon of Trope roll giddily upward, his nervousness abated. At least he was effecting his own delivery. After glancing at his grim Kieri passengers, he realized that for the moment their lives were in his hands, and that they were apprehensively aware of their dependence on him. By their looks, they'd found it far easier to trust K/R Caranicas, whatever the triune's spiritual state. But in his passengers' uncertainty Seth found a partial antidote for his own, and he determined to outface them and set them down uncracked.

Underlying the mists of Trope were wide, yellow-orange plains crimped with ridges of beige and umber: They looked as if they'd been applied to the planet with a palette knife. Greens and blue-greens were rare; the world had very few seas or inland waters, and its forests, judging from the evidence of an aerial overview, must consist predominantly of flame- or earth-colored foliage.

Seth banked the transcraft, and Anja, Trope's faintly blue sun, blinded him with a long stab of light. Abel had advised him to wear tinted goggles on the surface, but in the transcraft Seth let these collapsible plastic eye coverings hang unused inside his collar. Outside his collar, strung horizontally on a thin silver chain, was the ebony dairauddes that Narthaimnar Chappouib had given him, as a gift from Lady Turshebsel to the Magistrate of Trope. It swayed annoyingly whenever Seth moved. The sooner he was able to transfer it into the keeping of the Tropish administrator, the happier he'd be. . . .

Soon the transcraft had an escort. A pair of remotes swept up beside them on either flank, to accompany them into the southern hemisphere. They looked like delicate metal mosquitoes, spike-nosed and spindly-limbed, but their tensile strength was obviously every bit as staunch as the transcraft's, for they sailed with plucky, economical grace. Seth momentarily feared that the mosquitoes were near enough to provoke a collision, but an attempt to drop out of their embrace proved that they were locked in formation at calculated intervals impossible to close. No danger of either collision or escape. Meanwhile, deserts of yellow-red parchment fled by at dizzying speed, rising inexorably. From what he had seen of Trope so far Seth would have judged the planet an uninhabited desert. The pilotless mosquitoes seemed to be its only native life form.

A voice crackled over the transcraft's radio in precise and confident Vox: "Please permit our remotes to lead you in. Don't attempt to shake or outrun them."

"As you say," Seth responded.

Then, without closing the gap between their wings, the mosquitoes shot forward fifteen or twenty meters, and Seth followed in their wake, adjusting and readjusting to keep from falling farther behind.

A clockwork city flashed into view beneath them. It lay in the lee of a tablerock, or plateau, upon which was visible a complex pattern of strange, rust-colored edifices and bone-white walkways. The mosquitoes peeled away on either side, and both the clockwork city and the acropolis on the tablerock disappeared behind the transcraft before Seth could adjust to the fact of their existence. At almost three-quarters the speed of sound, the transcraft continued skimming southward.

"You've overflown Ardaja Huru, our capital, and Huru J'beij, the tablerock on which we have our administrative facilities," said the melodious Tropish voice over the radio. "Make a circuit and land atop the butte, please."

"Where, exactly, on the butte?" Seth asked.

"Do you require a landing strip?"

"No," Seth answered. "Our vehicle's capable of both hover and vertical descent."

"Then you may put down on the landing terrace in front of the J'beij—the great building running the western length of Huru J'beij."

The radio cut off, and Seth banked the transcraft into a stiff southerly wind to return to Ardaja Huru and its sheltering tablerock. Douin and Pors were rubbernecking like tourists—which, indeed, they were. For his own benefit as well as theirs, Seth slowed and swung wide, bringing them in so that they could get a leisurely panoramic vista of both the city and the government complex.

Ardaja Huru—as much mechanism as living entity—shone in the desert like the intricate, perfect bones of an extinct land leviathan. It was clockwork and skeletal at once, ordered but spare, so pruned of excess and ornament that the wind might have scoured it into this shape. The metals comprising its structures were the color of red-clay bricks. The pedestrian wheels clicking through its heart and the transport cars circumnavigating both its oval perimeter and its many interlocking circular courts might very well have been sophisticatedly wind-driven. The trees lining the city's thoroughfares and standing like sentinels on its terrace levels burned in the sun like torches. Ardaja Huru seemed to be alive principally by virtue of the movement of its parts rather than by that of its people, for its people were mostly invisible—indoors, below ground, somewhere out of sight.

More than this, Seth and the Kieri envoys had no time to deduce.

Huru J'beij, the butte behind the city, filled the transcraft's windscreens, and Seth was suddenly busy shifting into virtual hover and easing the vehicle across a magnificent expanse of blood-red rock toward the government buildings on the plateau. These had more substance than the structures of the city, as if they'd been hewn rather than delicately carved—but even they seemed outgrowths of the land. Unnatural outgrowths, like tumors or lepromata, but physical extensions of the planet, nonetheless. The landing terrace, which Seth now saw, was a circle of whitened stone in the midst of all this encompassing red.

Seth put the transcraft down within that circle, shot the turret back, and unstrapped in the stingingly cold air. A surprise, this coldness—even though, intellectually, he had known that Trope's desert uplands were chilly and that the atmospheric mix would sustain all three of them. Had he waited to throw the turret back, doubt might have intervened. He knew himself just well enough to understand that hesitation rather than conscience frequently made a coward of him. . . .

"A prayer for all of us," said Porchaddos Pors. "I thank God that this place is blessed with a proper coldness."

"And I, too," acknowledged Clefrabbes Douin.

They descended to the terrace and stood in the canting shadow of the J'beij, a monolith of rust-red stone and metal. Ten fluted columns fronted the great building, buttressing the long winglike awning of rock capping its portico. The J'beij was almost as large as the *Dharmakaya,* and behind their transcraft, for a distance of perhaps a kilometer, stretched flat table-rock lined with bone-white walkways, intermittent buildings, and an occasional structure resembling a gazebo of stone. Far to the east Seth thought he could see a flotilla of mosquitoes—remotes—glinting in the afternoon sun on the plateau's landing field.

A pair of Tropiards were standing in the portico of the J'beij. Tall figures in cloaks, they neither approached nor retreated.

Seth was disappointed to find that he could still tell nothing about their eyes, for their garments hooded them, putting half of each man's face in shadow. They might call their planet Trope and their humanoid species gosfi—an ugly, ugly word in Seth's estimation —but at this distance they were more aesthetically pleasing replicas of Earth-born humanity than either Douin or Pors. (This, Seth knew, was an ethnocentric bias, but he was powerless against it, at least after long incarceration in The Sublime with the Kieri.) The clay-colored cloaks the Tropiards wore seemed to betoken . . . Seth's imagination galloped off higgledy-piggledy, and his hands began to sweat again. Above, the sky flowed like thin blue lava.

One of the Tropiards beckoned to them, after which he and his companion turned and retreated toward a hidden doorway.

Wordlessly, exchanging uncertain glances, Seth and

the two Kieri envoys followed these monkish figures beneath the portico and between a series of tall metal stelae depicting what Seth supposed to be episodes from the heroic Tropish past.

There were seven of these stelae on each side of the aisleway, staggered rather than directly opposite one another—but they were not especially informative about the facial features of the gosfi because the figures in each panel almost invariably had their heads averted or their eyes shielded. One figure recurred from panel to panel, but in every case it was depicted without eyes. The engraver had simply—and purposely, no doubt—failed to include its organs of sight.

A door of buff stone and red-gold metal admitted the three offworlders into the vast interior of the J'beij.

White predominated here, accented on the walls and vitricite partitions with hanging tapestries. Seth took a deep breath. The ceiling was a good four stories from the floor, and the tapestries—whose designs resembled wiring diagrams, or the convolutions of a human brain, or maybe even the intricate layout of Ardaja Huru—hung at various heights all the way to the ceiling. Individual floors did not exist as such. Instead, arranged at different levels above the main floor were transparent scaffolds to which you could ascend by lifts or narrow, helical stairways. The Tropiards employed on these scaffolds seemed to hang dreamily in the air.

Despite the enormousness of the J'beij, and the number of platforms distributed like pieces of kaleidoscopic glass throughout its interior, its gosfi occupants were few. The cabinets and consoles on the various levels were probably self-sustaining types of equipment, for information storage or arcane telemetric tasks.

Light flooded the J'beij, emanating from everywhere at once. But when one of the Tropiards turned to urge Seth's party onward, letting his hood fall aside, it was still impossible to see what kind of eyes he had.

He was wearing a pair of slitted eye coverings. Tropiards elsewhere in the J'beij were similarly outfitted. Everyone appeared to be costumed and masked.

Grabbing Seth's arm, Pors spoke earnestly in his own tongue: "You represent not merely yourself, Master Seth, but Lady Turshebsel and the entire Kieri state. Have a care about your presentation or we'll all suffer. Don't speak until the Magistrate has spoken to you. Remember, too, that—"

Seth shook off Pors's hand and glared at him angrily.

"A reminder," Douin said placatingly. "Nothing more, Master Seth."

The three companions followed their guides deep to the center rear of the J'beij, where the Tropiards halted beneath a scaffold unlike all the others. Its floor was carpeted with a material of luxuriant plum. Where all the other platforms were open but for safety rails and discontinuous banks of silent equipment, this one had opaque, papery walls. Indeed, Seth realized, it formed the base of a genuine *room*.

One of their guides climbed a set of transparent steps and disappeared into the boxlike structure. The other guide, still hooded, faced about and stared at them appraisingly.

"Lord Pors and I have complete trust in you," Douin said. "For that reason, we don't intend to accompany you into the Magistrate's presence. We'll wait for you here or wherever else our hosts are kind enough to permit us to rest."

Seth swung about on Douin in perplexity and fear. No one had said anything to him about his confronting the Magistrate alone.

"Wait a moment! I don't want to usurp your own involvement. What will the Magistrate think if you and Lord Pors don't present your credentials?"

"Master Abel informed his people by radio that you—an Ommundi Company representative empowered by Lady Turshebsel to act as her agent—would be our sole intermediary in this matter."

"Why would Abel do such a thing?" Seth whispered urgently.

"He told the Tropish deputy magistrate that it's the custom of Ommundi Company negotiators to deal with government representatives on a one-to-one basis. With our blessing, Master Abel also said that Lord Pors and I were merely your onworld seconds."

"Neither of those things is true!"

"They are indeed true," Pors contradicted Seth. "Here on Trope—as little as I care to acknowledge it —you command as well as speak for us. This has been our intention from the beginning."

"You didn't tell me I was going to meet with the Magistrate alone!"

"What difference can that make?" Douin asked. "You knew you were to be our envoy, that you were to do the speaking."

"But not that I'd be abandoned on the Magistrate's doorstep!"

"Remember to give him the dairauddes," Lord Pors advised, ignoring Seth's accusation. "Begin with that."

"Yes," Douin interjected. "That may calm you down."

"If I command as well as speak for you," Seth reasoned desperately, "then I command you to accompany me to this audience."

"Your command authority doesn't extend so far as that," Pors countered. "Do well, Master Seth. I think they're ready for you."

At the top of the helical stairway the cloaked escort gestured to Seth, then disappeared into the room again.

"*What's this about?*" Seth demanded. "*What're you doing?*"

"You know your mission already," Douin replied, purposely misunderstanding his first question, ignoring the second. "You have our prayers."

"The dairauddes," Pors added. "Don't forget it."

When the Gla Tausians withdrew from Seth, he

went hesitantly forward because there seemed to be nothing else to do. Why had Abel isolated him with Lord Pors and Master Douin? And why, now that they'd all set foot on Trope, were the Kieri—both experienced administrators and envoys—isolating him still further by prodding him into this important meeting alone? Seth's heart thudded, his hands clenched and unclenched at his sides, and a sense of inadequacy climbed his constricted throat like an ill-digested meal. The taste of it was brackish and insipid at once.

At the base of the stairway stood the Tropiard who had not unhooded. As Seth passed him, he noticed the alien's impersonal stare—an impersonality heightened by the slitted goggles he wore—and his impossibly smooth, coffee-colored flesh. Also, he was tall, taller by a head than Seth, and he seemed as perfect and as unreal as a mannequin.

"The Magistrate expects you," the Tropiard said in Vox. His mouth—a thin, smile-shaped scar—scarcely parted to speak these words.

Neither acknowledging this greeting nor looking back to determine the whereabouts of his companions, Seth climbed to the Magistrate's chamber. At the top of the stairs he pivoted and entered the sanctuary of the highest official of the most advanced nation on all of Trope. Günter Latimer dead and Abel inaccessible in the *Dharmakaya,* Seth crossed the threshold and faced a being of prepossessing power and appearance. . . .

Chapter Five

On the wall behind the Magistrate of Trope, a white banner. In the banner's center, a large blue circle. Separating Seth and the Magistrate, a wine-colored table made of stone and featuring on its surface a number of inset panels. Sheets of bronze plastic, these panels rippled in the light like tiny lakes. A similar substance capped the elevated chamber, concealing it from the eyes of any in the J'beij who might be employed on still higher platforms.

Neither Seth nor the Magistrate spoke. As they stood facing each other, the alien by the doorway silently departed.

The Magistrate wore an immaculate white jumpsuit. About his neck was a silver chain from which hung a soft, brown amulet. Seeing it, Seth put his hand to the dairauddes he had brought with him from Gla Taus. The Magistrate duplicated this gesture, tenderly caressing the leather amulet; and, almost immediately, Seth felt that the man—a gosfi—was trying to put him at his ease, settle his nerves, establish a bond.

But like all the other Tropiards Seth had seen, the Magistrate wore a pair of slitted eye coverings which interposed a disconcerting barrier. They concealed and excluded, giving him the spooky aura of a thief or an executioner. Seth was forced to concentrate on the features he could clearly see: dark skin, smiling lips, a head with the softly polished look of worn stone. Also, considering the height of the Tropiards who had guided them in from the landing terrace, Seth was surprised to find that the Magistrate was not quite so tall as he. Although not a small man, neither was the Magistrate a primeval giant.

"I am Ulgraji Vrai," he said in perfect Vox.

Seth dropped to one knee before the Magistrate, as Latimer had taught him to do before an important head of state on a planet in the Menkent system, and obediently recited his brief genealogy.

"Isoget of Günter Latimer," the Magistrate repeated. "And younger isohet of a pair separated by fourteen E-years. Is that correct?"

"Yes, Magistrate."

"Please rise, Seth Latimer." Seth stood. "Now, please, would you explain for me the significance of such terms as 'isoget' and 'isosire'?"

Seth concisely explained them.

"Then you have but a single birth-parent, and that birth-parent in your case was perpetually *j'gosfi?*"

"I don't understand," Seth replied.

"*J'gosfi.* You would say male, I think. A more precise translation might be sapient male: *j'gosfi.*"

"Yes, then. My isosire—my birth-parent, as you would have it—was perpetually male. I would add that he was perpetually sapient, too. At least until he permitted the priests in Feln to—" Seth stopped.

"To what, Seth Latimer?"

"His death might have been prevented, I meant to say." Seth glanced nervously behind him, his thoughts turning to the Kieri ministers who had just deserted him.

"A difficulty, Kahl Latimer?"

"My—" He could scarcely get the word out. "My seconds await me below, Magistrate, and I fear—"

"You fear they're uncomfortable. Very well. I'm now dispatching the men who guided you here to see to their comfort. One of them speaks exemplary Vox. He'll show your seconds about Huru J'beii before escorting them to a private dormitory for visitors. You and I, meanwhile, are alone to conduct our business, Kahl Latimer."

Seth waited for Magistrate Vrai to call aloud, to

push buttons, to clap his hands, to do anything that would indicate he was "dispatching" a guide to Pors and Douin. But nothing like that happened.

—*Shall we get on with that business, then?*

The Magistrate was examining Seth with the expression of a praying mantis. He hadn't spoken aloud. His lips hadn't moved. Instead, the words that Seth had just "heard" had opened inside his brain like tiny fire roses.

"You registered my message?" the Magistrate said aloud.

Seth neither moved nor spoke. Something wonderful and terrifying had occurred.

"As the guardian of the Mwezahbe Legacy, Kahl Latimer, I'm a rational being. But even before you set foot in the J'beij, I'd had the irrational certainty that I would find you a creature after my own mind. Isn't that a presumptuous clairvoyance? After all, we're quite literally from two different worlds." Magistrate Vrai began rapidly snapping the long middle finger of his left hand against his palm, a reflexive mechanism that Seth supposed was the gosfi equivalent of human laughter. "And yet . . . and yet I believe I've just established the complete reliability of that clairvoyance, no matter how irrational it may strike you."

"What did you do?" Seth asked.

—*What did I do?*

There it was again, a kind of lovely violation. A windfall of microscopic seeds penetrating Seth's gray matter and instantly germinating. His own startled consciousness was briefly evicted in order to let this other burst through.

"Please," Seth said. "What are you doing to me?"

"Testing a hypothesis," the Magistrate said aloud. "You're an offworlder, but one descended from a solitary male birth-parent. We have this last in common, Kahl Latimer. In addition, despite your origins on another world, you're able to receive my . . . *cerebrations,* let's call them. That further testifies to the bond between us. Somehow I don't believe your Gla Tausian friends will experience a like receptiveness."

Seth wobbled in the knees. The air in his lungs was thin and metallic tasting. This unforeseen capacity of the Magistrate to plant messages in his brain frightened him. It implied other capabilities: insight, knowledge, power. Guilt welled in Seth. Why? What was reprehensible in being fearful in the presence of the unknown?

—*Being men of one mind, we shouldn't have to deprive the Kieri too long of your company.*

This was torture. Although it didn't in the least hurt, it bewildered and disoriented.

—*Being men of one mind, we should obtain agreement quickly.*

"You flatter me," Seth managed, his voice raw in the otherwise silent chamber: raw and intrusive.

Taking pity on him, the Magistrate told Seth aloud, "Kahl Latimer, it's exactly as I've said. I believe we have many things in common. Despite our physical differences, despite the differences in our backgrounds, I believe we're creatures of like motive. Don't you feel this, too?"

"No," Seth responded.

The Magistrate's long middle finger began to snap against his palm. "Am I too esoteric for you? Have I embarrassed you?"

"No. Neither."

"What, then? You're exceedingly nervous."

"I'm exceedingly nervous," Seth agreed.

"Why?"

"You were thinking with my mind. Can you see into it? Do you know my thoughts, the range of my fears?"

"No," said Magistrate Vrai. "I've spoken to you in a manner that you would call telepathic, yes—but I don't blithely pull information from your head, if that's your fear."

"Momentarily it was."

"Then put it aside. I've thought a little about a

telepathic community, Kahl Latimer, and my belief is that it would most likely create either a thoroughly paranoiac or a thoroughly homogeneous unit of individuals. Complete suspicion and hostility in the one instance, total harmony and concord in the other. I don't care much for either alternative."

There it was: Seth's excuse to broach something of his purpose in coming to Trope.

"But isn't it true," he began tentatively, "that you have a telepathic group of the second type here in the very nation you rule? A body of people in total concord?"

"You mean the Sh'gaidu, do you not?"

"Yes, Magistrate."

Magistrate Vrai lowered himself into a chair of a pale-gray, glassy substance, then swiveled about to face the banner hanging on his wall. "With regard to their state government, Kahl Latimer, the Sh'gaidu have adopted the first attitude, that of suspicion and hostility. Perhaps, in the past, we've given them cause." Face averted from Seth, he tilted his elegant head back. "You come immediately to the point."

"Not so soon as I might have, Magistrate." These words, once out, sounded like a rebuke, but Seth had intended them . . . innocently.

His thoughts flew back to Gla Taus. On the morning that he'd entered the laulset pool with Lady Turshebsel, Lord Pors had explained a little of the complicated case of Trope and its troublesome Sh'gaidu subculture. Later, aboard the *Dharmakaya*, Seth had tried to learn still more about the Sh'gaidu from both the Point Marcher and the various library tapes. The truth, however, was that information about Trope was scant, and information about the Sh'gaidu dissidents almost nonexistent.

Basically, the Sh'gaidu were an embarrassment to the state because their entire orientation as a people was shamanistic and mystical rather than rational and technophilic. For innumerable revolutions of Trope they had stymied their government's best efforts to bring them to heel, drawing upon formidable spiritual resources to resist state domination. As a consequence, small as the sect apparently was, its vitality was an affront to Tropish ideals and a dangerous beacon to young or disillusioned Tropiards who had failed to lay to heart the statutes of the Mwezahbe Legacy. This last was the rational code by which the Tropish state professed to operate and into whose rigorous teachings it scrupulously initiated its children. The Sh'gaidu, as Seth understood the matter, represented a basic and unacceptable challenge to this code. Moreover, the state feared the Sh'gaidu because in their insistence on the mystical unity of all gosfi they had developed full interencephalic communication among their own number: an exclusive sort of telepathy.

Magistrate Vrai swiveled about in his chair—it resembled a glass tulip, a truncated corona for a seat —and beckoned Seth toward him. "Here," he said, rising and moving away along the other edge of the table. "Please sit down. Ordinarily my own advisors stand, but you've traversed many lights and I want you to be comfortable."

Seth assumed the Magistrate's chair, easing himself down.

"I'll walk about, Kahl Latimer, as you outline your proposal."

Uncertain where to begin, Seth scrutinized his gloved hands. The proposal he intended to make was already known in part to the Magistrate because of earlier sublimission exchanges between Trope and various taussanaur officials aboard the *Dharmakaya*. How he acquitted himself in the voicing of this proposal, however, would determine whether the Magistrate accepted or rejected its terms. Prospects for success seemed good, else the Tropiards would never have permitted them to come. Little comforted by this fact, Seth decided to speak bluntly.

"We wish to remove the telepathic Sh'gaidu from your planet to Gla Taus in order to—"

"No, wait a moment!" The Magistrate, who had been strolling toward the banks of white communication consoles at the other end of the room, turned and let his hands play distractedly with his amulet. "The Sh'gaidu, Kahl Latimer, are no more telepathic than any of us here in the J'beij. What they have is . . . well, a shared intuitive ability. Because they follow the spurious *Path of Duagahvi Gaidu,* they're like so many interwired robots. They share one another's preprogrammed world view. That, not telepathy, is the secret of their community. Sometimes I think they're a group of spiritually leveled individuals."

This phrasing recalled to Seth the attitude of Lord Pors toward the pilot of their light-tripper. Caranicas, the Kieri had implied, was little more than a robot interwired with the astrogational components of its ship.

Seth shook off the incongruous recollection. "How many Sh'gaidu are there, Magistrate?"

"Perhaps a few more than three hundred."

So few! Seth was astonished to think that a tribe no bigger than that could so disastrously tie up the machinery of the state. Was it Pure Reason that had prohibited the Tropiards from annihilating the Sh'gaidu?

"I think I understand your surprise," the Magistrate told Seth. "In the past, the Sh'gaidu numbered considerably more, perhaps into the modest thousands, and the state instituted both vicious and subtle pogroms against them. I'm the first of five magistrates since Seitaba Mwezahbe to resist a policy of harassment against dissenters. In the case of the Sh'gaidu, who are fairly recent in our history, I've actively sought a more reasonable solution to the problem, often against the bellicose counsel of my administrative deputy and the leaders of Trope's Thirty-three Cities. It's my *duty,* Kahl Latimer, to find a humane solution."

The Magistrate turned and strolled away from Seth

again, trailing his fingers along the edge of the wine-colored table.

"We Tropiards—we gosfi, to be more accurate—are not a prolific species. We live long lives, bear few young, and evolve only by preserving individuals —even individuals who would thwart the evolutionary goals of the Mwezahbe Legacy and the Tropish state. Three hundred lives have real meaning here, Kahl Latimer. And now it's my understanding that you wish to take our exasperating three hundred Sh'gaidu back to Gla Taus with you. Why? How can this profit you?"

Seth picked up a thread he had dropped earlier. "The government of Kier is attempting to open up an uninhabited territory called the Ilvaudsettan, or the Obsidian Wastes, in the northern polar region of their world. The pioneers and technicians in this territory require supplies that Kier itself seems incapable of yielding. Outside of Feln and Sket, its two major cities, life is often at the subsistence level. This need has caused the Kieri government to look to Trope, Magistrate. Isn't it true that the Sh'gaidu economy is based on a self-contained agricultural system?"

"Quite true. They eat only what they grow."

"Well, then, Lady Turshebsel, Liege Mistress of Kier, wishes to deed to the Sh'gaidu—forever—a sizable quantity of land in a subtropical region along the southernmost margin of Kier. This area is called the Feht Evashsted. The land here, generously manured with volcanic ash, is very fertile. The volcanism, however, is a thing of the past and poses no present danger."

"Why does she wish to give the Sh'gaidu such desirable holdings? Why don't the Gla Tausians open up *this* area—rather than the inhospitable polar region where supplies are scarce?"

As Seth explained the Kieri susceptibility to heat and the fanatical aisautseb prejudice against colonizing any area south of the Feht Evashsted, Magistrate Vrai came back to his chair, pushed a console key, and summoned a bronze plastic panel in front of Seth out

of its inset well. This panel rose from the surface of
the table and opened like a book before the two men,
revealing what appeared to be an animated satellite
image of Gla Taus. The Magistrate pushed another key
and the planet grew larger in the dim bronze screen.
Then light illuminated the image from behind, and the
entire northern hemisphere was revealed, almost as if
in three dimensions.

After the Magistrate had frozen this image in place,
Seth pointed out the Feht Evashsted, the Obsidian
Wastes, and the waterways by which Ommundi ship-
ping could transport agricultural products from the
proposed Sh'gaidu commune to the pioneers working
their way northward from Old Ilvaudset.

"You see, Magistrate, Kieri priests forbid the development of the Evashsted Sea and its islands because they regard these places as hell on earth.
Only demons would wish to go there, and only the
most vile would make use of its products. My isosire
was murdered for proposing the development of the
area to Lady Turshebsel, a progressive ruler who re-
grets the opportunities being squandered because of
the backwardness and superstition of the aisautseb.
Opening the Feht Evashsted to the Sh'gaidu is only an
interim solution to a much larger problem, but the
aisautseb have grudgingly approved this plan because
they regard this coastal region as only an antechamber
to Hell rather than as Hell itself, and because no Kieri
will be required to go there. At present, only misfits
and exiles live in the Feht Evashsted."

The Magistrate was leaning over Seth's shoulder,
peering at the image of Gla Taus on the rippling
panel. "For which reason you believe the Sh'gaidu
will be at home there, too?"

"Oh, no, Magistrate; not because they're misfits.
Lord Pors tells me that the Sh'gaidu thrive in an en-
vironment similar to the Feht Evashsted's."

"The land they hold," said the Magistrate, standing
erect, "lies about a thousand kilometers northeast of
Ardaja Huru. At one time it was considered worthless,

though the protogosfi of Trope's prehistoric past may have found the basin hospitable. There's some evidence to support this conjecture. No matter. Seitaba Mwezahbe didn't approve the basin as a site for one of the Thirty-three Cities of the Tropish state, and the Sh'gaidu inherited it by default."

"The land's no longer considered worthless?"

"The Sh'gaidu made it otherwise. In doing so, they've earned the envy as well as the disapproval of many Tropiards."

Seth's nervousness had departed. The Magistrate's words had rekindled his enthusiasm: "Magistrate, all would benefit by the removal of the Sh'gaidu to Gla Taus. The Kieri find new allies in their assault on the Obsidian Wastes, Trope is disencumbered of an embarrassment, and the Sh'gaidu escape the persecution of their fellow Tropiards."

Magistrate Vrai—Seth noticed to his chagrin—winced at the word persecution, but didn't chastise him for using it.

"What of the Latimer isohets, Seth and Abel?" he asked instead. "How do they benefit?"

"We earn our passage home by succeeding in our mission to you. At present, you see, the *Dharmakaya* is effectively in Kieri hands."

"You gain nothing in the way of material wealth?" Seth was startled. "No, Magistrate."

—*You gain nothing in the way of material wealth?*

Again, the gentle, uncanny mind rape that made him feel warm and devastatingly petty at the same time.

"No," Seth replied again. "I get to go home. Nothing more than that, Magistrate—but it's everything."

The Magistrate absentmindedly played his console keyboard—whereupon the bronze panel in front of Seth closed like a book, collapsed upon itself, and settled back into the table's surface. Then Vrai walked to the opposite end of the room, his fine, dark hands clasped at his back.

"What material would you require, Kahl Latimer?

Assuming, of course, that the Sh'gaidu accept our offer."

Seth stood. *"Our* offer," the Magistrate had just said. That meant that he, the younger of Günter's two isohets, had singlehandedly carried the first phase of their mission to Trope to a successful conclusion! His nervousness returned. His gloves, he saw, were wringing wet.

"For the initial evacuation from their basin—" Seth stumbled, thinking through what Pors and Douin had repeatedly told him about their likely needs.

"They call it Palija Kadi," the Magistrate said, misinterpreting his hesitation. "It means the Great Wall. Nonetheless, Palija Kadi is what they also call the basin itself."

"For the evacuation of the basin," Seth said, virtually ignoring this, "we'll need trucks or vans and drivers to operate them. The *Dharmakaya* is large enough to transport all three hundred Sh'gaidu to Gla Taus. Once there, the Kieri government will provide them with everything they'll require to become self-sufficient in Feht Evashsted."

"Trucks. Drivers. That can be arranged. We also have sufficient shuttlecraft to convey the evacuees to your light-tripper."

"Good," said Seth, elated.

The Magistrate crossed his office's rich carpet of plum and paused at the head of the stairs. "Come. Let's see what arrangements have been made for your friends."

Together Seth and Magistrate Vrai descended into the vast cathedral of the J'beij, where the young isohet marveled again at the clear hanging scaffolds, the ornamental tapestries and banners, and the strange radionic cabinets and equipment banks manned by silent Tropiards.

Chapter Six

Somewhere amid the crisscrossing pathways of the government building, Magistrate Vrai introduced Seth to another Tropiard who spoke Vox. This person was attired in a jumpsuit the color of day-old cream and a pair of disconcertingly white goggles. He stood at least a quarter of a meter shorter than Seth, and although his body appeared a weak and breakable thing, his movements had the punishing rigor of an ineptly handled marionette. He bowed, nodded, and gestured as if too tautly strung.

"Seth Latimer, this is my administrative deputy, Ehte Emahpre."

A jerky, birdlike nod.

Seth noticed that Deputy Emahpre was wearing an amulet similar to the Magistrate's. A pouch of dark brown embellished by a small amber gem. Seeing another amulet, Seth was reminded that he had not yet given the Magistrate the dairauddes that Pors had repeatedly told him to present *at once*. This realization stung and befuddled. His answering nod to the Deputy was awkward, without follow-through, and his attention to the little man disintegrated into the fragments of his broken pledge to Pors. Still, this was not the right time to remove the ceramic weapon and hand it to his host. . . .

"Deputy Emahpre," the Magistrate was saying, "is the most incorruptible and self-confident of my advisors."

Even this failed to focus Seth's concentration. He wanted to be free of the moment, but hoped, too, that

Pors and Douin would not appear before he could hand over their bothersome little gift. Günter Latimer had understood the mechanisms of such trifling protocol. So, perhaps, did Abel. But for him the demand on his patience was a minor horror. Hadn't he accomplished the first phase of their mission without any such meaningless formality?

"The most annoying thing about our relationship," the Magistrate was saying, lightly snapping his fingers, "is that Deputy Emahpre's incorruptible thinking almost inevitably leads him to conclusions quite different from my own."

Emahpre politely demurred. "Not inevitably, Magistrate."

"But often. Quite often."

Although the Magistrate continued snapping his fingers banteringly, Seth slowly awoke to the fact that conflict as well as respect bound the two administrators. Wasn't it true that Abel often laughed as he seined a relationship of grudges? Apparently gosfi psychology permitted a similar tack among Tropiards. Seth was alert again. He wished to survive.

He listened as the Magistrate explained to Deputy Emahpre what had just occurred between Seth and him. He listened as the Magistrate declared his intention to accompany Seth and the two Kieri envoys to Palija Kadi to speak with Duagahvi Gaidu's Pledgechild about the proposed removal. And he listened as Emahpre, taken aback by this declaration, began expostulating with Vrai in their own tongue.

"For our visitor's sake," the Magistrate interrupted his deputy, "I would prefer that you speak in Vox."

The Deputy glanced at Seth, as if surprised to find him still there, and then obeyed the Magistrate: "You needn't go to Palija Kadi yourself," he said more composedly. "The decision of the Pledgechild may be secured through me or some other intermediary, Magistrate. The danger to you is such that—"

"I've decided to go, Deputy Emahpre."

"Why?" Emahpre inquired.

"It's my word that determines in which direction Trope moves, and the Sh'gaidu are Tropiards—even if they sometimes seem to disown us, and we them."

"Sometimes!" Emahpre exclaimed. "They've rejected both union with us and repatriation as enfranchised citizens."

"My responsibility requires that I go to them directly with this proposal, Deputy Emahpre. My *position* requires it."

Seth watched Emahpre strut away along a bank of consoles as if to regroup his wits. Even if he walked like a marionette, he was obviously far from being the Magistrate's puppet.

Jerking about and jabbing a finger at Vrai, he said, "Your word need not arrive in the Sh'gaidu basin in your own person in order to be implemented. If you're killed there—"

"I won't be killed."

"If you're killed there, Magistrate, you will have sacrificed yourself—the leader of Trope—not to state ends, but to private ones which I'm totally unable to fathom."

Seth asked, "Are the Sh'gaidu prone to violence, then?"

"Precisely the opposite," Vrai declared.

"Precisely what they're prone to is still a matter of conjecture," the Deputy rejoined. "Which is precisely why they remain under state surveillance."

The Magistrate approached his deputy with his hands spread, then halted an arm's length away and dropped them to his sides. "Alone among magistrates I've dealt humanely with this people. Why should they wish to kill me? I don't fear them, Deputy Emahpre, and I intend to go."

"Why?"

To Seth the question had the ring of insubordination. The Magistrate, he saw, reacted almost as if he had been slapped, turning his face and then walking a step or two aside.

Still, Vrai did not resort to Tropish: "I've come to

my position"—a strange, gravid pause—"honestly, Deputy Emahpre, and I intend to fulfill its responsibilities to their most exacting letter. Tomorrow morning I accompany our visitors to Palija Kadi. No more about this, please."

"Very well," said Ehte Emahpre crisply. "But it's *my* intention to go with you. Until the morning, then, Kahl Latimer."

He performed a bobbing bow and stuttered off into the open labyrinth of the J'beij.

Outside it was far colder than Seth had remembered. The sky was a dolorous purple behind the massive red-brown planes of the buildings, and a wind came careering along the plateau from the northwest. Seth saw that their transcraft was no longer on the landing terrace. His heart misgave him, and he gasped the Magistrate's sleeve.

"We'll go to Palija Kadi in a Tropish aircraft!" the Magistrate shouted in response to his unspoken query. "Yours has been towed away to clear the landing terrace for other vehicles!" He pointed to the east.

Among the silver-strutted remotes on a distant landing field Seth saw the *Dharmakaya*'s transcraft. It was too big for the playmates it was grouped with, even though it looked alien-seeming and tiny because of the distance.

Relieved, Seth shouted, "Where are we going?"

"Our dormitory for state visitors! Your seconds are already there!"

The dormitory on the eastern edge of Huru J'beij didn't much resemble the J'beij itself. It was faceted like a huge piece of garnet, with tall rectangular windows resembling the panels in the Magistrate's command table. Following his host, Seth entered a foyer glassed about like an aquarium. He turned around to find that the sky was not discolored by the dormitory's tinted windows. He could see out without hindrance, but no prying Tropiard could see in. Nor could the wind rattle the immense panes visoring the front of the dormitory.

Anja, Trope's mercurial sun, hovered above the J'beij. A deepening purple spread over everything as Anja descended beyond the acropolis.

"Here," Seth said, removing the dairauddes and handing it to Magistrate Vrai. "I've been remiss in failing to give this to you before now. Once it belonged to Lady Turshebsel. Her chief advisor among all the aisautseb, Narthaimnar Chappouib, placed it in my keeping on the day before we left Gla Taus as a gift to you and an emblem of our cooperation in the endeavor ahead." The phrasing was Pors's, but Douin had rehearsed Seth in its delivery a hundred times.

Magistrate Vrai accepted the dairauddes, then turned it in his hands as if it were a flute and he an inexperienced musician.

"Is it true, then," he asked, "that the administrative head of Kier is perpetually sh'gosfi and that her shamans are exclusively male?"

"The priests are men," Seth replied, puzzled. "And Lady Turshebsel is of course a woman. Is that what your question means?"

The Magistrate, without answering, hefted the dairauddes. He took a sighting through it as if it were an abbreviated telescope. He inserted his finger in the wider end. He tapped it in his palm. He blew, to no purpose, across the smaller end. He plugged the wider end with the tip of his thumb and again blew across the smaller opening, this time producing an ear-splitting whistle. He shook the dairauddes like an old-fashioned thermometer. He twirled it gently on its chain, as if it were a winding tool. He pointed it at Seth.

"What is it?" he finally asked.

"A dairauddes, Magistrate. That's what the Kieri call it. A literal translation is—" Seth caught his breath. The Kieri had played a vicious trick on him. Or, if not the Kieri, then Chappouib and all the aisautseb. For an entire E-month he'd been carrying about with him, almost unquestioningly, a specimen of instrument that—in bloody orchestration with others like it—had slain his isosire. Was he buying his trip home in the coin of Kieri mockery?

"Yes?" the Magistrate urged him.

"A literal translation is demon killer, Magistrate Vrai." He was too confused to weep, but the impetus was there somewhere, biding its time. "It's a *spiritual* weapon, they say."

The Magistrate handed it back to Seth. "I'm sorry, Kahl Latimer, but the statutes of the Mwezahbe Legacy don't permit me to accept such a gift. The Magistrate of Trope never goes armed."

"Not to carry, then, Magistrate. To keep as a memento among your other possessions. As I say, this is a spiritual weapon."

Seth looked despairingly across the tablerock at the J'beij. Trope's small, orchid-blue sun was balancing on the northern end of the building's long entablature. The sky around it seemed to be in a state of lush, organic rot. To return to Pors without having presented the dairauddes . . .

"But it's wounded you, this weapon, hasn't it?"

"Magistrate?" Seth asked.

"Never mind, Kahl Latimer. I can't accept it, not even as a memento to put in a museum case. Not only does the Legacy forbid me the possession of weapons, it likewise prohibits me from collecting or wearing the products of superstition or religious ritual." Vrai suddenly grasped the amulet hanging at his breast. "With one exception, that is, and by this we all acknowledge the ultimate mystery of origins."

Seth started to replace the dairauddes about his own neck.

The Magistrate's cool hand checked him. "No," he said. "Wear this in its place." Fumbling briefly at the chain, Vrai slipped the amulet over his head and placed it in Seth's free hand. Then, gesturing, he urged Seth to don it, which the young isohet did bemusedly.

—Being men of one mind, we may safely share what's most important.

Seth closed his eyes. He had registered the Magistrate's cerebration as a series of piquant, encephalic pin pricks—even though he knew full well that the brain has no nerve endings.

"Magistrate, what have you given me?"

"This ornament we call *dascra gosfi'mija*. It means treasure of the birth-parent. I wish you to wear mine. Perhaps its bestowal will atone in some small way for the insult your seconds are likely to perceive in my refusal of their Liege Mistress's spiritual weapon."

"I can't speak for their possible response, Magistrate."

"Of course you can't. In the meantime, wear this. I must have something from you in exchange—*not* the dairauddes—and you must agree to keep my gift with you at all times until your departure from Trope, when you must give it back into my keeping. Our exchange will betoken the bond between us during our mission to Palija Kadi. We are men of one mind."

Discomfited, Seth replied, "Magistrate, I don't know what you mean when you say that. I don't feel it as you seem to feel it, and I believe you should know my confusion. What we have in common, I think, is a desire to settle our own private concerns through the Sh'gaidu. That's all."

—I must have something in exchange, the Magistrate cerebrated sharply, as if Seth hadn't even spoken.

"But I—"

"This will do, I think." The Magistrate stepped forward and with quick fingers unclasped still another chain at Seth's neck. Was he retrieving the amulet he'd just given? . . . No, not that. Seth saw that clutched in Vrai's right hand were the collapsible eye coverings that Abel had told him to wear on Trope.

"But those are for the sun, Magistrate. I may require them tomorrow in the Sh'gaidu basin."

"If you do, we'll provide you with *anjajwedo*—slit-

goggles, you might say—like our own. Yours I must
have in exchange for the amulet." He put Seth's goggles around his neck.

The sky's orchid rot had quickened to a kind of
overarching bruise. Deeply melancholy, this hurt
stained the entire twilight landscape.

"I trust you utterly, Kahl Latimer. I'm sensitive to
emanations. I know you for a good man. Moreover,
we have at least one thing else in common besides the
Sh'gaidu."

Seth waited for clarification.

"We each wish to go home," the Magistrate cryptically obliged him. "We each wish to go home."

Chapter Seven

The first-floor "room" in which Douin and
Pors had been lodged was in reality an elevated platform with a pair of papery screens for walls. Another
side was open to a corridor, and the fourth and final
wall was glass: a prodigious dormitory window that
the Kieri envoys had opaqued by some subtle interior
fine tuning. Bronze in color, this window shimmered
against Trope's mournful twilight.

Entering, Seth saw three sleeping pallets sunk like
shallow graves into the carpeted platform. Pors and
Douin sat in tulip chairs near the window, hunched
over a small plastic gantry playing a Kieri counter
game called *naugced*. It was comforting to see that
they had retrieved their effects kits from the transcraft before coming to the dormitory; Seth's, too. He
pulled off his clammy gloves and tossed them toward
the only pallet not already littered with Kieri hair
clasps, pumice-soap bundles, and ministerial caps.

This would be the first night since his boyhood in the Lausanne Paedoschol that he had slept in a room with someone other than Günter Latimer or his own isohet. How strange that his bedfellows should be Gla Tausians, jauddeb, *aliens*. A scent as of bitter cinnamon pervaded the area, and Seth knew this to be an intimate Kieri scent. Although Pors was smoking *fehtes*, a rare Feht Evashsted "tobacco" said to have strange effects on jauddeb metabolism, the smell in the room derived less from the burning cigarette than from the simple presence of Pors and Douin themselves.

They had turned their corner of this Tropish dormitory into a Kieri geffide.

Seth tossed the dairauddes onto his pallet after his gloves, and Douin, who was awaiting Pors's next play, looked up.

"Master Seth!" he cried, rising.

Pors also looked up, and Seth was momentarily startled by the haggardness of the Point Marcher's expression. His face had an indrawn, cadaverous look that Seth couldn't attribute solely to fehtes and fatigue. But Pors returned his attention immediately to the naugced game, thus freeing Seth of the need to explain why the ebony demon killer was still in his possession.

He determined to speak first of his success: "Magistrate Vrai is going to accompany us tomorrow to the Sh'gaidu commune. He's going to intercede on our behalf with the Pledgechild—which, it seems, is the title of the Sh'gaidu leader."

"Excellent!" Douin exclaimed.

"I also met Vrai's administrative deputy, a Tropiard named Ehte Emahpre. He says that he's going, too."

"We also met Deputy Emahpre," Douin said. "He showed us a portion of the J'beij and a little of the tablerock. He has no very good opinion of the Sh'gaidu, I'm afraid."

"Ekthep ath agronomithz," Pors mumbled. "Which ith all we want them for." He finally ran a counter along one of the struts of the naugced gantry. Then he, too, rose.

Bewildered by Pors's appearance and unintelligibility, Seth confessed his only failure: "Magistrate Vrai wouldn't accept Lady Turshebsel's gift. He said that the Mwezahbe Legacy prohibits him from having either weapons or religious artifacts. The dairauddes is both."

"Where is it?" Pors demanded.

Seth gestured toward his pallet. Pors, in turn, gestured brusquely at Douin, who walked with calm dignity to the sunken bed, knelt beside it, and picked up the spurned Kieri offering. It was with great difficulty that Pors maintained *his* composure, however, and when he next spoke, expanding his barrel chest to keep the words from spilling too quickly out, Seth realized what had caused the unsettling change in his looks and diction.

"Thith ith an inthult to uth," he began. "Thith ith . . . Mathta Douin, fetch him afta my thurrogathz! I won't continnoo like thith!" And Pors turned abruptly on his heel and faced the great bronze window.

"There's a lavalet at the end of the corridor," Douin told Seth, still kneeling. "He wants you to bring him his surrogates."

"His dentures?"

Douin merely nodded, embarrassed for the young isohet and chagrined that his Point Marcher had chosen this way to chastise Seth for a foreordained failure. Seth was amused, sorrier for Douin's discomfort than for the supposedly degrading task Pors had just set him. Never had he imagined that the Kieri had perfected orbiting vehicles before stumbling upon the necessary prophylactic measures to preserve an individual's natural teeth. Maybe someone had knocked Pors's out for him. Considering the Point Marcher's disposition, that seemed highly likely. . . .

Seth left the sleeping area, walked down the corridor, and entered his first Tropish lavalet.

A transparent pedestal surmounted by a circular

ceramic basin dominated the room. Against one
wall was a wide marble shelf upon which stood three
wingbacked lavatory chairs, stone strategically uphol-
stered with a velvetlike fabric the same shade of
plum as the Magistrate's carpet. Chromium pedals
protruded from the base of each chair. . . . Did male
Tropiards stand or sit when they had to make water?
The chairs seemed ill designed for the upright,
face-on technique, nor were there any urinals or
canted troughs to accommodate such an approach. . . .
Whatever your business, you apparently had to sit.
Seth mounted the shelf and pushed a pedal with his
foot. A blast of air rather than water cycloned about
in the hopper, creating an echo as if from the fathom-
less catacombs beneath Huru J'beij. That was all.

Satisfied that the contraption would neither devour
nor emasculate him, Seth eventually sat and relieved
his bladder. Toilet training in the Lausanne Paedoschol all over again. He remembered that training only
because one of the male warders had delighted in
telling him what a troublesome case he had been.
The bastard . . .

Water rather than air flowed through the pedestal of
the wash basin. Seth used a half-melted bar of
pumice-soap to scrub his hands, then shook them over
the basin and wiped them lightly on his pantaloons
because he saw no towels or air-blowing devices on
the walls. Perhaps Tropiards dripped dry.

Lord Pors's "surrogates"—which Seth had seen
upon entering—were hanging by a thread of dental
floss from a circular tray above the basin. Out of the
Point Marcher's mouth, they were . . . well, australopithecine. *Obscenely* australopithecine. At least to
Seth's eye. The sort of thing that a fossil hunter—not
a modern dental technician—would cast. But this
was a homocentric prejudice that did him little credit.
Really, what most disturbed him (Seth tried to tell
himself) was having to tote the damn things back to
Pors on a thread. He would've been no happier if the
dentures had been designed for human use. But who,

then, would? The task was just as demeaning as Pors wished it to be, although, it seemed to Seth, the Kieri lord surely lost as much face by exposing himself without his dentures as he saved by wreaking this petty and absurd punishment.

Carrying the teeth, Seth returned to Pors and Douin. Their naugced game was forgotten. Pors impatiently took the surrogates from Seth, unwound the thread of floss, and positioned them firmly in his mouth. When he spoke, he was once again intelligible:

"There's no excuse for his refusing the dairauddes! If he wished to insult us, he might just as well have pissed on our boots!"

"He didn't wish to insult us," Seth replied. "And the insult you propose may not be possible for Tropiards."

This made no impression on the Point Marcher. He stalked along the window, halted, stared at Seth, ruefully shook his head.

"It's senseless to worry about this," Douin told him. "We want to take the Sh'gaidu back to Gla Taus with us. The ultimate disposition of a ceramic blowgun is a simple irrelevancy."

"Not to the aisautseb!"

"The aisautseb aren't here."

"No, Master Douin, but *we* are. And by Chappouib's command we're their agents on Trope, as Master Seth is principally Lady Turshebsel's."

Seth suddenly asked, "Have either of you seen any female Tropiards? Any . . . well, women?"

Chappouib's Hawks of Conscience looked at Seth in surprise. Neither Kieri appeared to regard this question as meaningful; and, briefly, Pors and Douin were united again—in their annoyance at Seth's interruption.

"The lavalet facilities would suggest—" Douin began.

"Yes, they would," said Seth. "But were either of you introduced to a Tropiard who responded to a feminine pronoun? We bring jauddeb and human prejudices to our understanding of the lavalet facilities."

"This is their government complex," Pors snapped. "Their ruling hierarchy is masculine, as it is in Kier —with the exception of our Liege Mistress, may God protect her."

Douin put in, "Why do you ask, Master Seth?"

"I'm not sure, really. The Magistrate seemed pleased that I am an isohet: the male child of a single male birth-parent. *J'gosfi,* male sapient, was the term he used." Seth glanced toward the corridor behind him. "In the lavalet, though, it occurred to me that— except for height differences—everyone in the J'beij resembled the Magistrate. Do female sapients exist on Trope? That lavalet's not much evidence either way."

"We've seen nothing of Ardaja Huru or any of the other Tropish cities," Pors said. "Of course there are female sapients."

"I don't know," Seth demurred.

"It makes no difference!" Pors cried. "We don't wish to . . . to poke with them. We wish to put them in the Feht Evashsted as farmers." He strode to the naugced gantry and found the butt of his forgotten cigarette on one of its struts. One quick inhalation set the fehtes tobacco glowing again and the smell of bitter cinnamon drifting lazily toward Seth.

"Another possibility," Seth said, "is that female sapients on Trope are forbidden the sight of foreigners and offworlders."

Pors looked at Douin. "This is useless speculation. Nights on Trope are short, and we'd best take our rest." He inhaled deeply, then expelled the pale blue smoke in a lacy, dissolving plume.

That was when Douin caught sight of the amulet hanging from Seth's neck. He approached to examine it.

"Every Tropiard wears one of these," he said, "much as devout Kieri wear their dairauddes. Where did you get this, Master Seth?"

"It was the Magistrate's."

"He gave it to you?"

"He insisted that I keep it until we've completed our mission to Palija Kadi, where the Sh'gaidu live."

"You should have refused to accept it," Pors said sourly.

"What is it?" Douin asked, still supporting it in his palm.

"A *dascra gosfi'mija,* or treasure of the birth-parent. He demanded that I give him my goggles in exchange."

"Was he dissatisfied with his own?" Pors asked, blowing out more smoke. "They all resemble jongleur-thieves, wearing those masklike goggles of theirs. Why would he want your pair?"

"In exchange," Seth said. "He had to have something in exchange."

"So long as it wasn't our dairauddes," Pors carped. But the amulet had begun to interest him, too, and he approached to grasp and heft it. "What *is* the birth-parent's treasure, Master Seth? The pouch feels as if it's laden with powder or fine sand. Do you know what it is?"

"No, Lord Pors. The Magistrate didn't say."

"Let's look, then."

Seth and Douin exchanged doubtful looks.

"Come, Master Seth. Remove it, please. It won't hurt to find out exactly what sort of treasure you're packing about for our host." Pors's garments reeked of fehtes—but his teeth were, or had been, clean.

"I'm afraid to do that," Seth said.

"Why?"

Seth told the Kieri about the Magistrate's ability to make messages flower in his mind. "I'm afraid he's also capable of reading my thoughts. He denied that he had this power, but if the Sh'gaidu possess it, as we've come to believe from the old Interstel reports, then why not Tropiards, too? What if . . . what if the Magistrate should *see* us opening his gift to me and ex-amining its contents?"

Now Pors and Douin exchanged a glance. Their expressions, although full of meaning, were unreadable to Seth. A new uneasiness gripped his heart. He was among strangers.

Pors stubbed his cigarette in the palm of his hand, indifferent to the burn. Fehtes was supposed to offer the Kieri a degree of metabolic immunity to intense heat, but Seth had not known it might make a smoker unmindful of burns. The Point Marcher, understanding that Palija Kadi would be much warmer than Huru J'beij, was smoking in preparation for their journey there. The inhaled drug had numbed not only his anxiety about this trip but also his sensitivity to pain.

"Let me see the amulet," he said. "If the Magistrate gave it to you, he's also given you its contents. At least for the time being."

Seth relinquished the *dascra gosfi'mija*. Pors carried it to the ledge of smooth white stone traversing the dormitory's window. Seth and Douin followed him. At the ledge Pors removed a tiny pin from the neck of the pouch and carefully laid the pin aside. Then he spread the lips of the amulet, shook it gently, and fanned a pattern of grayish-green dust across the ledge. Enough dust, thought Seth, to fill a pair of good-sized human thimbles. Little seemed extraordinary about the substance, whatever it was, but if Pors indulged a sudden whim and swept the stuff away merely to demonstrate his contempt of it, what would happen to them? Even a thoughtless puff of breath would irrevocably scatter the substance. Seth, frightened, refused to breathe—but Pors turned to Douin with an exasperated shake of the head and gestured at the powder.

"Tropish gold?" he asked. "A rare mineral? A religious hallucinogen?"

"The Tropiards have no religion but reason," Douin responded.

"Then what by the unholy Evashsteddan must it be?"

Averting his face, still half afraid to breathe, Seth

said, "It *may* have religious significance. The Magistrate said that by wearing the *dascra gosfi'mija* Tropiards acknowledge the ultimate mystery of origins."

"Dried semen?" Douin hazarded in complete seriousness. "Wouldn't that qualify as a birth-parent's treasure?"

Pors made a noise of amused disgust. "Gosfi semen? Why not a powder of well-pestled gosfi ova?" He made the noise again. "Master Douin, your imagination indicts you for a morbid dreamer."

"I was simply attempting—" the literary man began.

"We don't know what it is," Seth told the Kieri. "Nor do we have any way to analyze the substance. I'd feel much better if we returned it to the amulet. Suppose the Magistrate knows its quantity by weight. We may have all indicted ourselves not as dreamers but as losels and snoops. What footing do we gain by that?"

"None," Douin admitted immediately. "You're right. You've gained us what footing we have by earning the Magistrate's trust, and we've imperiled that trust by strewing this substance about as if it were ground pumice."

"I would hardly call it strewn," said Pors testily, gesturing at the ledge. He took two small pieces of paper from his jacket, swept the substance onto one piece with the other, and carefully funneled the powder back into the amulet, which he then closed, pinned shut, and handed to Seth. "Wear your precious treasure, then. If this attire brings the Sh'gaidu to Gla Taus, it little matters to me what sort of foulness you wear around your neck."

Seth donned the amulet again. He watched as Lord Pors retrieved the dairauddes from his, Seth's, pallet and then laid it reverently in the padded interior of a small leather case. Pors placed the case beside the pallet he had earlier claimed, and slumped back into his tulip chair.

"Do you wish to complete the naugced?" Douin asked him.

"Who leads in counters?"

"I do, my Lord."

"Then the naugced can go to Hell with Master Seth's isosire."

Seth, stung, glanced indignantly at the Kieri lord. But before he could act upon his anger, Douin stepped forward and intercepted him. The Point Marcher, meanwhile, appeared completely unaware of the effect of his words. His posture betrayed his weariness. His mouth had fallen open, and his australopithecine dentures glittered in a film of saliva.

Thith ith an inthult, Seth thought at him mockingly, desperately coveting the Magistrate's ability to cerebrate.

Douin said, "The nights here are indeed short, Master Seth. We'd better get what sleep we can."

How could anyone sleep in those gravelike indentations on the floor? For that matter, how could he sleep in the same room with Pors and Douin? The contemplation of both prospects chilled Seth.

"I'll be back shortly," he told Clefrabbes Douin. "I need a few minutes alone."

Douin knelt and lifted something from his pallet. Approaching Seth, he said, "Here, you must be hungry. Take this with you. I'll leave the lights dimly glowing for your return."

Seth took the gift. Like a pear encased in a rind the color of Anja at sunset, it was a specimen of Tropish fruit. Holding it, Seth abruptly exited the room, strolled through the echoing darkness toward the dormitory's foyer, and, once there, bit into the fruit. Warm and juicy, tasting a little like a Concord grape despite its size and texture, it appeased his hunger and somehow seemed to dissipate his wrath.

After he had finished the fruit and wiped his hands on his flanks, Seth studied the starscape. One of the stars was the *Dharmakaya.* Abel, his isohet, was inside it. Seth missed him.

Chapter Eight

In the morning he was the first to open his eyes. He caught sight of a cloaked Tropiard studying his companions and him from the doorway. This alien, having ascertained that Seth was awake, slipped into the ill-secured chamber and knelt at his side with several small squeeze flasks and a bundle of fruit. Pors and Douin awakened after the Tropiard had entered.

"Drink," he urged in Vox, his goggles indeed giving him the appearance of a thief. "You'll be departing for Palija Kadi in only a moment."

Seth obediently accepted one of the squeeze flasks and drank. The liquid oozed into him, viscous and bittersweet, thirst- as well as hunger-slaking in spite of its honeylike consistency. He was reminded of milk and tart pineapple, smoothly blent. Pors and Douin accepted the breakfast offerings of the kneeling Tropiard, too—undoubtedly one of the aliens who had met their transcraft yesterday afternoon—and their meal was quickly concluded. The Tropiard indicated that they should carry the fruit with them.

"What are they?" Seth asked.

"*Mwehanja,*" the messenger said, and it was impossible to miss his emphasis on the suffix.

They gathered their gear together and followed this tall, almost swashbuckling ghost out of the dormitory onto the tablerock. The shock of the cold air was as spirit-stiffening as it had been yesterday. How big and clean Trope seemed this morning, the sky like distilled water and the plains below the butte like an immense,

brick-red apron. Ardaja Huru was huddled against
the plateau's northern flank, invisible, and they walked
past the rough-hewn buildings and the strange stone
gazebos—which Seth supposed to be entrances to
tubeways down to the city—as if they were the only
living creatures on the planet.

In the circular terrace where they had landed the
transcraft there awaited them a Tropish vehicle surmounted by a set of saucerlike wings. It combined the
appearance of an ancient cargo airplane with that of a
modern helicraft, albeit one without rotors, and its
skin shone silver-white in the morning sun. Two small
figures stood near its nose, a bubblelike enclosure
tinted, yes, a gleaming bronze; and using the figures to
establish proportions, Seth judged the airship at least
fourteen meters in length. It scarcely looked capable
of flight. The Albatross, thought Seth. I'll call it The
Albatross.

Pors was smoking fehtes again. The smoke trailed
off behind him like an exhaust. He had spoken no
more than three words since awakening, and he
looked as fatigued as he had the night before.

Deputy Emahpre, who had met and talked with all
three offworlders, made the appropriate introductions.
Magistrate Vrai welcomed Pors and Douin to Trope
and made a brief set speech in which he declared his
world and Gla Taus "neighbors."

During these preliminaries Emahpre stared fixedly
at the amulet around Seth's neck. His gaze was per-
sistent and incomprehensible. Although the goggles
Tropiards wore made it hard to interpret their expressions, Seth feared that the little deputy's interest guar-
anteed his disapproval. You could read emanations
without being psychic. Both Emahpre and Vrai were
going to Palija Kadi, and neither was happy with the
other's decision.

All five men boarded The Albatross. Emahpre
went forward to take its helm, and a moment later
Huru J'beij and Ardaja Huru were dropping away beneath Seth as the airship rose vertically. He had pur-

posely come forward with the Deputy because the
pilot's compartment offered such a splendid window
on the landscape. He watched the portico and roof of
the J'beij dwindle in size, the prairie expand, and
blue-white streamers of sky creep into the peripheries
of his vision. The Albatross was aloft, and moving. Its
speed had increased to such an extent that the only
cure for dizziness was more altitude. Emahpre consid-
erately took them higher, and Seth turned his full attention to the feisty little Tropiard.

Without looking at his human passenger, Emahpre
said, "You're the only person since Vrai's assumption
of the magistracy with whom he's shared his *dascra*.
Did you know that?" Both the statement and the
query were accusations.

"No," Seth said. "I didn't."

"You came by it terribly easily. When I met you in
the J'beij yesterday afternoon, he hadn't yet given it to
you, had he?"

"No, he hadn't."

"Vrai has made an egregious blunder, Kahl
Latimer. An administrative, a cultural, and perhaps
even a spiritual blunder—even if my phrasing does
smack of Sh'gaidu superstition."

"Is it your place to second-guess the Magistrate? Or
to speak aloud to an offworlder the substance of such
second-guessing?"

The Deputy's chin jerked toward Seth, then swiveled back. "Yes, most definitely."

"And to voice your disagreements with him to others?"

Emahpre remained silent.

"I didn't ask him for the *dascra*," Seth said. "I told
him I didn't feel the same sense of union with him
that he seemed to feel with me."

"Indeed?" Emahpre's voice was frankly incredulous.

"I don't even know what this is," Seth protested,
covering the amulet with his palm. "I don't know what
I'm—"

"If you were a Tropiard," Emahpre said, overriding

him, "it would be a different matter. The bond would be mutual and absolute, whether you deserved the *dascra* or not. But you're a foreigner, an offworlder. It gives you an unjust advantage. You've become the manipulator of his peace of mind."

Seth said nothing.

The Deputy reiterated, "An unjust advantage."

"It's not one I wish to exploit. It's not one I asked for. —Deputy Emahpre, what exactly has the Magistrate given me?"

"The treasure of the birth-parent," the Deputy replied curtly.

"The Magistrate told me that. He didn't tell me what that treasure is, though. I have no idea."

"*Jinalma.*"

"Sir?"

"I said *jinalma,* Kahl Latimer." The Deputy's head bobbed once. "Looking at you and your friends, looking at the moist places through which you perceive the world, I don't know how well you're likely to understand."

"I don't yet know what you're talking about."

"Would you disrobe before a being of another sapient species and stand before that being naked?"

"I did so on Gla Taus, Deputy Emahpre. The Kieri priests believe that the naked do not lie. Therefore, I stood naked before the Liege Mistress of that land and spoke to her from the absolute truthfulness of my heart." Seth still recalled, however, that his outer garments had been stripped from him before he could prevent that indignity. . . .

"Naked before a"—the Voxian word arrived tardily —"*woman?*"

"Yes. It happened not altogether of my own free choice."

Seth could not understand how the conversation had moved in this direction. What was the Deputy trying to establish?

"This is a demeaning experience for you?" he asked.

"Only when it's compelled," Seth replied. "Any

compelled action is demeaning, I think. Uncompelled nakedness holds no shame. Although my jacket and my pantaloons were taken without my consent, it was I who removed the final garment, my breechclout. Momentarily, I must confess, I was very uncomfortable." By this addition Seth felt that he was redeeming the half truths that had already inadvertently slipped out. He waited.

Ehte Emahpre turned his face to Seth and with a single slashing gesture of the hand and arm removed his slit-goggles. His eyes coruscated. They were olivine crystals set in a head of mottled beige stone. Despite the startling beauty of Emahpre's eyes, Seth helplessly recalled Pors's false teeth. Like them, these eyes had an unreal quality. Moreover, he was sure that he should never have been granted this intimate glimpse of them. The solitary photograph he had found in the *Dharmakaya*'s tapes had not lied. Nor had it done justice to the reality.

"I am naked before you," Emahpre declared.

"But why? I didn't—"

"To explain to you the truth about the Magistrate's gift. Tell me what you behold."

"Eyes. Eyes like fire." Involuntarily he glanced away. Far below he saw a splintering of light from one of Trope's cities of the plains. Or maybe it was a jabbing afterimage thrown across his retinas by the Deputy's eyes. The planet, after all, was nothing but a barren, blood-brown stone.

"Our eyes are a living form of crystal, Kahl Latimer. The Magistrate's *dascra*—indeed, the *dascra* of any bereaved gosfi—contains the birth-parent's eyes. That's the treasure we speak of."

Seth looked disbelievingly from the amulet to Emahpre's face. Last night Lord Pors had emptied onto the ledge of their dormitory room not a dicelike pair of eyes but a mysterious grayish-green grit. . . .

"*Jinalma*," Emahpre repeated. "Each amulet contains *jinalma*, Kahl Latimer. That's our word for the dust into which a Tropiard's eyes disintegrate within three or four days after his death. It's this substance that goes into the *dascra,* not the crystalline eyes themselves."

"And by this you acknowledge the mystery of ultimate origins?"

"Not really, no. We observe, under compulsion, the only Old Custom not forbidden Tropiards by the statutes of the Mwezahbe Legacy. Through our *dascra* we preserve a dramatic tie to our irrational past. I hardly believe that such a prescribed ritual gives any of us a deeper understanding of 'ultimate origins.' Instead, we glorify the strides we've made away from those origins." Emahpre put his slit-goggles back on and snappishly averted his face.

"Why do you cover your eyes?"

"Why do you clothe your nakedness?"

"We don't, not always. When we do, it's for warmth and protection. Also, according to my isosire, since humans are bipedal creatures, we clothe ourselves to minimize the distractions of what would otherwise be a continuous genital display. Aren't those the reasons that gosfi go clothed?"

"Essentially," Emahpre admitted.

"But that doesn't explain why you cover your eyes."

"Before Seitaba Mwezahbe established the Tropish state, Kahl Latimer, our eyes were thought to contain our souls. A gosfi's soul is his own, as a man's thoughts are, or ought to be, his own."

Seth was still not satisfied. "And do the eyes of a gosfi also have evolutionary import as a sexual signal?"

A birdlike twitch of the head. "Very astute, Kahl Latimer. Yes, you're correct, they do."

But the deputy no longer appeared anxious to discuss the matter. He shifted in his chair, traced his finger along a line of weird digital readouts on the pilot's console, and, so suddenly that Seth's stomach capsized, dropped The Albatross to a lower altitude. Even in a rational society, it seemed, you could still discover moodiness among the put-upon guardians of the state.

How odd. The eyes of gosfi—like the tails of peacocks, the manes of lions, and maybe even the breasts of human females—had evolved in part as sexual signals. Simultaneously, however, they were organs of higher perception and repositories of the gosfi soul. In order to preserve civilization, Ehte Emahpre seemed to be implying, a Tropiard's eyes had to be able to see without themselves being seen. He had uncovered for Seth to apprise him of the full meaning of the Magistrate's gift, yes—but the sexual connotations of this act were nullified by Seth's belonging to a sapient species with other origins and other procreational signals. Still, the Deputy was not pleased by what he had done, or had been forced to do, and the atmosphere in the pilot's bubble grew as achingly chilly as it had been earlier that morning on the tablerock.

Keeping his own counsel, Seth saw that sharp-edged buttes and ridges had begun to push up out of the prairie to the far northeast. These gradually underwent severe metamorphoses, shaping themselves into hills. And behind these hills appeared hazy, nickle-red mountains, girdered and columned like no mountains he had seen before. They looked as if they had been carved from copper pyrite.

"And what did you give the Magistrate to complete the bond?" Emahpre suddenly asked. But he answered this question himself: "A pair of goggles, an Earthman's goggles. How appropriate."

"The Magistrate chose them himself," Seth said defensively.

Emahpre didn't look at him. "It won't be too much longer before we reach Palija Kadi. I'd like to have the pilot's bubble to myself until that time."

"Very well." Seth lifted himself from his chair and made his way into the cabin where Vrai and the two Kieri had been engaged in desultory conversation for the past hour. The cabin smelled of fehtes tobacco, and of close confinement, and of a strange, pervasive nervousness. . . .

The nation Trope, with its thirty-three camouflaged, clockwork cities, was not the only political entity on the planet Trope, but it dominated the entire southern hemisphere and lay a narrow ocean away from a vast continental mass partitioned by either local decree or various topographic barricades into countries. The people of the nation Trope had held themselves aloof from these feuding, primitive states for well over nine hundred years. They wanted no part of the northerners' warfare, no part of their resources, no part of their unregenerate superstition. Trope, the nation, had come to its present level of technological achievement with only the most minimal kind of help from its northern neighbors, whom they had long ago dubbed *Nuraju,* or the Mad Ones.

Now, despite the development of space travel and the discovery of other worlds with quasi-gosfid populations, the Tropiards held themselves aloof from Interstel and all its licensed trade companies. The habit of aloofness had become engrained. Further, who was to say that the agents and the constituency of Interstel did not represent an insidious, alien variety of the *Nuraju?* Technological achievement, the Tropiards reasoned, was not by itself proof against the viruses of barbarism and superstition.

Madness—*nuraj*—was almost a property of nature. To defeat it, one required not only full consciousness but the unflagging regulator of rationality. If such deliberate regulation seemed to counter or thwart the processes of nature, it did so *only* seemingly; otherwise, reason would never have been able to assert its preeminence in the first place. Indeed, once the evolution of consciousness had given the gosfi sufficient self-knowledge to recognize their emerging rationality, it was the natural *duty* of reason to establish its primacy.

Such was the philosophy of Seitaba Mwezahbe,

founder of the Tropish state. Although the Mwezahbe
Legacy did not demand the absolute annihilation of
nuraj—pointing out, reasonably enough, that various
forms of madness were profitable in their proper context—it did expressly discourage the cultivation of
trance states, superstition, religious fervor, passive ac-
ceptance, sexual excess, and violence. The wearing of
the *dascra gosfi'mija* looked back to pre-Mwezahbe
days, primarily as a means of providing a nominal continuity with the past, but it also defined the limits of
nuraj in the daily lives of obedient modern Tropiards.

That was why (Seth slowly gathered, talking with
Magistrate Vrai as Deputy Emahpre piloted The
Albatross) the Sh'gaidu were such an embarrassment
to the state. Born Tropiards, they flouted the statutes
of the Mwezahbe Legacy. Born Tropiards, they be-
haved no better than the *Nuraju* of that backward
northern continent where stupidity, strife, and superstition were endemic. They had no excuse. They shamed
their paisanos by their intransigence. They exploited
the tolerance of Ulgraji Vrai, whose inclination was
to recognize their gosfihood even in their flouting of
the Legacy. Given his head, the Magistrate confessed,
Deputy Emahpre would have solved the Sh'gaidu
question decades ago, by wiping them out of Palija
Kadi as unfeelingly as a soldier on bivouac might clean
his dinner bowl with a crust of bread.

Such a solution would have been easy for the state.
For centuries Trope, the nation, had possessed a well-
equipped land- and sea-going force whose primary
responsibilities were the surveillance of the many unpredictable continents to the north and the defense
of their own country against *Nuraju* invaders. Periodic
sea skirmishes with the crazier of the Mad Ones had
kept the enemy at bay until the advent of such sophis-
ticated Tropish weaponry that, today, the *Nuraju* seldom ventured more than a few kilometers from their
coasts. For them and for their rational adversaries
to the south, the world had been halved. What singleminded Tropiards had put asunder, the *Nuraju* had

neither the technological capacity nor the insane bravado to try to unite. Hemisphere against hemisphere, like a spongy rubber ball sliced nearly but not altogether through. In such a case, the appearance of wholeness is a cruel deception.

In the decades since the Tropiards' discovery of Interstel, however, the armies of the state—substantially diminished in numbers—had remained in readiness as a planetary defense force. Separated or not, all gosfi were siblings. The only way for Trope, the nation, to protect itself against incursions from beyond the Anja system was to assume the larger guardianship of Trope, the planet. But Interstel put out trade and cultural feelers rather than rude, acquisitive tentacles, thereby gradually mollifying the suspicion of the Tropiards, and the result was regular sublimission contact between Trope and various scattered representatives of Interstel. Trade and diplomatic alliances still hung fire, but Vox had been introduced to Tropiards in all Thirty-three Cities as an essential ingredient in their educations—for union with Interstel had seemed inevitable if not imminent. Meanwhile, several units of Trope's planetary defense force were assigned to perpetual bivouac around Palija Kadi, there to keep the Sh'gaidu—victims of a divine but dissident madness—under unrelenting watch and guard.

Then, by a quirk of far-reaching simultaneity, the Latimer isohets had found themselves stranded on Gla Taus just as the Kieri Liege Mistress was deciding to take a new tack with the aisautseb, and just as the Magistrate of Trope was actively looking for a humane solution to the disposition of the Sh'gaidu. The taussanaur aboard the *Dharmakaya* had arranged a parley with Magistrate Vrai on Trope; and Seth, conscripted against both his understanding and his will, had come seven sublime light-years and many hundreds of mundane kilometers to tie together the strands of this intricate and mystifying web. As The Albatross descended toward the upland basin of the dissidents, Seth silently prayed that he might somehow succeed.

For Abel's sake. For his own sake. And perhaps even for the sakes of the persecuted Sh'gaidu and the haunted Magistrate Vrai.

The interests of the Kieri, even though he admired Clefrabbes Douin and didn't really wish Porchaddos Pors any ill, no longer seemed particularly compelling to him. Gla Taus was a nightmare he wanted to forget. . . .

"Magistrate, tell me about Seitaba Mwezahbe," Seth said. He and the others had been silent for a time, lost in private reveries, and his words made everyone in the passenger section start into grudging alertness.

"Mwezahbe was our first magistrate," Vrai responded. "He founded Trope, lifted it out of the wallow of our prehistory."

"A mythological figure?"

"Indeed not. The first true Tropiard. A multiselved genius. His legacy to us was civilization itself."

Alone with the Magistrate and the two Gla Tausian Hawks of Conscience, Seth sat in a white swivel chair in the belly of The Albatross. He watched as Vrai hefted himself from his own chair and took a purple fruit from a rope basket hanging in the center of the airship's fuselage. Pors was directly opposite the Magistrate, and Douin occupied a fold-out bunk above Pors. Strange flowers hung in other baskets about The Albatross's interior, and light spilled in from a stipple-glass rectangle in the curved ceiling. Vrai, eating the *mwehanja,* returned to his place. Shifting dapples from the skylight played catch-as-catch-can on the bulkheads.

"How long ago was this?" Seth asked.

The Magistrate took a thoughtful bite of his fruit. After chewing for several minutes he said, "A little more than nine hundred years, Kahl Latimer, although I'd best explain that although Trope makes its revolution around Anja in about 453 days, our day is only three fourths as long as a standard E-day. This means that our year is not quite so long as a terrestrial year. Do you understand?"

Pors struck another cigarette into bittersweet flame, his third since Seth had retreated from the pilot's bubble.

Distracted, Seth replied, "I understand."

"Can't we wait until we reach Palija Kadi?" Pors asked. He blew a puff of smoke and nodded deferentially at the Magistrate. "I intend no rudeness, Magistrate Vrai. It's simply that Master Douin and I are used to having a few moments of undisturbed contemplation before undertaking an enterprise of this importance. Also, I'm beginning to feel the heat, even through the skins of our airship."

"Maybe if you—" Seth, who had been on the verge of advising the Point Marcher to stub out his cigarette, caught himself.

Vrai nodded politely at Pors, and the conversation, which seemed at least as vital to Seth as a few final moments of fehtes-blurred thought, was apparently dead. The Point Marcher had killed it.

—*We record modern history from the first year of Seitaba Mwezahbe's magistracy. This, then, is the year* 912.

Seth started again. To bypass the obstacle posed by Pors, the Magistrate had cerebrated this message. A windfall of microscopic seeds burying themselves in Seth's mind and instantly sprouting . . .

—*I'm the sixth magistrate of our planet, Kahl Latimer, for we live what you would probably consider gratifyingly long lives. We do so without the biochemical assistance and the genetic tampering which we believe you must use to enjoy even a fraction of our longevity.*

"But," Seth said, freshly dumbfounded, "but—"

Pors looked at him contemptuously, and even Douin, propped on an elbow in his bunk, seemed confused by the tardiness of this bit-off objection. They had "heard" nothing of the Magistrate's message.

—*Every Tropiard undergoes a series of evolutionary*

*developments within his own person. These are pre-
ceded by biochemically induced events which we call
auxiliary births. Their purpose is to offset our lack of
prolificity as a species by ensuring that each individual
effects in himself a process of 'natural selection' culmi-
nating in the emergence of his strongest and most viable personality. The ability to cerebrate seldom
appears until after the fourth or fifth auxiliary birth.*

"Except among the Sh'gaidu," Seth said aloud.

"Master Seth, you're talking to yourself," Clefrabbes
Douin informed him gently. "Has the heat reached
you, too?"

Flustered, Seth glanced apologetically at the Kieri
in whose geffide he had lived for over a Gla Tausian
year. "No, Master Douin, forgive me. A stray thought
that escaped before I could stop it. Nothing more."

Douin nodded dubiously and lay back. Pors was
smoking with his eyes closed, gauzy dragon wisps
curling from his nostrils and half-parted lips. And the
Magistrate was still gnawing contentedly at the purple-
skinned fruit he'd taken from the hanging basket. His
concentration on the fruit was heroic, superhuman.

*—The Sh'gaidu may indeed be exceptions to this
rule. I confess this to you mind to mind.*

This time Seth said nothing.

*—But you have just asked about Mwezahbe. He
was a genius without benefit of auxiliary births. He
midwifed the births of his own successive selves, in
fact, without resorting to biomechanics. And just as
Mwezahbe was many geniuses, each Tropiard is a series of progressively more enlightened consciousnesses
in the same body. Unlike Mwezahbe, however, we
must undergo the encephalic reorganization of the evo-
steps, or our auxiliary births, in order to approach perfect rationality. The goal itself, of course, is never
attained.*

Perfect rationality. The irrationality of this goal
seemed transparent to Seth. Did the Tropiards wish
to achieve godhood through these cryptomystical auxiliary births of theirs? Did they not see the contradic-

tion inherent in the desire? There sat Magistrate Vrai, licking his fingers of the last bits of pulp from his sunfruit and simultaneously transmitting verbal thought patterns to Seth; and, against the bizarre conjoining of these behaviors, he was telepathically prating of . . . dear God, perfect rationality.

—*Each individual possesses the capacity to become a multitude of individuals; the possible permutations of the mind are uncountable. In his lifetime a Tropiard may become as many as seven completely different people, concluding his evo-steps with a consciousness as far above his first as intellect is above instinct. Mwezahbe taught us how to prepare for and successfully pass through these biochemical auxiliary births. Having contributed what they could to the state, Kahl Latimer, our old selves die and fall away.*

Like snake skins, thought Seth.

The cerebrations continued: —*I've served as Magistrate of Trope for forty-three of our years. In my lifetime I've passed through five auxiliary births, each time working out my neonatal potential for the general good, as we all do. The* dascra *provides continuity not only with the distant past but from one life to the next.*

The Albatross was sinking, slowing. Seth could feel these changes in both his ear canals and his gut. A faint whine accompanied them, and the whine shimmied audibly through the hull of the airship. Pors's eyes were open again, and Douin swung his feet over the edge of the bunk, dropped to the floor beyond the Point Marcher, and took up a swivel chair. Seat harnesses were available, but Emahpre's piloting was so adroit they seemed unnecessary.

"May I ask the Magistrate a final question before we put down, Lord Pors?" Seth asked. "We're almost there, I think."

"Go ahead," Pors replied, stubbing his cigarette in his palm.

"How do Tropiards choose their magistrate?" Seth wanted to remark on how infrequently leadership in

Trope changed hands, but to have done so would have alerted the Kieri to the fact that he had recently acquired information new to them. How, they would wonder, had he come by it?

This time Magistrate Vrai started. He looked at Seth as if his cerebrations had been betrayed. They had not, not by any means, but even the mask of his goggles didn't conceal the fact that his dark face had flushed a deeper shade of brown.

"How do Tropiards choose their magistrate?" Vrai repeated aloud.

Seth nodded, puzzled by the hesitation.

"Each magistrate selects his own successor," the Magistrate said, striving for forthrightness. "Only his decision matters."

"Why?"

"Because as the head of a nation based on the statutes of the Mwezahbe Legacy he is the gosfi embodiment of reason."

"Other Tropiards have no say in the selection?"

Vrai swiveled his chair so that he and Seth might take each other's measure with locked eyes. He seemed to feel that a gauntlet had been dropped. The mahogany flush in his face had not gone away.

"If I put to referendum the question of whether the sun is hot or cold, and if the populace overwhelmingly responds that it is cold, does this vote alter the basic truth of the matter?"

Seth was appalled by this tactic, one that his isosire would have ridiculed instructively. The Magistrate was trying to throw dust in his eyes: a blast of pseudo-Socratic *jinalma*. It didn't even graze the issue.

"Magistrate—" Seth started to protest.

"Come forward if you wish to see Palija Kadi from the air!" Ehte Emahpre shouted from the pilot's compartment. "Come forward, friends!"

BOOK THREE

Chapter Nine

Ulgraji Vrai led Seth and the two Kieri envoys forward to see what they could of the Sh'gaidu holdings. Kaleidoscopic patterns of light ran through the pilot's bubble, inducing Seth to lift the lightweight hood of his tunic against the glare—the Magistrate had his goggles. Pors, without invitation, sat down next to Emahpre while the others hunched forward to peer at the tilting landscape.

"I'm going to make a circle over the entire area so that you can see the surrounding cliffs as well as the basin," Emahpre said.

The Albatross, shuddering gently, banked to the right.

The Magistrate pointed. "Those are the permanent encampments of our surveillance force—there, along the cliff edges."

Seth and the others looked down. Small, dome-shaped structures resembling toadstools sprouted from the rocks. A number of squat land vehicles were parked in a dusty semicircle beside one of the toadstools. Farther along the cliff face, more craftily concealed, Seth spotted a camouflaged panel truck with its front end pointing toward the basin.

"What's that?"

The Magistrate had also been staring at the van. Seth's question seemed to jolt him from a reverie. "A van," he answered vaguely. "A troop-controller van, nothing extraordinary . . ."

When The Albatross banked again, they saw the blindingly white figures of the soldiers themselves.

Their chromium helmets flashed like silver platters. Perched on rocks, sitting in open truckbeds, strolling among the domes, they were terribly conspicuous from the air. The Sh'gaidu, Seth thought, must also be aware of them. What must it be like to live—minute to minute, hour to hour, day to day—with such clumsy prying? The state lacked even the grace of subtlety.

"Do they know we're coming?" Seth asked.

"Last night," the Magistrate replied, "I communicated with Commander Swodi of the surveillance force. He sent a soldier to the crofthouse to inform the Pledgechild of our visit. According to Swodi, she agreed to receive us."

Seth noted the pronoun. He asked, "Could she have refused?"

"Be civil," Douin rebuked him. "Remember where you are."

But the Tropiards had apparently heard no sarcasm in Seth's question, and Emahpre said, "She would have received us without notification. Now, however, she knows something is in the offing. She will have spent her time since last night anticipating our motives and devising counterstrategems."

"Our motives aren't fungi, Deputy Emahpre," Vrai said. "They're not corrupt things that grow in the dark."

Emahpre addressed his passengers as if Vrai hadn't spoken: "I'm going to land on the roadway on the basin's northern end. Look for the crofthouse and the towers. The galleries are carved into the eastern cliff walls. You can also see the bridges linking the galleries to the basin's floor."

A road came out of the high rocks to the east and made a dusty, buckled ribbon through the formations grading into the lower, or northern, part of the Sh'gaidu holdings. Seth imagined that state vehicles would have no trouble getting down that road when it came time to evacuate the basin. Meanwhile, the bridges that Emahpre had mentioned were immense,

coral-colored structures of astonishing intricacy; they
made stairways from the eastern cliff face to the cultivated fields dominating the basin, and they crossed
or intertwined at various heights like möbius strips of
stone. The galleries in the eastern cliff face were
themselves intricately balustrated with rock resembling twisted coral. From the air, the panorama was
breathtaking.

Palija Kadi, the basin, raged with orchestrated
color. Cleanly divided and terraced, the fields lapped
almost to the tumbled rocks from which the walls of
the basin arose. The crops undulating in these fields
were mint green, cabbage red, Anja blue. They rippled under a wind whistling across them from the
north and coursing them with graceful shadows.

The Albatross banked again.

Almost directly below the airship Seth saw terraces
stepping upward in a wide semicircle to the huge wall
enclosing the basin on the south. Unlike the other
cliff faces, this wall was smooth rather than rugged,
bone white rather than coral red. Emahpre brought
The Albatross down a hundred meters or so and, after
sweeping along inside the great southern wall, piloted
them northward over the basin itself.

A tower jutted upward from each corner of Palija
Kadi. The one in the southeast corner, rising from a
field just below the southern terraces, pricked at The
Albatross like a spear. Made of saplings bound
together to form stilts, with a closed platform atop the
stilts, the tower swayed supply in the wind. A moment
later the forward motion of the airship eclipsed it
from view.

Hanging onto the back of Emahpre's metal chair,
Seth glimpsed in the middle of the basin a vast, circular clearing. In the center of this clearing, a circular
stone building thatched over with crimson reeds. Positioned at regular intervals about the building, lovely
blue-green trees that reminded Seth of the cypresses
in Lausanne. Descending crookedly to the building
from the eastern cliff face, a prodigious rock bridge

that extended so far into the basin as to halve its eastern hemisphere. When The Albatross flew over this bridge, the airship's bizarre shadow was thrown into one of the western fields bordering the circular clearing.

As they approached the roadway at the northern end of the basin, the stilt tower in the northeastern corner resolved itself out of the morning glare.

"What are the towers for?" Douin asked.

"Those are *kioba Najuma*," the Magistrate said. "The Holy One's lookouts. It's from these towers that the Sh'gaidu claim they'll see Duagahvi Gaidu returning from her odyssey through the continent of crazies to which she supposedly betook herself in search of converts. They believe she's still in the land of the *Nuraju*."

"But the towers don't clear the top of the basin," Douin pointed out.

"A matter of no concern to the Sh'gaidu," Emahpre said. "Nor is the fact that Gaidu herself disappeared nearly a century and three quarters ago, sixty-two years into the rule of Orisu Sfol, Magistrate Vrai's predecessor."

"Look!" cried Pors.

The Albatross was beginning to ease its ungainly bulk down toward the roadway, and clustered beneath the descending craft were small humanoid figures. Looking up, they nearly blinded the occupants of The Albatross with their gemlike eyes. Flashes of emerald, amber, and topaz detonated in their faces, each explosion pinwheeling brilliantly. Seth turned his head, but peripherally he could still see the small, naked figures running and dancing on the roadway.

Children. Sh'gaidu children.

They were the first children Seth had seen on Trope, the first gosfi to appear before him naked, and the first to come forth without eye coverings. No wonder the Deputy was outraged by these people: They had no shame.

As The Albatross settled lower and lower, the children prudently scattered. Then The Albatross was down. No one aboard had had to strap himself into a chair, and a side panel behind the pilot's bubble clicked back so suddenly that the heat of Palija Kadi roared in.

"We've indeed come to Hell," Pors whispered.

Nevertheless, he and the others exited. Anja hung low in the east, precarious above the galleries. The sky was a lavender parchment burning inward from its edges. The excitement of the naked children, the fever of their curiosity, trembled in the air. Resolute, the Magistrate gestured Seth, Douin, Pors, and Emahpre after him, then struck off through the gamboling children toward the Sh'gaidu crofthouse.

Seth found himself turning about to look at the ragtaggle group scrambling along with them. Several of the children seemed to be trying to make out his face inside the hood of his tunic. Their eyes had a genuine monarchial fire.

Despite their nakedness, however, it wasn't easy to determine the sex of these children. They more nearly resembled females, for between their legs they had no conspicuous rope of flesh to identify them as males. Still, the external genital configuration was slightly more complicated than the soft, split mound by which Seth had long ago learned to recognize the parts of a young human female. There was this, but something else as well. A kind of dark fleshy button at the top of the cleft, like the head of a tiny animal indecisively peeping out. . . . And none of the children, Seth noted with some wonder, had navels. It seemed highly possible, though, that the gosfi umbilical cord might attach to the unborn child somewhere in the perineal region. No one had yet claimed, in any case, that gosfi—whether Tropiards or Sh'gaidu—sprang entire from their birth-parent's foreheads. . . .

Was this what Ulgraji Vrai and Ehte Emahpre looked like under their jumpsuits? Seth refrained from asking. The lavalet equipment in the dormitory on the tablerock, however, suggested that their morphology might well be similar to that of the Sh'gaidu children. This speculation gave rise in Seth to the private hypothesis that Tropiards and Sh'gaidu alike were . . . well, androgynes. Hermaphrodites. Yet—in Vox, at least—the Magistrate and Deputy Emahpre had consistently employed masculine pronouns for the citizenry of the state and feminine pronouns for the dissident Sh'gaidu. Why?

Meanwhile, the children bobbed and darted along beside their party of clothed interlopers. Trailing his comrades, Seth watched Emahpre shake a jerky arm at the children, shoo them away, threaten to cuff those who got too close. Pors was similarly protective of his person, although less overt in his gestures of warning and reproach.

"Kwa tehdegu!" Emahpre shouted. *"Kwa tehdegu!"*

For the most part, the children were unimpressed. They made mocking moues and performed temper-provoking dances, jigging along beside the newcomers on the narrow path leading to the crofthouse. On both sides of this path grew shoulder-high grains with ribbed stalks and enormous red-gold leaves.

Seth turned about and caught sight of a young Sh'gaidu as tall as Deputy Emahpre. She—yes, *she*—did not commit herself to the mindless revelry of the younger children. She followed along about ten meters behind Seth, maintaining a predetermined distance and a measured pace. Her skin, although a deep brown in color, had the unblemished texture of fine writing paper. Her eyes were a luminous tiger-eye green, hard and faceted. Seth found it difficult to look away from her. Her gaze ensnared. Worse—rut-driven even on a world where humans had no niche or claim —Seth experienced an involuntary but torturous erotic stirring.

Idiot, he chastised himself. Miscegenetic goat.

But, helplessly, he kept glancing back at the young Sh'gaidu. Was there no cure for his libidinous feelings outside of their actual expression? The children romping about him had less substance than ghosts, for his whole attention, now, belonged to the creature pacing behind him, even if he found himself stumbling to keep his eyes on her. Ridiculous.

In Vox the term for coitus between individuals of distinct sapient races was *paragenation*. The prefix in this coinage meant "wrongly, incorrectly, unfavorably, harmfully." All the connotations were bad.

What if you played a mental trick on yourself and insisted on thinking of this striking person as male? Seth asked himself. Would that remove your horns? If the Tropiards employ our Voxian pronouns arbitrarily, and it looks as if they do, then there's nothing to prevent you from alternating among pronouns at whim. Think of her as him. The objective reality of the situation won't be violated, will it? *Will it?*

Seth glanced at the Sh'gaidu following their party. *He* maintained a predetermined distance and a measured pace. *His* skin was a deep luminous brown. *His* skin had the unblemished texture of fine writing paper. *His* eyes were tiger-eye green. . . . Looking at *him*, though, Seth found it almost impossible to think of *him* as anything but *her.*

Besides, Seth's sexual orientation didn't preclude contact with males. Abel, his own isohet, had been his lover for four or five years. And what disturbed Seth about the carnal aspect of his relationship with Abel was not its homosexuality but its narcissism. Or, more honestly, his suspicion that Abel had introduced him early to their unique variety of autoeroticism because Abel's self-love was so great that it had to have an object outside itself. Or, then again, perhaps Abel had merely been seeking to possess their common isosire in his, Seth's, person. Günter Latimer had always held himself aloof from their "love play," tolerating it as a natural outgrowth of their isolation and their propinquity.

Seth halted on the pathway. It was dizzying to think about both his own and his isohet's possible motives —but, yes, there had been times that he had felt used by Abel, and times that his disgust after servicing his own and Abel's passion had turned him unaccountably surly and fractious. Where did the anger come from, where the guilt? In the Ommundi Paedoschol he had dallied with boys and girls alike, with seldom a hindrance and never a rebuke, and that had been a happier, more innocent time. . . .

"*Kwa tehdegu!*" the Deputy was shouting. But the children delighted in discomfiting him and didn't retreat any farther than necessary. The Magistrate, on the other hand, paid them no heed, just strode calmly forward, halting when a child danced into his path and continuing when the way was clear again. Douin followed the Magistrate's example, but Pors, sweating greasily, mopped his brow with a linen kerchief which, each time his hand came away from his face, he shook in annoyance at the children. Seth was being left behind.

"I speak no Tropish," Seth told the young Sh'gaidu in Vox, amazed not only by the allure she held for him but also by his own foolishness in speaking to her. "I speak no Tropish but—"

"I speak Vox," she said. "My name is Lijadu."

Several meters still separated them, for she had halted when Seth had halted. Behind her, strange crops waved and heat shimmers danced on the ticking hull of The Albatross. Dumbfounded, Seth gaped.

"How do—" he began. "How do you happen to speak it?"

Farther up the pathway, Porchaddos Pors turned and hailed Seth impatiently: "Come on, envoy, let's get out of this sun! You delay us!"

"There'll be time to talk in the Sh'vaij," Lijadu said. "Our assembly place, I mean. What the Tropiards call our crofthouse."

"*Sh'vaij?*"

"Chapel of The Sisterhood—that's an approximation."

"Sh'gaidu, then, must mean The Sisterhood of Gaidu," Seth said.

"Unless you're a Tropiard who's uncompromisingly j'gosfi. In which case—almost *every* case outside Palija Kadi—it means something like The Bitches or The Harlots of Gaidu. Bitches is your word for . . . for a certain kind of female animal, isn't it? In any event, the terms in Vox are all approximations."

"Master Seth," Douin shouted, "please come on! The Pledgechild has arrived, and you're to speak with her on our behalf!"

Seth looked toward the crofthouse—the Sh'vaij—and saw that all the dancing children had disappeared, probably into the fields. Approaching the Magistrate's group from the circular building, tottering down the path, came the Pledgechild. Slightly behind her, a less ancient adult dutifully kept pace. Although both were partially concealed from Seth's view by the clot of intervening bodies, he easily discerned that unlike Lijadu and the children, these Sh'gaidu were clothed.

They wore colorful sarilike garments. The old woman carried a staff. Their feet were bare, and their eyes, brilliant in the sunlight, were naked. Had they been dressed in jumpsuits and slit-goggles, however, it would have been impossible to distinguish them by gender from Vrai and Emahpre. In fact, the aged Pledgechild appeared to be the tallest figure on the path. Pronouns, and sexual distinctions, and all that went with them, seemed hopelessly muddled here on Trope.

"I'd better get up there," Seth told Lijadu, as if the moment demanded a formal leavetaking.

"Go on," she said. Her voice was toneless.

When Seth arrived among the others, the Magistrate was making introductions. He and the Pledgechild knew each other by reputation, certainly, and his public relationship with the Sh'gaidu was respectful if not friendly. Both Emahpre and Pors looked put out, the Deputy because he despised what the Sh'gaidu stood for, the Kieri because he was suffering from the heat. Douin patiently endured.

"Welcome, Kahl Latimer," the Pledgechild said to

Seth in excellent Vox. "Let me apologize for the unruliness of the children." She smiled. "They're always very excited by airships."

Her eyes, Seth noted, were neither emerald nor amber nor topaz, but a deep black, like certain rare varities of fire opal. Her skull was a faintly brown egg, as if long hours under Anja had leached the melanin from her skin. Her sari seemed to be dyed or printed with frondlike patterns of crimsons and even darker reds. The person behind her was similarly attired, but her skin was browner and her amber eyes were shot through with an unsettling milkiness. Only she of the two wore an amulet.

"This is Huspre," the Pledgechild said, indicating the milky-eyed woman with the *dascra*. "She's my right hand."

Huspre nodded, and Seth returned the nod.

"Her sojourn outside Palija Kadi occurred many years ago, for which reason she has only a very limited command of Vox. Some of the young people taught me, you see, but Huspre is not quick with languages. I don't press her to learn. Here, in any case, there's little necessity—unless one must speak for the Sh'gaidu with outsiders who come on mysterious visits. I knew that might happen one day, and so it has." The Pledgechild's fingers were drumming on her staff: laughter. "Yes, I knew in my heart that one day we would be visited."

The Deputy nodded at Huspre. "She speaks the Ardaja dialect, doesn't she?"

"Yes, of course. But Huspre's not much talker even in our own tongue."

"Well, when she *does* talk," Emahpre said irritably, "either the Magistrate or I will be able to translate her words for our visitors. You needn't apologize for her lack of proficiency in Vox."

"Oh, I intended no apology," said the Pledgechild.

"May we go in?" the Magistrate asked, gesturing toward the Sh'vaij, which still lay a good eighty or ninety meters above them. He was clearly trying to head off

an unpleasantness between the Sh'gaidu leader and his
own chief lieutenant. Pors looked grateful for the tactic Vrai had chosen.

"Indeed, indeed," the old woman said. "I would
have waited for you there, but I feared the children
were proving troublesome. Airships excite them, as
do the disembarked passengers of airships." She made
a limp-wristed motion at the grain field to her right,
and Seth saw several children squatting among the
stalks, peering out with weird, mischievous faces. Two
or three retreated at the Pledgechild's feeble gesture,
but most held their ground. "Very fond of airships,"
she informed her visitors again, then turned and
limped unassisted toward the circular assembly building. Her staff, rather than Huspre, was her support.

Seth grabbed Douin's elbow and detained him.
"That girl back there," he said, nodding at Lijadu,
"speaks Vox."

Douin, obviously surprised, glanced at her. She had
not moved. Her eyes glittered intimidatingly. "You're
sure?"

"I spoke with her, Master Douin."

"She looks little more than a child."

"She told me that Sh'gaidu means The Sisterhood
of Gaidu. The dissidents—everyone in Palija Kadi—
are females. Girls and women, Master Douin."

"*Everyone?*" Douin was incredulous.

"So it seems. These are the female sapients Pors
was certain existed on this world. Moreover, the
Sh'gaidu are the only female sapients in Trope. Everyone else, every citizen of the Thirty-three Cities, is
j'gosfi, male."

Douin pointed into the waving red-gold foliage of
the monarchleaf. "But there are children here, several
children. How——?" He clipped this question off.
"They're hermaphroditic," he declared with sudden insight. "Each gosfi has the reproductive apparatus of
both the male and the female."

"The bodies of the children suggest as much."

"Ah," said Douin, taken aback by this discovery. "Ah."

"What will be the response of Lady Turshebsel and the aisautseb if we take back to Gla Taus three hundred Tropish women? How will they react to a tribe of female settlers in the Feht Evashsted?"

Douin covered his eyes and considered. "Master Seth?"

"Sir?"

"The answer, I think, is that the Tropiards—the gosfi—aren't properly either male or female. The Sh'gaidu *call* themselves female, but in truth they're no different anatomically from the civil servants in the J'beij or the soldiers of the surveillance force. And vice versa, of course. I'm speaking solely of their physical makeup." He uncovered his eyes and peeked familiarly at Seth. "Do you see?"

Seth looked at Lijadu, who still had not moved. She was regarding Douin and him with such intense concentration that he felt uneasy. Perhaps, if reports about the telepathic abilities of the Sh'gaidu were true, she was actively tapping their minds or at least psychically amplifying their whispered conversation. No matter. She was lovely. He was lovely. *Lijadu* was lovely.

"Their physical makeup is of no consequence," Seth snapped, surprising himself.

"That's what I've just said," Douin replied. "Since it's of no consequence, neither Lady Turshebsel nor the aisautseb can object to the fact that we have returned to Gla Taus with three hundred gosfi. *Gosfi,* Master Seth; not men or women, but *gosfi.* Diplomacy is the art of the possible."

"Their *psychology* is of the utmost importance, though."

"We'd best go on, Master Seth. The others are entering the building. This accomplishes nothing." Douin gently disengaged himself from Seth's restraining hand and made to follow the Magistrate's party.

Seth caught his elbow again. "My isosire used to say that we are what we pretend to be."

"Yes?" Douin waited.

"The Sh'gaidu pretend to be female, the Tropiards male. Therefore, each *is* what it pretends. We'll be taking the members of a single culturally and psychologically determined sex back to Gla Taus with us, and we'll be taking females, only females." Seth's heart misgave him. The entire mission suddenly struck him as a fiasco of grand proportions. Was this a misbegotten chivalry? Would he have objected to carting off three hundred self-proclaimed j'gosfi? Yes . . . no . . . he honestly didn't know.

"Master Seth, you're agonizing needlessly. On Trope the terms male and female are virtually meaningless as jauddeb and humans understand them. The problem is as much linguistic as sexual, don't you see?"

"I don't know."

"In any case, the Sh'gaidu won't be compelled to do anything they don't wish to do. If they don't want to settle in the Feht Evashsted, why, then, we'll simply go home without them."

"And Abel and I? And the *Dharmakaya?*"

"Ah, Master Seth, that I can't say. I speak neither for Aisaut Chappouib nor for our beloved Liege Mistress." This time he succeeded in breaking Seth's grip and in escorting the young isohet toward the Sh'vaij.

The breeze blowing through the basin was fresh if not cool, and on the intricate coral-colored bridge looming ahead of them Seth saw a gaggle of children watching their progress. When he glanced behind him, Lijadu was gone. He and Douin attained the clearing of the crofthouse, an apron of well-swept, brick-red rock. Whisk patterns were visible in the clearing's fine gravel, but Douin, determined to get him inside the Sh'vaij, gave Seth no time to examine them.

"Wait a moment, strangers!" a voice cried. The language was Vox, and the voice—Seth already knew it —was Lijadu's.

He and Douin turned. Lijadu emerged from the

right-hand field below the crofthouse and pointed
around the building's curve to where the circular clearing joined the great stone bridge to the cliffs. Seth and
Douin looked, but could not see what Lijadu was trying to indicate.

"Here she comes," Lijadu called. "Little Omwhol
wants you to see her flock. —Come, then, child."

A moment later a very young Sh'gaidu came around
the curve of the assembly building shooing eight or
nine hissing beasties in front of her. To Seth, they
resembled miniature dragons. They went on four legs
and distractedly waved double sets of feather-scaled
wings behind their small, beaked heads. Waddling
and flapping, they hurried across the apron of the
Sh'vaij and into the western fields. Omwhol, the child,
caught one of them and carried it to Seth.

As she was handing it to him, Lijadu stepped onto
the apron and spoke: "They don't bite. They're
gocodre. Take it. Omwhol was only recently given
charge of them. She's very pleased with herself."

Seth knelt and accepted the gocodre from the child.
Captured, it didn't struggle. Transferred into his hands,
it didn't try to fight free. Its skin was leathery, patterned copper and coral. What most disconcerted Seth
about the creature was its eyes: They were tiny chryso-
beryls. In the matter of physical optics, evolution on
Trope had stuck to a profitable tack and carried it
through to the level of creatures with intelligent self-
awareness.

The animal flopped in Seth's hands, altogether un-
expectedly. He caught it. Omwhol's little fingers were
snapping in amusement. Douin stepped back.

"See," Lijadu said. "This one is j'gocodre, male. It
had no choice in the matter. It hatched that way."

Seth released the beast, and it scampered away after
its broodmates. Omwhol skipped off, too, unperturbed
that her charges seemed to be getting beyond her tiny
sphere of influence.

"We had no choice in the matter, either," said Seth,
rising. "But we *weren't* hatched."

Lijadu regarded him peculiarly, he thought, for vouchsafing this information. Then she entered the cool immensity of the Sh'vaij.

"Come with me," she said from inside the doorway. "The Pledgechild and the others have preceded us to her cells. I'll take you there."

Chapter Ten

Even after he had thrown back his hood, it took a moment for Seth's eyes to adjust. Horizontal window slits ran about the interior of the Sh'vaij, just below its ceiling, but the building's thatched eaves blocked the passage of direct light. The place was dark and quiet. Gradually, however, both architectural and gosfi forms resolved themselves out of the dimness.

Directly opposite Seth, far across the nave, he saw an imposing, sloped wall. He recognized it immediately as a replica of the wall enclosing the basin on the south: bone white, slightly convex, smooth and blank. In the Sh'vaij this wall served as a sacramental backdrop for what appeared to be a low altar set with unlit candles and fronted by a reed mat. Someone—an anonymous Sh'gaidu—was lying supine on the mat, almost like an offering. Her stillness suggested death.

Carved wooden benches lined the walls of the assembly building. Upon these sat a number of adult Sh'gaidu, most of whom were clothed in colorful garments. They sat singly, apart from one another, either engaged in deep meditation (Seth decided) or else communing mind to mind. Their eyes were open—it seemed the gosfi had no eyelids, in any case—but the lack of fire in these organs bespoke a turning inward of the sense of vision: These people were scrutinizing their own souls. It then occurred to Seth that perhaps they were praying for the person who now lay before the replica of the basin's wall. . . . The Pledgechild, Magistrate Vrai, Deputy Emahpre, Lord Pors, and Huspre were nowhere to be seen.

Lijadu said, "The Pledgechild's rooms are behind Palija Dait, that wall you see there. You would say the Lesser Door. Palija Kadi, of course, means the Great Door."

"You regard that wall and your entire basin as *doors?*" Douin enquired.

The young Sh'gaidu found a blue-patterned garment on a bench to her left and fastened this serenely about her torso. "We regard them by the names they bear," she said. The pastel blue against her warm, brown flesh in no way diminished Seth's desire. He cursed his desire, and she said, "Come pay your respects to my birth-parent Ifragsli, who died four days ago."

She set off toward the wall. Douin and Seth fell in behind her, their boots scuffling obtrusively on the rock floor. At Palija Dait, Lijadu knelt beside the body of her birth-parent and leaned over it with a hypnotic swaying motion.

The corpse was redolent of a strange perfume, like the bouquet of certain brandies. It was draped with a white cloth to the neck, and its face was completely concealed by a death mask of caked red clay. Most startling to Seth was the fact that the Sh'gaidu, using a moist, emerald-green pigment, had daubed eyes on the death mask. Subtly iridescent even in the gloom, these eyes looked challengingly real. Lijadu stopped swaying, leaned forward, and kissed each painted eye in turn. Then, nimbly, she rose.

"Ifragsli's *dascra'nol* ceremony is this evening. Each of you from Huru J'beij is invited to attend."

"This was your birth-parent?" Douin asked.

"My mother, you would say," Lijadu told Douin.

"She scarcely appears an old woman," the Kieri noted. "What brought about her death?"

"Thirty-seven days ago she fell ill, and swooned, and lay for many days in a coma which we were only rarely able to penetrate. The Pledgechild and I stayed with her until her death. Afterward, we prepared her for her last passage through Palija Kadi. She has only this morning come down from the *kioba Najuma*—the tower—to the southeast of the Sh'vaij. Now her final vision is ripe, and her eyes about to crumble into dust. This evening's ceremony will reveal that vision."

"But the death itself?" Douin asked. "What caused it?"

"The Pledgechild, who is herself heirbarren, has told me that Ifragsli died of . . . anticipation."

"How does one die of anticipation?" Seth asked.

"I'm not sure," Lijadu said. "The Pledgechild says that self-aware creatures neither feed on time nor allow it to feed on them. We create time out of the vigor of our beings, she says, and were our spiritual vigor perfect, we would create time infinitely. Ifragsli was a woman of great character and vigor. Time flowed in her veins rather than blood, and it seemed her heart would sustain her forever. But thirty-seven days ago this changed. She grew anxious of the future and her anticipation of it poisoned the vigor by which she lived."

Seth felt for the *dascra* that Magistrate Vrai had given him. Although it was concealed inside his tunic, he could still put a hand on it. "Will Ifragsli's eyes now become your own?" he asked. "Will you wear her *dascra gosfi'mija?*"

"No, not I."

"But she was your birth-parent, wasn't she? Aren't you supposed to inherit her *jinalma?*"

"I have the Pledgechild's eyes."

This statement made no empirical sense to Seth. Lijadu's eyes were tiger green, pierced with spearlike yellow flaws, while the Pledgechild's eyes were an

opalescent black. Then Seth understood that Lijadu
had framed a kind of metaphor.

"I'm the Pledgechild's heir," she said, confirming
his reasoning. Her voice conveyed a quiet pride.

"But not the Pledgechild's offspring," Douin said.
"How does that happen?"

"Ifragsli offered my life to the Pledgechild because
she is heirbarren. The Pledgechild accepted me, and
now I'm her child."

"And what of your birth-parent's *jinalma?*" Seth
asked, pleased to be repeating this esoteric Tropish
term precisely because he knew Douin would not
understand it. "Who will receive the dust of Ifragsli's
eyes?"

"All of us," Lijadu said. "The *dascra'nol* will tell."

"All of you?"

"Because Ifragsli bequeathed me to the Pledgechild,
it's now as if my birth-parent were among the heirbarren while she lived. The *jinalma* of the heirbarren
—if they so will it—goes into the familistery urn, a
closed amphora which the Pledgechild keeps in her
rooms. Once a year the Sh'gaidu partake together of
the *jinalma* of those who lost their heirs or who died
without ever having given birth."

"How?" Seth asked. "How do you partake of this
jinalma?"

"Here in the Sh'vaij the familistery urn is carried to
each member of the sisterhood. As it passes, each
rememberer—is that the word you would use?—puts
her hand into the urn and touches a moist finger to the
sacred dust. Then she does this." Lijadu sucked the tip
of her finger, her eyes grown briefly cloudy. She was
back, alert, as soon as she had dropped her hand.

Cannibalistic communion, Seth thought. He looked
down at Ifragsli's corpse; the shroud and the death
mask made him shudder, and the embalming fragrance was beginning to burn his nose. The bedaubed
eyes haunted him. He realized that beneath the red
clay of the death mask Ifragsli had no eyes at all.
Either the Pledgechild or Lijadu had cut them out of

her head in preparation for this ceremony called the *dascra'nol*.

"Master Douin, Master Seth, we're waiting for you." Porchaddos Pors stood at the right end of the wall, having just emerged from a nichelike doorway there. He was neither smoking nor wiping sweat from his brow, and the surprising coolness of the Sh'vaij had restored his spirits. He sounded only modestly put out with them for their tardiness. "The Pledgechild would like to ask us about our mission, I believe, and you had best not keep her waiting any longer, Master Seth." Pors retreated into the tall, narrow passage.

"Go ahead, both of you, please," Lijadu said. "I'll follow in a moment." She knelt again beside her birth-parent's corpse. "Go on, Kahl Latimer."

Seth and Douin entered a tiny, wedge-shaped room lined from floor to ceiling with shelves. The shelves, in turn, were lined with countless clay urns, of all shapes and sizes, so that the room nearly overpowered them with a smell simultaneously clumsy and delicate—as of damp cement and wet tea leaves. Seth caught Douin's elbow again.

"She called me Kahl Latimer, Master Douin."

"Which, along with the Tropish honorific, happens to be your name."

"I never *told* her my name. And when the Magistrate introduced me to the Pledgechild, Lijadu wasn't close enough to hear."

"Lord Pors has just called you by name."

"He called me Master Seth. He didn't call me by my surname."

"Well, what do you think it means?"

"It means she either picked my name from my head or learned it by way of telepathic cerebrations from the Pledgechild."

Douin was cold-bloodedly matter-of-fact: "What do you think we should do about it, then?"

"I don't know," Seth admitted.

"Neither do I." Douin led him toward a door standing slightly ajar just ahead of them. "So let's just join the others."

The Pledgechild's audience room was cramped but well lit. A large, rectangular window looked out on the terraces rising to the base of Palija Kadi, the Great Wall. The Magistrate, Deputy Emahpre, and Pors were seated together on a wooden bench against the wall facing this window—looking very much like naughty schoolboys dragged in for disciplining. The Pledgechild faced her visitors in a backless wooden chair resembling an elevated footstool. She was to the right of the window, near a small amphora stand, and her hands toyed compulsively with an odd, carefully carved Y-shaped stick.

A scepter? A divining rod? A wand? It didn't appear to be any of these things, really, for at the end of each prong was a kind of circular clip bespeaking a practical if arcane purpose for the instrument. Seeing Douin and Seth enter, the Pledgechild gestured them to a second bench with her Y-shaped toy, and they obeyed as if she were Lady Turshebsel herself.

"I was telling your friends," the old woman began, aspirating her words, "that it's unfortunate your journey to the basin has coincided with the removal of a dead sister from one of the Holy One's lookouts. We're in the midst of preparations for her *dascra'nol* ceremony. We can conduct no talks involving the welfare of the community until we've seen tomorrow through this sister's eyes and laid her respectfully to earth."

Emahpre was outraged, and only as tactful as his indignation would permit him to be: "Commander Swodi sent a soldier to you last night to inform you of our coming. You might have conveyed this message to the soldier, who would have reported to Swodi, and so on to the Magistrate. It would have been easy for us to delay our visit to the basin for a day."

"Ah," said the old woman. She raised her Y-shaped scepter and looked through its circular clips at the Deputy, as if through a lorgnette. "But you would have been suspicious of my motives, I'm afraid. You would have wondered what I was plotting. Is it so bad you arrived early?"

"The Magistrate's time is valuable," Emahpre retorted.

The Pledgechild lowered her stick. "It may also be valuable for you to witness the *dascra'nol*. Gaidu once told me that there's no such thing as a coincidence. And last night I dreamed of her. Again."

Seth suddenly understood why the Pledgechild wore no *dascra:* She was the rightful heir of the departed messiah, but that messiah had disappeared without a trace nearly a century and three quarters ago. Therefore, the Pledgechild had had no way to recover the Holy One's eyes and commit their *jinalmā* to the obligatory amulet. Lijadu, of course, wore no amulet because her birth-parent had only recently died, and because Ifragsli had in any case bequeathed her to the heirbarren and still living Pledgechild. If you paid attention, it wasn't impossible to dope out the relationships among these people.

From nowhere Huspre appeared before Douin and Seth to give them each a bowl of water. A Sh'gaidu much younger than Huspre came through a door in the other side of the Pledgechild's reception cell and presented Magistrate Vrai, Lord Pors, and Deputy Emahpre with similar gifts. She had balanced all three glazed bowls so deftly that not a drop was spilled. Both Huspre and the newcomer wore *dascra*, Seth noted, but they had tucked the amulets inside their loose garments to keep from accidentally dipping them in the water bowls.

Emahpre was the last to be served by the newcomer. As she was backing away from him, the Deputy swore viciously in Tropish and thrust his bowl away from him so that it fell to the floor and shattered. Water splashed his boots, and shards skipped across the floor in every direction.

"*Gosfithuri!* he cried, looking to Vrai. "*Gosfithuri!*"

Pors and the Magistrate also stood, by necessity,

and Seth found himself on his feet with everyone else. Only the Pledgechild remained seated, apparently unperturbed by what seemed to Seth a wholly gratuitous outburst. The Deputy gestured at the woman who had just attempted to serve him and repeated a third and a fourth time the same urgent word. The young Sh'gaidu accused by this term merely stared at Emahpre, her dignity not only intact but radiant.

Meanwhile, the Pledgechild, Vrai, and Emahpre engaged in a discussion in their own tongue. While they were talking, Lijadu entered the cell through the door by which the young Sh'gaidu had also entered, and Seth's eyes went to her like smoke seeking an upward passage. Lijadu, Huspre, and the woman at the center of this mysterious brouhaha knelt together to pick up the pieces of the broken bowl.

Unmindful of his status as envoy and guest, Seth put down his own bowl and hurried to help them.

Emahpre's voice grew louder, almost abusive, and finally the Magistrate overrode him with such authority that, briefly, no one else seemed capable of speech. The only sound was the clicking of earthenware shards as Seth and the others dropped them into a bowl which Lijadu was holding. Seth kept his head down. They were almost finished cleaning up, but he wasn't yet ready to confront the enigma of the prevailing situation. Then the Deputy pivoted and strode past the Pledgechild, heading for the musty little pantry bordering her reception cell.

"*Emahpre!*" Magistrate Vrai barked. "*Emahpre, asul tehdegu!*"

But the Deputy didn't return, and they could all hear his boots ringing on the stones of the Sh'vaij as he departed.

The Pledgechild waved her Y-shaped dowel as if blessing the ensuing silence. "*J'gosfi nuraju,*" she said eloquently, and even Seth understood her: They had all just witnessed the departure of a crazy man.

"Please accept my apology for the behavior of

Deputy Emahpre," the Magistrate said, returning to Vox. He was trembling.

The Pledgechild graciously inclined her head—but Seth, rising from the floor with Lijadu and the others, saw that against the taut material stretched over the old woman's knobby knee her fingers were drumming helplessly. It made him want to laugh, too.

Half appalled by his own boldness, he asked, "What does *gosfithuri* mean?" He looked at the person who had suffered Emahpre's verbal abuse. She was as unruffled as the Pledgechild.

"Pregnant," Lijadu said. "It means pregnant. Before the turn of the year, Tantai will bear a child."

Seth looked again at Tantai. Her stomach was indeed swollen inside her simple garment. *Gosfithuri.* Heavy with life. Tantai and Huspre, after obtaining the Pledgechild's permission, exited the cell. Lijadu remained.

Still shaken by Emahpre's unexpected mutiny, Magistrate Vrai averted his face and strolled a few steps aside.

Seth asked him, "Did Deputy Emahpre leave because of Tantai's being . . . *gosfithuri?*"

"Master Seth, this is none of our affair," Lord Pors cautioned him.

But the Pledgechild said, "Oh, the Deputy was indeed offended. Good Tropiards regard the *gosfithuri* among them as either criminals or bearers of a contagious disease."

Vrai turned about. "Our visitors aren't interested in a sociological treatise, Pledgechild. They've come to you with a proposal of considerable importance."

"During the gestation of a child," the old woman continued, undeterred, still addressing Seth, "the body insists on a sh'gosfi orientation. Pregnancy is therefore either a willful crime or an unfortunately contracted disease. Although the state has been making babies in bottles for almost two centuries, Kahl Latimer, crimes or accidents still occasionally happen. The criminal, or the afflicted one, is sequestered away from her fellows until she is delivered of her child. Once delivered, he is rehabilitated, cured. The child is invariably j'gosfi, of course. In this way the keepers of the Mwezahbe Legacy perpetuate their code of reason."

"We have compassion for the *gosfithuri* among us!" Magistrate Vrai said. "We set them apart to protect them. We don't subject them to the indignity and danger of serving those who are well." Then, as if embarrassed by both his passion and his phraseology, he sat down and stared at the floor. Nearly inaudibly he emended his final words: "Of serving those, that is, who are not themselves vessels of new life."

"So, yes, Deputy Emahpre left because Tantai is pregnant," the Pledgechild reiterated for Seth's benefit. "On Trope reasonable persons are offended by pregnancy. It represents an alternative that has recently been denied them by law."

Magistrate Vrai protested self-assuredly, lifting his head: "I must tell you, Pledgechild, that I believe you summoned the Sh'gaidu called Tantai for the purpose of discomfiting us. Hoping to precipitate a scene that would humiliate us before our visitors, you had Tantai rather than Huspre serve my deputy and me."

"One doesn't always get what one hopes for."

"Then you admit your deceitfulness in this?"

The old woman gestured with her Y-shaped scepter. "Tantai and Huspre attend to me under ordinary circumstances, Magistrate, and simply because Tantai is *gosfithuri* is no reason to deny her the joy of that service. I admit only that I give you no special dispensation for your prejudices, particularly if I must do so at Tantai's expense. Judge my motives however you choose. I little care if Tantai's ripening beautifully with child has offended your snippety compatriot."

Seth could see that Pors and Douin were as uneasy as he was. The old woman had pushed the Magistrate into a corner. There seemed little way he could get out of it without demeaning himself in his own eyes or else sabotaging their mission with a sharp rebuttal.

Then Lijadu said, "The Deputy's anger will cool.

This evening he and our other visitors will attend Ifragsli's *dascra'nol*. In the morning there'll be time for proposals and discussions."

The Magistrate regarded Lijadu with steep surprise. Although she had spoken before in his presence, only now was he registering that she had an idiomatic command of Vox. She might just as well have demonstrated a talent for water-walking or flying.

"In the meantime," Lijadu continued, "I would ask the Pledgechild to entertain our guests with a recitation of her dream vision. This vision, Magistrate Vrai, which the Pledgechild often dreams, details a meeting between Seitaba Mwezahbe, First Magistrate of Trope, and Duagahvi Gaidu, the Holy One who led her outcast people to Palija Kadi."

The Magistrate looked from Lijadu to the Pledgechild. "The lives of Mwezahbe and Gaidu at no point coincided," he said.

"Viewed from the perspective of dream," the Pledgechild countered, "all lives are coincident, and not accidentally so, either."

"Please relate your vision, then," Lijadu pleaded. "You dreamed it again last night, didn't you?"

"I did," the old woman confessed.

The Magistrate said, "I must tell you, Pledgechild, that if your arbitrary vision establishes the First Magistrate as a straw man for Gaidu's convenient shredding, you will merely estrange us further. It will do you no good to tell it, and neither our visitors nor me any good to hear it. I won't have our time wasted. We came here with a proposal whose significance—"

"But we can't discuss that proposal yet," Lijadu interjected earnestly. "I've asked the Pledgechild to relate her vision, Magistrate, because I think it may *improve* your temper."

"Improve my temper?" Clearly, the Magistrate didn't like the implications of Lijadu's phrasing.

"Gaidu scarcely speaks, you see," Lijadu went on. "Mwezahbe carries the entire debate, if it's to be called that. In many ways, the dream vision offers every

Sh'gaidu a challenging test of her faith and every
Tropiard an articulate defense of the Legacy by which
he lives."

"Then why should the Pledgechild wish to recite it?"
Vrai asked. "Why abet the enemy and perplex the
faithful?"

"I'm bound by the *Path of Duagahvi Gaidu* to recite my dreams for the people," the old woman replied. "Their content doesn't matter. I receive and
report, and if the substance of my vision seems a threat
to our beliefs, I must speak that which threatens and
disturbs. This was my pledge to Gaidu before she
left us for the *Nuraju*."

Magistrate Vrai turned to Seth. "What do you
say, my bond-partner? If you don't wish to hear, we'll
join Deputy Emahpre in our airship until it's time for
the *dascra'nol*."

"I'd be pleased to hear the Pledgechild recite her
vision." Despite the old woman's intimidating gaze,
Seth knew that he'd answered not from queasiness
or fear but from a genuine curiosity about the workings of her mind and of the society of her sh'gosfi-by-
choice disciples.

Chapter Eleven

By some tacitly reached understanding Seth
was permitted to sit down beside the Magistrate, while
Pors and Douin settled themselves on another bench
with their water bowls. Huspre left the cell, and Lijadu
propped herself on the window ledge to the left of the
Pledgechild's amphora stand. The old woman laid her
scepter in her lap and cleared her throat.

The sound was startlingly masculine. No matter. Seth had already realized he couldn't distinguish the voices of Tropiards as "male" or "female." Each individual had a voice uniquely his or her own. To Seth's ear, for instance, Deputy Emahpre had the high-pitched but musical voice of a woman. Lijadu, on the other hand, spoke with a pleasing adolescent huskiness.

"I call my dream vision—or, rather, it demands to be called—'The Messiah Who Came Too Late,'" the Pledgechild said. "Last night was the third time I've dreamed it this year, and it's always the same."

And she began:

A light comes on inside my mind. I see Seitaba Mwezahbe and our Holy One together on a lofty glass scaffold in the building that Tropiards call the J'beij. The light in my mind goes out. When it comes back on, I see the messiah and the magistrate standing in each other's company atop the wall we know as Palija Kadi. For the remainder of my dream, these two places alternate so rapidly that only the figures of Mwezahbe and Gaidu themselves have any real outline. Time doesn't exist for them. Gaidu has not gone back to the era of the First Magistrate, nor has he come forward to the advent of the Holy One. Instead, they have met at a flickering intersection of their intellects and souls.

When Mwezahbe speaks, however, he attempts to define the moment in terms of measured and identifiable units. It's as if I'm dreaming a vision that Mwezahbe has dreamed before me.

"Welcome, Gaidu, to the year 223," he says. "This is the last year of my life, three and a half centuries before your own birth. It's only in this way that we'll ever be able to talk, for very shortly in your own lifetime you'll disappear from your people and suffer a violent death.

"Each of us has striven to alter and improve the lot of our followers, I as maker and lawgiver, you as apostate. Many of those who come after me will wish to kill you. One will undoubtedly succeed. Still, I don't wish to punish you for your apostasy by threatening you with a death that you won't believe in. What sort of punishment is that? Instead, your punishment must consist of a single, soul-destroying revelation.

"You see, my late-arriving adversary, your life hasn't been your own."

Gaidu does not respond. She stands before the First Magistrate in a state of silent receptiveness, attempting to read the multifaceted personality behind his concealing goggles. She herself is naked.

"You were a statistical probability," Mwezahbe continues. "All my life I've encountered resistance to my Legacy, minor insurrections that failed out of sheer, short-circuited *wrongness*. But I knew that one day a few would rebel because irremediably touched to the heart with an ancient sh'gosfi madness that we've labored, first, to mute and, finally, to forbid; they would elevate superstition over science, and mysticism over the probing empirical mind. The Tropish state being what it is, Gaidu, I knew that any future rebellion would evolve in the form of a movement more religious than political, and that a madwoman would become for the apostates a new focal point of authority. I've known all along that you would come, and that your advent would cast you in the role of a savior."

But our savior answers Seitabe Mwezahbe nothing.

"The domination of the sh'gosfi—as a people rather than as an essential aberration of the light—will be cramped and short-lived," the First Magistrate declares. "It has no future. It evolved in the first place only out of a failure of full self-awareness, and its purpose was to provide the necessary contrast by which we could come to recognize and pursue the path of an aggressive, thoroughgoing rationality. I'm the embodiment of that recognition and that pursuit. It was for me to codify the way to both, and I did so, much to your hapless disadvantage, long before you arrived on the scene to challenge my success.

"Holy One, the simplest and most decisive truth about your advent is that it will be inopportune. You will have come too late to undo the good that my reign inaugurates and gives enduring passage."

Gaidu's eyes bejewel the darkness of my dream, but still she keeps her peace, letting Mwezahbe accuse and chastise.

"Gosfi of reason—*j'gosfi,* by very definition—function beyond the limits of worship, Holy One. They cry out for ideas to respect, for rulers who will capture not only their imaginations but their intellects. Therefore, they have subordinated themselves to my Legacy, which has freed them from the irrational fears and the animal longings of their baser selves. In being bound to reason, Gaidu, there is no slavery and no despair.

"But the beginnings of your ministry, over four centuries hence, will dazzle and enslave only those who have failed to assimilate the statues of the Legacy. From the state you'll siphon off only those still backward enough to demand a focus of veneration rather than a fount of inspiration. You will have gained the souls of harlots, perverts, and madwomen, the very ones too feeble to abide by the truths that commit their souls into their own keeping. These are the ones who will be looking for a Great Mother to save them from themselves, the sh'gocodre of legend who hides her crippled broodlings under the monumental tents of her double wings. For your own purposes, then, you will have come too late. Can't you recognize your failure, Gaidu?"

Although the eyes of the Holy One gleam, she doesn't speak.

"As one who would provide an alternative authority by ensnaring gosfi souls, you've timed things badly.

"Perhaps, however, you could argue that you will perform miracles to bring about your Sh'gaidu Millennium. But we have created a society in which the miraculous is looked upon with all the grand and mighty suspicion of the intellect. Even that which momentarily appears worthy of the mind's dread has explanation, and derives from this fact a mystery of its own. It becomes even more miraculous for having an empirical basis.

"If there exists an unsolvable riddle, it may well be death, or entropy, or the spirit's waste. But we deny that you unriddle these final conundrums. You shroud them in the tattered dress of superstition and answer them with obfuscating riddles of your own.

"How, then, can you discover to any gosfi a metaphysics more incisive and transcendental than the state's? Our miracles, because grounded in a method quantifiable and exact, are so much more certain than yours. And because we have deprived you of the weapon of miracle, Gaidu, you've presented yourself to the Tropiards of the Thirty-three Cities too late to make use of it."

Now I'm thrashing in my sleep, angry for my Holy One and desirous of rebuking her inquisitor for his lack of courtesy. A light goes on and off in my brain. Now I'm on a scaffold in the J'beij, now on the very edge of Palija Kadi overlooking the laser-singed fields of the basin. I see the ruin that's to come, and I wish to wake up. But Gaidu holds me in my dream. With the violence of a rape she opens me to the relentless arguments of First Magistrate Mwezahbe.

"Why don't you answer me?" he asks. "Do you

believe yourself the spirit-of-mystery made flesh? Do you mean to imply by your silence that you must work through mystery to attain your ends? *Mystery*. Is this the metaphysical cloister in which you take refuge? Well, it won't do, Gaidu. It won't do. Even you must realize the inadequacy of your stratagem.

"Mystery made flesh! The mystery of your birthing—if mystery you insist upon—lies in the fact that insentience may somehow generate life, that the organic may somehow derive from the inorganic, that flesh may contain spirit. But you're not unique in being the product of such a wondrous quickening. Not by any means. What feeling, fiery creature doesn't illustrate and embody the same mystery, Holy One?

"Answer me! Open your soul to me! How are you, Gaidu, more miraculous—in essence, not simply in degree—than the smallest mite that hatches, gluts itself on blood, and dies? Answer me!"

At this point I'm in torment. I even begin to fear that Mwezahbe has pushed our savior to the utmost extremity of self-doubt. But she remains serene. She grants my dreaming self a brief glimpse into the calmness of her heart. Otherwise, she knows, I would come raging out of my sleep like a j'gosfi warrior dutifully fulfilling the madnesses of reason.

Mwezahbe resumes his inquisition: "We both know that your coming coincides with a point in history not especially vulnerable to your message. Who's to blame for that? You know as well as I, and this knowledge, by itself, is partial punishment for your apostasy, Holy One. However, there's more, and it's my intention to reveal to you that which must condemn the worthiness of your entire ministry and so inflict upon your soul a punishment suitable to your betrayal.

"My Legacy has sought to provide for the

weak, the mind-crippled, and the pathologically
sh'gosfi, either by curing them or by offering them
an outlet for their weaknesses. One such outlet
will be your Sh'gaidu community of misfits and
mystics. Therefore, on a modest if misleadingly
successful scale, the experiment at Palija Kadi will
survive for some time. But eventually you'll find
yourselves outdistanced by the programmed evolution of a million Tropiards working through
their intellects and their auxiliary births toward a
transcendental gosfi condition. On the day that
we attain to this condition, Holy One, your people will have long since perished. The Sh'gaidu
will have simply disappeared from the face of
the planet.

"Holy One, you came too late.

"Had you come earlier, before my own lifetime, nothing I could have done would have erad-
icated your image. The nation would be either
wholly sh'gosfi or divided against itself in the self-
destructive polarity of desperate males and un-
merciful madwomen. Probably, however, the
former—for I wouldn't have yet appeared to lift
all Trope from the grip of ignorance and superstition. Your own view would have prevailed, and
sh'gosfi nationwide would have bravely resisted
the imposition of my upstart authority. Martyrs
by the thousands would have arisen to die for
your holy illusions.

"And I, Seitaba Mwezahbe, would be relegated
to the role of Second Messiah. A second messiah
is an anomaly, Holy One. She is either *Nuraju*
or charlatan. She has no official status and only
the adherents she deserves. Her Elect are a piti-
ful and deluded group, and that's why she has
them. In fact, it may be that she requires her
Elect far more desperately than they require her.
Though they're too weak to live entirely by their
own wills, a few will gain the strength to desert
her. Others will deny reality their whole lives,

and these few pathetic specimens of gosfihood she will ambiguously exploit, their needs feeding hers and hers theirs in a melancholy symbiosis.

"Meanwhile, the religion of her rebellion has become a cauldron wherein the disenchanted, the deranged, and the desolate are salutarily boiled away. The real substance of the state remains behind, purified.

"And those who are boiled off, Gaidu, what of them? What do you really care for them beyond their usefulness as psychic grist? Is it possible for you even to formulate an answer? If so, try. Answer one who has granted both freedom and dignity to his people—for I've done that by administering to their worldly needs, giving them fathomable mysteries, and vanquishing forever their terror of the dark. All this I did from the challenge of doing it, and from love, and from a secret but not unnatural desire to be known forever as a powerful benefactor.

"But what of *your* motives, Holy One? What are they? Are they too dark to voice? Speak, I command you!"

Gaidu torments me in my sleep by refusing to respond to these provocations. I would answer for her, sing her praises, but my tongue is a hibernating animal in my mouth, no more able to awake than I.

"You came too late," the First Magistrate repeats. "I fear the source of all your strength lies in a monumental pettiness yearning toward the honor that three million Tropiards give me alone. If not, speak. Give me your thoughts, or else vanish into time like the phantom you are."

Here the Pledgechild stopped. She lifted her Y-shaped scepter, studied it intently, then placed it back in her lap. Everyone in her reception cell waited for her to go on, expectant of some conclusion or commentary.

"Is that all, Pledgechild?" Porchaddos Pors asked. "Does the vision have an ending? Does your messiah answer Mwezahbe anything?"

The old woman looked up. "You may judge for yourself, Kahl Pors. My dream vision always concludes in the same way."

"Tell it," Lijadu urged from the windowsill.

"Oh, I don't intend to stop so close to the true end, my little Lijadu." The Pledgechild pointed her stick at Seth and Magistrate Vrai, one prong to each of them. "It's at this point that Gaidu makes her reply, you see, and although she doesn't attack Mwezahbe verbally or disparage Tropish ideals, her behavior would perhaps strike a good Tropiard—particularly a distinguished successor to the First Magistrate—as unseemly. I spell this out explicitly before I proceed."

"Do you want my permission to finish?" the Magistrate asked.

"Oh, no," the old woman replied. "I must finish every recitation I begin, as Lijadu, despite her unnecessary urgings, well knows. But if you don't wish to hear it, Magistrate, you may join Emahpre in your airship."

Vrai hesitated only a moment. "I'll stay," he said.

"Very well," the Pledgechild replied. "My vision concluded last night as it always concludes."

Mwezahbe, with a nervousness I can feel, waits for Gaidu to make a succinct and intuitive rebuttal of his attack. The Holy One senses the First Magistrate's apprehension, his fear that he has not woven tight some threadbare place in the fabric of his argument. But, strangely, she also senses that Mwezahbe longs for the rebuttal he fears. . . .

At length she turns toward the First Magistrate and spreads her arms wide. In the next instant— there in the J'beij, here on the summit of our wall —she steps forward into the body of Seitaba Mwezahbe. She allows herself to become one with the dream flesh of her inquisitor. For a brief moment the two are a unity, drinking in starlight through the same fiery eyes and sharing a pulse beat that reverberates in time with my own. Together, they are whole and seamless.

So is the world.

But Mwezahbe begins to shake his head, discomfited by the surrender of his autonomy. When he can stand it no longer, he backs away from Gaidu's all-encompassing embrace, thereby denying his nuclear union with her. I can read his feelings. Exhilaration undercut with shame. He has been immersed against his will in sh'gosfi consciousness, and although the immersion has not deprived him of his self, he feels disoriented and shamefully aflame.

"Return to your time," he commands our Holy One. "Very shortly in our own eras, each of us will die, nor do I believe we'll meet again. That which created us has little use for dialectics. Farewell, sibling and fleshsharer."

Gaidu touches the First Magistrate with her mind, wordlessly, and tilts her head so that the stars may remove her from my vision. A nimbus captures her, a brightness shivers in her veins, and she is gone. Then Mwezahbe, too, disintegrates, and all that remains in my vision is a heavenly panorama of all of Palija Kadi: cliffs, fields, bridges, and Sh'gaidu communicants. Our crops are on fire, and the roar of their burning ascends through the night like the cries of a million tortured spirits.

No one moved. Seth could hear the roaring of the fires. Outside, however, through the window, only the wind-stirred Sh'gaidu crops. Lijadu's tiger-green eyes intercepted his. Her stare was unsettling. How could you interpret the meaning of such a stony, inhuman appraisal? Guiltily, he looked away.

The Pledgechild rescued Seth with a question:

"Does the ending of my dream vision displease you, too, Kahl Latimer?"

"Displease me?" Seth shook his head. "No, Pledge-child, not at all. In many ways Gaidu's response to Seitaba Mwezahbe is more eloquent than his lengthy inquisition."

"It's that eloquence that displeases Magistrate Vrai," the old woman said. "That, and the merging of j'gosfi and sh'gosfi in a union whose significance is not simply sexual."

Vrai said, "If Gaidu triumphs in your vision, Pledgechild, she triumphs because your own sleeping self controls the direction of your dream. That's self-evident."

"Is it?"

"The vision has an aesthetic rightness, I suppose, viewed from the Sh'gaidu perspective—but it doesn't reflect reality, and the flames at the end are history rather than prophecy."

"In which instance it *does* reflect reality," the Pledgechild countered. "In its other parts it symbolizes rather than reflects the real. Do you expect self-consistency of a dream?"

"Dreaming is a sh'gosfi enterprise, Pledgechild."

"You never dream?"

The Magistrate looked uncomfortable. "Of course. Dreams are a natural outlet for the irrational, a fail-safe against madness."

From the corner of his eye Seth saw that Lijadu was studying him. Her interest made his earlobes burn, even as it quelled the randy ardor that had earlier tormented him.

The Pledgechild, as if in sympathy with Lijadu, swung her attention from the Magistrate to Seth. "Do you love anyone, Kahl Latimer?" she asked.

The question rocked him. "Love anyone?" He could feel not only Lijadu's and the old woman's eyes upon him, but also those of the Magistrate and the two be-mused Kieri envoys.

"I ask because love is an emotion—a fixation, if

you like—that often has no rational source. Sometimes we love as helplessly as we dream. Do you, then, love anyone, Kahl Latimer?"

"I loved my isosire," Seth replied after a moment, glancing at Pors. "My birth-parent. And I love my isohet, my older sibling, Abel." Would this admission convict him in the Sh'gaidu's glittering eyes as a narcissist? Did they have any concept what isosire and isohet meant? . . . Would his genuine love for Abel absolve him of the charge of narcissism? After all, he did finally love someone outside of Seth Latimer, even if his love object happened to be genetically identical to himself. Abel was a person, as he was a person.

"Is this a rational love?" the Pledgechild asked.

"You have no right to interrogate Kahl Latimer in this way," the Magistrate said. "He's a guest on Trope and a guest here in Palija Kadi."

"I don't mind," Seth said.

"Well, then?" The Pledgechild waited.

"Well, I would suppose that pure reason would rule out love as a human, or a gosfi, or a jauddeb, possibility. Instinct at least preserves the possibility. I don't believe I'm a full-fledged devotee of either system."

"You define the Sh'gaidu 'system' in terms of instinct?" the old woman asked.

"Perhaps as a ritualization of it, Pledgechild."

"Then how would you define the Magistrate's 'system'?" The last word emerged from her lips like something contaminated.

Seth put a hand to his chest and glanced at Vrai. "Perhaps as an attempt at instinct modification," he hazarded.

"Not as a negation of instinct?"

"That wouldn't be possible, would it?"

The Pledgechild began to rise from her backless chair. Lijadu, springing lightly from her place on the windowsill, hurried to assist the old woman. Everyone else rose out of deference to the Sh'gaidu leader, who, freeing herself from Lijadu's hand, put her scepter down and tottered the few remaining steps between her chair and Seth.

Seth watched in amazement as the old woman's almost predatory black eyes approached. Her thin arms opened wide. A moment later he was captive in their embrace, rigid under the uncomprehending gazes of the Magistrate, Pors, and Douin. The Pledgechild held him in this way for at least a minute, then released him and went unassisted into the tiny room opposite the pottery-storage niche. No one spoke or attempted to sit down again.

"Why did she embrace you?" Douin finally asked Seth.

"I don't know," Seth said, shaking his head. Lijadu was still watching him, her eyes as indecipherable as alien runes.

Pors said, "Her embracing Master Seth concerns me far less, Magistrate Vrai, than the Pledgechild's leaving. We've made no substantial progress, and the better part of the afternoon lies ahead."

"Forgive her," Lijadu said. "Her recitation of the vision has sapped her strength. She must rest. This evening's *dascra'nol* ceremony will also be fatiguing for her."

"What would you have us do now?" the Magistrate asked.

Huspre reentered the reception cell, with her milky eyes and her mismatched facial features—as if at infancy someone had split her head from crown to chin and then inexpertly realigned the halves.

"You may remain here if you like," Lijadu said. "Huspre will bring you food. Or you may tour the basin with me and eat later. Or you may return to your airship on the roadway."

"I wouldn't care to tour the basin," Pors declared.

"We'll eat something, then," the Magistrate said.

Lijadu spoke to Huspre in Tropish, and Huspre retreated into the Pledgechild's adjoining room, only to come back a moment later laden with baskets of bread and fresh uncooked vegetables. Huspre refilled everyone's water bowls from the amphora on the stand next to the Pledgechild's chair. Then, with Lijadu's help, she distributed the bread and colorful vegetable stalks into another set of bowls. Tantai, the pregnant Sh'gaidu, was conspicuous by her absence.

"I'd like to see the basin," Seth said, anxious to escape the others. "If I could take a piece of bread with me, I'd need nothing else."

"Very well," Lijadu said. "I'll show you."

"Kahl Latimer," the Magistrate blurted. Seth turned toward him. "Do you require your goggles against the sun?" He touched the chain by which they hung inside the bodice of his jumpsuit.

"No," Seth said. "I'll be fine." But he wondered if the Magistrate's sudden concern for his eyes was in reality a warning to protect the *dascra* that lay inside his own tunic.

Pors said, "Master Seth, where will we meet again?" The Kieri was also apprehensive about his departure.

"I'll bring him back to the Sh'vaij," Lijadu said.

Pors nodded. He was already eating a breadstick Douin had not taken anything yet, and he approached Seth to embrace him paternally, as if bestowing a benediction to his leavetaking.

The Magistrate said, "We'll either be here, Kahl Latimer, or in the airship with Deputy Emahpre."

Seth pulled free of Douin, patted him on the shoulder, bowed courteously to Magistrate Vrai. He ached to be outside. Except for a few businesslike walks in the open air, he'd been confined to walled and roofed-in places for nearly two months: Douin's geffide, the *Dharmakaya,* and, if only briefly, the J'beij and the crofthouse here on Trope. Anja was an alien sun, true enough, but he desired its blessing far more than Douin's, and relished the prospect of sweating from the sunny heat rather than from a craven anxiety.

Lijadu beckoned him out of the Pledgechild's cell.

Chapter Twelve

It was almost noon. Seth saw everything as if by a magnesium flare. Anja balanced overhead like a pinwheel running alternately blue and white, and the entire basin had the magnified clarity of a rock garden beneath a still mountain spring.

Lijadu and Seth were walking toward the Great Wall, climbing the terraces that stepped upward to its base. Occasionally Lijadu paused to bend down a stalk and examine the fruit at its tip. As they walked and looked, Seth ate a Sh'gaidu breadstick, deciding gradually that he liked the taste.

In the fields were other Sh'gaidu, adults laboring with wooden or stone implements to chop out weeds or to prepare the ground for new plantings. Seth usually detected their presence by the stabbing glints of sunlight from their eyes as they turned among the stalks. . . . The heat didn't worry Seth, but the brightness did. Should he lift his hood for protection? On so warm a day that seemed scarcely justifiable. Lijadu, in her abbreviated sari, was practically naked. When she climbed, when she knelt, her limbs flashed brown in the sunlight: She was an uncanny brightness herself, and Seth had no desire to shield his eyes from her.

"I can't translate the names of all the plants for you," Lijadu said. "Everything here is specific to Trope, of course, as the plants of your own world are specific to it—but a few we call by descriptive compounds that do permit rough translation." She gripped the stalk of a shoulder-high plant and showed Seth the hard, deep-green cluster at its head. "This, for instance, we call emerald-eye, *lijadu*. I'm not named for the plant, or it for me, however. We share our name because of the appropriateness of the metaphor to both of us." She released the stalk and set off again toward the looming white wall whose bulk made Seth feel dwarfed to insignificance. It, too, was blinding.

Over Seth's shoulder, the Sh'vaij was far away. The cypresslike trees around it were small blue flames.

Ahead, hedges of amber, lilac, and crimson encircled the base of the wall, mounting toward it inexorably. Lijadu picked her way through these banks of living vegetation with a skill born of familiarity and practice. Seth was hard put to keep up, but fixed his eyes on the Sh'gaidu's supple legs so that admiration and desire eventually neutralized his windedness. Finally, at the wall, Lijadu reached out both hands and touched the warm white rock. Seth aped her stance, palms flat and head thrown back.

"Palija Kadi," Lijadu said. "The Great Wall. A portion of the buried heart of the planet. It was here long before the Tropish state, long before the protogosfi who first lived in the galleries." She nodded at the balustraded cliff face in which the Sh'gaidu apparently had their individual dwellings.

For the first time that day, perhaps because of an assisting wind, Seth thought he could hear the noise of vast machines whirring in the hidden chambers in the eastern wall. A kind of roar.

"Who were these protogosfi?" Seth asked.

Lijadu dropped her hands and faced him. "The ancestors of the people of Trope. The state, however, refuses to think on our origins here in Palija Kadi."

"Surely the state's explored gosfi prehistory, Lijadu."

"Excavations? Archaeology? Is that what you mean?"

"I suppose it is, yes."

"To a very limited extent the state's engaged in these things, on the grounds that to ignore the past is senseless. But for most Tropiards, including especially their own First Magistrate, prehistory is *was*.

Mwezahbe said that the state must look forward rather than back. The purpose of each individual Tropiard and the technocracy of which he's a part is to comprehend the significance of their *becoming*. They believe it's the becoming that defines them."

Seth attempted a pun in Vox, something approximating "It's the defining that becomes you."

"No, Kahl Latimer, it's the *being* that interests us, essence rather than process. We revere the protogosfi for what they were. The state ignores them because what they were is anterior to the evolutionary path which all good Tropiards follow obediently toward a doubtful transcendence. And the citizens of Trope don't care to dwell on that from which they've arisen."

"Why?" Seth asked. Lijadu's knowledge, sophistication, and aplomb both astonished and daunted him. They were not what he had expected from a member of a dissident, mystagogic commune. That she and her people would agree to leave this place for a world seven light years away began to seem more and more unlikely. . . .

"Because like humans and jauddeb, Kahl Latimer, every species of protogosfi to live on Trope was represented by two sexes. None were—as all modern gosfi are—physically hermaphroditic."

"Is that why Trope still holds itself aloof from Interstel?"

"Because humanity still has two distinct sexes? Probably. I don't know everything about the rational aversions of the present magistrate."

"He seems a decent person."

"He's much better than the last one," Lijadu conceded. "I'm grateful I never knew Orisu Sfol."

"But these protogosfi, Lijadu—how do the Sh'gaidu know about them?"

She gestured again at the eastern cliff. "We live where they lived. Or where several bands of the most successful protogosfid species lived, I should say. Tropiards refer collectively to our apartments in the rock as the galleries, but their true name—which even

the protogosfi who lived here may have spoken, Kahl
Latimer—is Yaji Tropei, Earth Womb. They prepared
these mansions for us millions of years ago, and died
becoming us. Their immediate descendants survived
and prospered through androgyny, but the technocracy
that succeeded this culture a mere nine hundred years
ago built itself on the suppression of the sh'gosfi im-
pulse in every one of its . . . *sons.*" Lijadu used the
Voxian word for "self-aware male offspring" with
what struck Seth as an admirable moral neutrality.
"Yaji Tropei is a painstaking feat of engineering, Kahl
Latimer, and you'll have a chance to see it before you
leave. We find it highly satisfying that our protogosfid
ancestors built the galleries many thousand millennia
before the First Magistrate codified the statutes of the
Mwezahbe Legacy."

Lijadu led Seth along the base of the great wall,
then abruptly down a series of stone-braced steps to a
terrace level where a regiment of stunted-looking
bushes grew. Their leaves were acid green and
palmate. They smelled keenly of an unnamable spice.
Lijadu stalked along this tier, found a plant to her
liking, and knelt beside it.

After glancing cryptically at Seth, she took the
plant's central stalk between her fingers and pushed
the clustering leaves aside. Revealed about halfway
down the stalk was a tumorlike pod about half the size
of her fist. Lijadu snapped this pod from the plant,
cupped it in her hands with an affecting gentleness.
She extended the pod to Seth, signaling with her chin
that he should accept her gift and cradle it in his
hands. He did so.

A moment later she said, "Return it, Kahl
Latimer."

Seth returned the strange seed pod.

Now Lijadu carefully peeled back the long hard
petals of the iridescent green exoskin. Working fastidiously, she reduced the pod to a miniature chalice, in
which there grew a round blue ball. Weblike filaments
anchored the ball in the chalice, but Lijadu cut these

away by scooping her finger around the pod's open interior. Then she let the casing drop and made a fist around the ball, utterly concealing it in her right hand.

"This we call the heartseed, Kahl Latimer. Do you know it?"

"No."

"Then watch." Lijadu undid her fist and held her palm out before her. The ball trembled as if something inside it were struggling to break out. "The heartseed grows for everyone on Trope, the sane and the mad alike."

Seth watched. As in time-lapse photography, the heartseed ballooned on Lijadu's hand. In scarcely a minute it had become a fragile cerulean-blue spheroid, the size of an ancient ecclesiastical censer and almost as aromatic. But it had no more substance than a soap bubble. Seth reached to touch it, and felt only a resilient silkiness.

"Of all the plants in Palija Kadi," Lijadu said, "only this one is not for food. Not for food, but for beauty."

Like the *mwehanja* Seth had eaten in the Tropish dormitory and again aboard The Albatross, the heartseed resembled the sun.

Lijadu stood, lifted her cupped hands to the sky, and pulled them down to release the sphere. It floated free, dipped on the wind, spun away above the colorful stairstep terraces toward the Sh'vaij. Finally it blurred with the afternoon brilliance, lifting on a thermal and pirouetting away into infinity. Seth squinted after it into the stinging light.

"Would you like to see the *kioba Najuma* from which my birth-parent kept watch after her death?" Lijadu pointed to the tower below them to their right.

When Seth nodded his consent, Lijadu led him along the same terrace level to another series of stone-braced steps descending to the north. Seth could see the boxed-in lookout at the top of the tower, and was surprised to discover that it was still a little *below* them. But Lijadu danced easily down the steps to the base of the tower, and Seth, no longer winded, followed.

From the tower's platform dangled a rope. Lijadu braced it for Seth so that he could shinny up it and through the opening into the lookout. Then, so gracefully that the rope hardly danced despite its being unbraced by anyone on the ground, Lijadu climbed up after him.

From the *kioba* Seth and Lijadu surveyed the intricate quilt patterns of the fields and terraces laid out beneath them. Neither spoke, although Seth went from side to side to experience each new view in turn. The curious roaring he had heard from Yaji Tropei— the galleries—seemed to have stopped. Looking over that way, he could see members of the Sh'gaidu sect moving behind the cliff's coral balustrades and pacing leisurely back and forth along the twisted stone bridges connecting the galleries to the fields. Palija Kadi was alive.

In the center of the lookout was a pole going from ceiling to floor. Pensively, Lijadu gripped this, then spoke:

"There are places of vision. We bring our dead to these towers and bind them to the pole-trees, as my own birth-parent Ifragsli was brought here and bound four nights ago. From here the dead look out on their lives and remember Daugahvi Gaidu. They remain here three days. Before their eyes crumble into *jinalma,* the dead are cut down and their eyes taken out in preparation for the ceremony we call *dascra'nol.*"

"And do you believe that from these lookouts the dead will see your Holy One returning from her sojourn among the gosfi of the north?"

"Not with hard, living eyes, Kahl Latimer, but with the essence giving those eyes life. The Sh'gaidu believe that the dead require a period of solitude in which their final visions may ripen."

"And what are these 'final visions' you speak of?"

"This evening you'll see." Lijadu stared out across the fields.

Although she wasn't even facing him now, Seth

began to feel that his mind was as transparent to her as a glass bell. He remembered that she had called him by his isosire's surname even though she'd had no chance to hear that name spoken aloud. He wondered if she were even now communing with the Pledgechild or with other members of the Sh'gaidu scattered about the basin. Vrai had said that a telepathic community—where reading as well as sending is commonplace—would be a community of either wholly paranoiac or wholly indistinguishable personalities.

That condition didn't seem to obtain in Palija Kadi. From what he had seen so far, Seth judged the Pledgechild, Lijadu, Huspre, Tantai, and the little girl Omwhol as complete and healthy persons; suspicion was not a conspicuous character trait in any of them. Were they, however, suspicious of the mission that had brought two high-ranking Tropiards and a trio of motley offworlders to their basin? . . . A guilt without a readily identifiable correlative began to well in Seth.

"Lijadu."

She turned toward him.

"Lijadu, Magistrate Vrai is able to speak to me mind to mind. Are you able to do that, too?"

—*We are.*

He accepted the admission, or the avowal, as if it had been voiced—even though Lijadu had been staring at him, mutely, for a long, disconcerting moment. He was neither surprised nor frightened. "Do your capabilities extend beyond simple transmission?" he asked. "Can you read as well as send?"

"At the moment, Kahl Latimer, you're uneasy rather than frightened. Would a straightforward answer banish your uneasiness or simply replace it with a gnawing fear?"

"You've answered my question, haven't you?"

"Yes, but not straightforwardly." Lijadu drummed the fingers of her right hand against her bare left shoulder. "And do you fear me?"

Seth considered this. "No, but—"

"You don't understand why the Magistrate is capable of sending but not of reading?"

Nodding, Seth acknowledged Lijadu's prescience.

"Sending is an intellectual capability. It's lineal in nature and active in origin. A Tropiard has little difficulty mastering the rudiments of sending because the Mwezahbe Legacy apotheosizes the very qualities that make the act possible."

"Whereas reading—"

"Reading is an intuitive capability. It's diffuse rather than lineal. It requires receptiveness rather than self-assertion. Our Holy One and her Pledgechild have taught us to esteem the sort of awareness that makes this capability as natural as breathing. Nor do we experience these capabilities solely in verbal terms. We also read emotional states."

"What do you read in me, then?"

"Anxiousness," said Lijadu, reaching out and touching his face. "A fierce desire to succeed balanced against an even fiercer desire to please everyone whom you've inwardly validated as a person. Hence, Kahl Latimer, your anxiety."

"I don't understand."

"That's also clear to me." She dropped her hand.

On the roadway below the Sh'vaij, with all the other naked children, Lijadu had seemed a child herself. Now, however, she radiated the wisdom and confidence of a goddess. How had she gained her knowledge not only of Palija Kadi but of the greater world beyond it?

A flight of vaguely saurian cranes, or cranelike reptiles, passed high over the basin. They trailed their astonishingly thin legs behind them like powder-blue streamers.

When they had gone, Lijadu said, "When she has attained twenty harvests, each Sh'gaidu must embark on a ritual sojourn to one of the Thirty-three Cities. In the year Tropiards call 908, Kahl Latimer, I journeyed to the city of Ebsu Ebsa. In the guise of a j'gosfi who had still not experienced his first auxiliary birth, I remained among the citizens of Ebsu Ebsa for three complete turnings of the sun. I've seen the world the Magistrate rules and I know firsthand its virtues and its shortcomings. I returned to Palija Kadi grateful that the state grudgingly permits our community to exist. Did it not exist, I would find a way to die."

"You're older than I am," Seth said incredulously.

"I'm twenty-three of Trope's years—but our years are shorter than yours."

"I'm twenty-one, Earth reckoning."

"Then, by an absolute measure, you're *my* elder, Kahl Latimer."

What should his reaction be? To discover that Lijadu was younger than he, and yet possessed of adult knowledge and self-assurance, seemed a slap at his own intellectual and moral progress. Moreover, on Trope, Lijadu was still a preadolescent. Chagrin blossomed in Seth, reddening his cheeks. At the same time, he wondered how Lijadu had emerged from her years in a Tropish city still a devout Sh'gaidu, if no longer a total innocent.

Tactfully ignoring Seth's chagrin, Lijadu began to recite her story: "Not long after the disappearance of our Holy One, Kahl Latimer, the Pledgechild established the ritual of a three-year sojourn among the j'gosfi. She stipulated that only fledglings who were well past the most impressionable period of their growth were eligible to go. The purpose of these sojourns was not only to expose the young Sh'gaidu to an alien way of life, but to give her an opportunity to search among our enemies for the departed Holy One."

"I thought she was supposed to have gone to the barbarian northern continent looking for converts."

"That supposition is a part of Sh'gaidu lore, but we've also always felt it possible that the state had taken her captive and confined her in one of the Thirty-three Cities. The hope of her captors, of course, would have been that the community here at Palija Kadi would disintegrate for want of leadership."

"Wouldn't you know if she were still alive?" Seth asked. "Wouldn't you receive her cerebrations, and she yours?"

"If she weren't physically impeded in some way, yes. But it's possible the j'gosfi subjected her to the violation of an auxiliary birth and so destroyed the personality by which we knew her."

"Couldn't you read the Magistrate or Deputy Emahpre to find out?"

"Tropiards are difficult to read, Kahl Latimer. They live close to the surface of their skins. It's hard for us to go any deeper into their inner lives than they go themselves. And yet, yes, we may possibly learn some very important things while Magistrate Vrai and Deputy Emahpre are here."

These words seemed to Seth to imply something ominous. He turned away from them and asked, "Isn't leaving the basin dangerous for a young Sh'gaidu? Doesn't the state know of these three-year sojourns in its cities?"

A flash of light winked above the western cliff face, a reminder of the perpetual presence of state troops.

"Oh, the state has known about them from the beginning. But it does nothing to discourage our seekers and pilgrims because it feels it can only benefit by our presence in the cities."

"How?"

"Occasionally it happens that a young Sh'gaidu surrenders to the workaday glitter of Tropish life. Bodily comfort prevails over spiritual rigor. The state finds this rewarding."

"What does your Pledgechild believe?"

"She holds that one day the defector will see, with a fiery clarity, the error of her choice. Besides, these defections are rare. Most of us come home, and we come home wiser than we went."

Lijadu related what it had been like to learn that the Sh'gaidu were not the only people on Trope pos-

sessed of a savior. The citizens of Ebsu Ebsa revered
Seitaba Mwezahbe as the communards of the basin
revered Duagahvi Gaidu. Moreover, years were counted
not from Gaidu's birth but from Mwezahbe's creation
of and inauguration into the office of magistrate. Lijadu
had not known that before. She had assumed that time
passed unregistered, except perhaps in the minds of
such eminences as the Pledgechild and her aged coun-
selors. Most miraculous of all, the Pledgechild had
actually known the Holy One. No one alive in the city,
however, had ever seen Seitaba Mwezahbe in person.
He was many, many years dead.

Still, for the duration of her sojourn in the clockwork metropolis of Ebsu Ebsa, where Lijadu had
earned her way taking the memory transcriptions and
compiling the evo-step genealogies of j'gosfi preparing
to undergo auxiliary birth, the knowledge that Gaidu
was not the center of the universe for everyone had
gnawed at her heart. She had suffered excruciating
agonies of the soul. It had seemed to her that the universe resolved itself into one great polarity: Mwezahbe
versus Gaidu. With which savior did one cast her lot?
Although the weight of time and numbers lay with
the Tropiards' First Magistrate, Lijadu had seen the
emptiness in the hearts of Ebsu Ebsa's populace, the
abysses yawning beneath their unreasoning obedience
to the Legacy.

On the other hand, what if Gaidu herself, whose
devotees numbered today in the meager hundreds,
had been nothing but a biochemical aberration of the
j'gosfi norm? Or the product of an abortive auxiliary
birth? Or merely a frail soul who had fallen into the
grip of a galvanizing *nuraj?* Throughout the whole
of her stay in Ebsu Ebsa, Lijadu had agonized over
these questions.

More than once she had nearly compromised her
identity, already well known to the city's leaders,
by hectoring complacent Tropiards about their un-
questioning j'gosfihood, by proselytizing them with
mock-sardonic references to the glories of witchery.

She had done these unwise things as if for their faintly illicit humor, as a high-placed Tropiard might indulge a weakness for scatology with his trusted intimates. Consequently, she was always relieved when her targets drummed their fingers in high glee instead of calling her down for a pervert or an apostate. In truth, doubtful of Gaidu's origins and mystagogic authenticity, Lijadu had envied these dull, reasonable persons their certitude. They were never plagued with sleepless nights. For them the Holy One was a joke, and Palija Kadi an insane asylum. The Sh'gaidu, meanwhile, were the freaks, cripples, and madwomen who worshiped the joke and inhabited the asylum. Wasn't it wonderful that the state had provided a reservation for these unhappy people? Well-adjusted j'gosfi had no need to associate with their like.

The *kioba* groaned as a breeze gusted across the basin. Seth felt himself swaying with the lookout. "How did you resolve your crisis?" he asked.

"Toward the end of my sojourn in Ebsu Ebsa I had a dream vision."

"Like the Pledgechild's?"

"Not very, no. The similarity lies only in the fact that our Holy One figures prominently in both.

"But in mine, Kahl Latimer, Duagahvi Gaidu appears at midday atop the central transport wheel in Ebsu Ebsa and turns her naked eyes on every person in the streets. At the sight of her, the eyes of unbelieving Tropiards melt behind their goggles and stream together through the stone canals and run-off conduits in a deliquescent flow of lava.

"Gaidu descends from the transport wheel and walks at the head of this scorching flood. With her staff, and with a winglike corner of her cloak, she directs this river of melted crystal out of the city and across the wasteland prairie called Chaelu Sro.

"The blind follow our Holy One, Kahl Latimer, but although for nearly three years I have doubted Gaidu devoutly, my eyes haven't melted from my face. I'm not one of those who are stumbling blind in her wake. Free to discard my j'gosfi eye coverings, I run along beside the stricken ones until I'm nearly abreast of the divine madwoman directing the flood.

"The flood seethes with fiery greens and interthreading filaments of ruby. It coils viscously across the barren Sro, responding to the slightest motion of the Holy One's body—as if endowed with a vision too powerful for its manifold contributors' disbelief.

"Helpless, the citizens of Ebsu Ebsa grope along the banks of the stream until new tributaries of lava begin converging from every horizon. Then the first-stricken are joined by the blind from every other Tropish city. Gaidu skips ecstatically at the head of these various streams, knitting them together with rhythmic jabs of her staff and graceful sweeps of her tattered cloak.

"I alone am a sighted witness to these events. Everyone else moves by touch-and-turn, turn-and-touch. And suddenly it's my lot to feel pity for the very ones who have for three years enraged and perplexed me.

"At last Gaidu leads all these converging rivers of crystal to the summit of Palija Kadi. Halting here, she commands both the tide and the groping Tropiards to ebb away from the precipice. As far as I can see, there are eyeless people among the molten streams knotted in dazzling patterns across the Chaelu Sro.

"Gaidu summons me to her. Bending at my side, she creates new eyes from the matter everywhere visible, and hands these scalding organs to me, and bids me distribute them to those penitent Tropiards who come forward to have their vision restored.

"Anja is low in the western sky, but it doesn't set. Even as the Holy One shapes her millionth pair of eyes from the receding rivers of crystal, Anja hangs on the horizon. I take the hot, hard eyes from Gaidu's hands and push them into the sockets of the blind.

"All that lingering twilight, Kahl Latimer, the Tropiards come to us. And when the plains of Chaelu Sro are again nothing but dust and red rock, I find that even our penitents have deserted us. I'm alone with the lovely woman whom I have doubted, prayed to, reviled, and prayed to again.

" 'Where are the people whose vision I've helped you restore?' I ask her.

" 'You are they,' Duagahvi Gaidu responds. 'Only in the labors of faith does faith evolve. The vision that we've restored, Lijadu, is your own.' "

Lijadu fell silent. Seth, moved by this strange recitation, studied her profile and tried to find in his own experience an apocalyptic vision comparable to the young Sh'gaidu's. But all that winked against the screens of his memory was a blood-stained, halting film of his naked isosire going up the side of the Kieri Obelisk. . . .

"Your vision was sufficient to allay your doubts?" Seth asked.

"Yes," Lijadu answered. "Because Gaidu herself sent it to me. I knew that her spirit lived even if her body had died, and I understood that one day even j'gosfi Tropiards would share in our fiery sh'gosfi vision. Knowing these things, Kahl Latimer, it was easy to return to Palija Kadi."

For you, perhaps, Seth thought. A dream, after all, was merely a dream, whereas his memory of Günter Latimer's death had had its birth in a lurid reality. How balance that cold fact against a mere vision in which the High Priestess of the Sh'gaidu had restored the sight of the blind? Persecution could come from many quarters; ideologies were its most nutritious fodder.

"What made my reimmersion in my faith possible," Lijadu went on, "was the realization that the polarity I'd insisted on seeing in Ebsu Ebsa—that between our Holy One and the First Magistrate—wasn't necessarily a polarity at all. J'gosfi and sh'gosfi are *orientations* toward the truth, Kahl Latimer, not embodiments or absolute negations of it. A sh'gosfi need not forfeit her identity if she learns to analyze her visions, nor a j'gosfi surrender his rational orientation if he begins to perceive the world through Sh'gaidu eyes of fire. What I learned to hate in Tropiards was the blindness that leads them to deny the existence of a choice. That's why I gladly came home."

"To be sh'gosfi," Seth said. "Otherwise you couldn't live in Palija Kadi. It seems to me you have to be what you are, sh'gosfi, just as Tropiards have to be what they are, j'gosfi."

Lijadu turned on Seth with quiet fury, her eyes coruscating. "We affirm our belief in free choice by being what we are! If we were j'gosfi, what kind of statement would we be making with our lives? That only one orientation toward the truth is possible! Does your own biologically determined j'gosfihood blind you to the situation on Trope?"

Seth gripped the pole-tree to which Ifragsli had been bound. "I don't know. I think of you as a woman, and—"

"That's inaccurate. This artificial language gets in our way."

"I think of you as a woman," Seth repeated, "and the idea of an exclusively female community seems . . . seems unnatural to me."

"What of an exclusively male community?"

Seth hesitated. "That, too," he said.

"But because of your biologically determined maleness, less so? Is that correct?" Lijadu gave him no time to answer. "I wonder what a female representative of your species would have felt. Of course, the state would never have permitted such a person to come. That's why you and your colleagues are here rather than the Kieri Liege Mistress and her sh'gosfid retainers."

Seth said nothing. What Lijadu had told him was undoubtedly true. Meanwhile, for Tropiards and off-worlders alike, Vox distorted, traduced, and turned topsy-turvey the reality of gosfi sexuality.

"We'd best go down," Lijadu said. She pointed into the northwestern corner of the basin, where a group of

Sh'gaidu laborers was working its way through a square of trellises supporting eellike, purplish vines.

They spent the remainder of the afternoon touring the arbors, terraces, vegetable gardens, and grain fields of Palija Kadi.

BOOK FOUR

Chapter Thirteen

As Anja set, the sky hemorrhaged. Dark blood seemed to tremble behind the tissue of dim stars overarching the basin.

"It's nearly time for the *dascra'nol,*" Lijadu told Seth.

They made their way down from a ledge above the Sh'gaidu vineyards, where Seth had examined the workings of a gravity-powered irrigation system. Indeed, there were water channels throughout the basin, cunningly laid out and braced.

An evening breeze kicked up. Around the Sh'vaij the branches of the stately cypresses were lifting together like ragged black fans.

Other Sh'gaidu were converging on the assembly building. From the fields, from the irrigation terraces above the basin, from the stupendous bridges climbing to the shadow-riven eastern cliff face. And up the same path by which Seth's party had reached the crofthouse earlier that day there now traipsed five tiny figures: Porchaddos Pors, Clefrabbes Douin, Magistrate Vrai, and Deputy Emahpre, all preceded by the Pledge-child's right hand, Huspre. At this bloody twilight moment, visible to Seth only from the waist up, they each wore aureoles of dust upon their heads and shoulders, and so resembled medieval friars slumming toward a grubby canonization. Palija Kadi, thought Seth, was a hotbed of dubious saints. . . .

Everyone foregathered on the apron of rock in front of the Sh'vaij, hosts, guests, young and old. The children, this evening, wore lightweight dalmatics with

162

embroidered sleeves and hems, but, like the adults, they were still barefoot. The adults wore the garments they had worked in. No one paused to eat, or drink, or chat. Seth wanted to confer with Douin, to tell him about the heartseed, Lijadu's dream vision, and all the pragmatic wonders of Sh'gaidu agriculture—but he couldn't get close enough to do anything but nod his head in greeting.

In a supple, almost choreographed procession the Sh'gaidu herded their children into the Sh'vaij ahead of them. One by one, people filed through the open doorway. As his own turn to enter approached, Seth could see that the building's interior was lit by ceramic lanterns positioned in a ring on the curving walls. Shaped to resemble heartseeds, these lanterns emitted a pungent incense, like roses and charcoal. Lijadu was behind Seth, and bringing up the rear were Huspre, the Tropiards, and the Kieri.

Inside, Seth whispered, "Where's the Pledgechild?"

"In her cell," Lijadu replied. "She'll come forth when everyone's passed the corpse and done Ifragsli silent homage."

The procession circled along the right-hand wall toward Palija Dait and Lijadu's dead birth-parent. Although several children tried to walk along the benches lining this wall, adults gripped their elbows, pulled them down, and made them adopt a mature propriety. At last Seth and Lijadu passed Ifragsli, her bedaubed death mask eerie in the shifting glow of the heartseed lanterns, and Huspre separated herself from her charges and disappeared into the Pledgechild's rooms behind the Lesser Wall.

A moment later Seth found himself seated on a bench against the left-hand wall, with Deputy Emahpre on one side of him and Lord Pors on the other. Lijadu had knelt in front of him. All the other Sh'gaidu sat either on benches or cross-legged on the stony floor. In the center of the Sh'vaij was a vast open area waiting for a performer to occupy it.

Seth began to understand what it meant to "die of anticipation."

And then, very briefly, he felt coursing through his blood an atonal humming, as if all three hundred Sh'gaidu had interthreaded their private cerebrations of mourning and benediction into one resonating chord. A silent hallelujah.

The Pledgechild stepped from her cell. Her patterned sari scarcely concealed her nakedness, her black eyes glittered, and before her, draped with a fluttering cloth, she bore her Y-shaped scepter. Huspre followed the old woman, solicitous but unobtrusive, as if fearful that her mistress might stumble and require her support. She carried a lantern of strange design.

At Ifragsli's corpse the Pledgechild halted and inclined her head in silent prayer. Then she turned and proceeded to the center of the Sh'vaij, the Chapel of The Sisterhood.

There the Pledgechild lifted her covered scepter like a crucifix, turned in a circle, and offered the blessing of this enigmatic instrument to everyone in attendance. Heads bowed as the old woman languidly swept the circumference of the Sh'vaij. Huspre, still holding her lantern, stared at the floor.

Seth leaned forward and gripped Lijadu's shoulders. "What's the Pledgechild doing?" he whispered.

Deputy Emahpre clutched Seth's arm and gently pulled him back. "That's a *saisei* she's holding. It's an ancient instrument, as old as the species, nearly, and if you watch you'll learn all there is to know about it." He offered this information as if it were abhorrent to him, then released Seth and rolled his head resignedly against the cold stone wall.

Lijadu glanced over her shoulder, but neither confirmed nor denied the Deputy's words.

Lowering the Y-shaped scepter, the *saisei,* the Pledgechild spoke to her congregation in a musical Tropish dialect. Seth could distinguish no individual words nor even any of the spaces among them. If entirely conducted in this dialect, the ceremony would remain impenetrable to him.

Then, in Vox, the Pledgechild said, "I wish to welcome five visitors to the *dascra'nol* of Ifragsli. For this brief hour they hold their hopes in abeyance to partake with us of the final vision of the birth-parent of my heir." The Pledgechild lifted the *saisei* again, spoke in oddly syncopated Tropish, and lowered herself to her knees in the middle of the Sh'vaij. Huspre hurried to assist her.

In the flickering darkness, three hundred pairs of gemlike eyes were fixed on the kneeling Pledgechild. Painstakingly, the old woman screwed the *saisei* into a hole in the floor. Squatting, one hand supporting her frail body, with Palija Dait directly before her, she spoke in Tropish again.

Emahpre, lantern light reflecting from his slit-goggles, leaned toward Seth. "She says that she intends to conduct the remainder of the ceremony in the language of her visitors. That the Sh'gaidu will in any case receive emotional cerebrations more powerful than mere words. And that the message of Ifragsli's living eyes will undoubtedly be as meaningful for us, her visitors, as for the assembled sisterhood."

"How does she know that?"

"She doesn't, Kahl Latimer. All this is . . . well, gibberish."

Lijadu shot the Deputy a look that obviously disconcerted him. He rolled his head toward the building's entrance and stared into the darkening fields. Erect and noncommittal, the Magistrate sat to Emahpre's right.

"Lijadu," the Pledgechild intoned, "I bid you step between the body of your birth-parent and her living eyes, that she may see you."

Lijadu rose, stalked across the Sh'vaij, stopped in front of Ifragsli's corpse, and turned so that she was facing the old woman. The Pledgechild responded by slowly drawing the cloth away from the prongs of the *saisei.* She then handed this cloth to Huspre, who was standing behind her.

Mounted in the circular wooden clips of the instrument were the dead Sh'gaidu's eyes, flashing now with mysterious emerald luster.

"Lijadu," the Pledgechild intoned, "you must let the spirit of your birth-parent enter you. You must respond to my questions as the spirit of Ifragsli dictates. You are no longer yourself but rather she from whose womb you derived your life. Do you understand?"

"Yes, Pledgechild." Lijadu stiffened. Her eyes locked with the disembodied eyes in the *saisei.*

"Who are you?" the Pledgechild asked ritually.

"Ifragsli," Lijadu answered, transfixed. Although she spoke aloud, her lips scarcely moved and her voice was someone else's.

"To whom do you bequeath the immortal dust of your eyes?"

"I stand among the heirbarren, Pledgechild."

"How so, if your fleshchild stands in your place?"

"I've surrendered her to our people."

"Willingly?"

"Yes, Pledgechild."

"Why?"

"That she may inherit the dascra gosfi'mija *of her catechist."*

"Heirbarren though you may be, Ifragsli, you are fruitful of soul. Whom do you designate to receive the *jinalma* of your living eyes?"

"All of you, and none."

Crouching before the *saisei,* her old, mottled head cocked to one side, the Pledgechild eventually asked, "How may you make your bequeathment to both none and all?" This question seemed an improvisation, so tardily did it follow Lijadu's—or Ifragsli's—final response.

"Time has run from my veins, and I can no longer say."

"How did time slip from you, Ifragsli?"

"I ceased to create it, and so died."

"But in your flesh only."

"In my flesh only," Ifragsli agreed through her fleshchild's lips.

"Why did you cease to create it, departed one?"

"My heart filled with the surplus I made, and the surplus gave me visions which could not be borne."

"And these visions caused your death?"

"Not the visions, but the time in excess of our present: The future made me die, for I couldn't grow into it."

"What of your three days in the Holy One's lookout?"

"Dead, I searched for Duagahvi Gaidu."

"And?"

"I couldn't find her, Pledgechild."

For the first time that evening the Sh'gaidu reacted to the exchange between their Pledgechild and Ifragsli's proxy: Bodies moved, and garments rustled.

The Pledgechild improvised: "The Holy One didn't appear to you in your place of vision?"

"No, Pledgechild, she didn't."

"Weren't you, then, purged of the evil visions that uncreated you in your surfeited heart?"

"I don't know, Pledgechild." Formerly rigid, Lijadu began to sway; her upper body, as if in mourning for the birth-parent she had become, to move dolorously from side to side.

"Ifragsli!" the Pledgechild snapped.

Lijadu ceased swaying. *"I don't know, Pledgechild,"* she repeated in what was apparently her dead birthparent's voice. *"Perhaps my eyes will tell."*

"Have we permission to read them, Ifragsli?"

"Please read them. Before they crumble into dust."

"We thank you for your permission, Ifragsli, and for your child."

"Lijadu belongs to the people of Palija Kadi. I can't withhold her. She belongs to Palija Kadi and to the islands of our exile."

Tilting back her mottled head and peering sidelong at her heir, the old woman again let the catechism lapse. Although Seth had no way of knowing what was traditional and what extraordinary, it seemed to him that nothing about this ceremony was going as planned. The Sh'gaidu, reading the emotional content of Lijadu's words, even if she framed them in Vox, shifted restively on their benches. The flickering of the heartseed lanterns embodied and shadowed forth their apprehensions.

"The islands of our exile?" the Pledgechild asked.

"Please, Pledgechild," Lijadu said, swaying again. *"I beg you to read my eyes and free me of my vision."*

The old woman gestured impatiently with her left arm. "You're of the dead, Ifragsli," she declared. "Go where the dead go while we read your eyes."

Obedient, Lijadu—or the spirit of Ifragsli inhabiting her—left off her worrisome swaying, stepped away from the wall. Someone near the left-hand door to the Pledgechild's rooms drew her down and out of Seth's sight. Lord Pors, Seth noted, was conferring in whispers with Douin, who sat immediately to Pors's left. They were using Kieri, and he couldn't follow their conversation.

Still squatting, the old woman fiddled unceremoniously with the clips supporting Ifragsli's eyes. A moment later Huspre, bearing the odd-looking heartseed lantern with which she had entered, knelt beside the Pledgechild to assist with these niggling adjustments. What magic were they brewing? None, it seemed to Seth. The entire pageant had degenerated into a dumbshow of mundane tinkering.

Then the old woman said, "Let the light of the heartseed shine through Ifragsli's eyes that we may know her final vision."

Huspre, having duckwalked around the Pledgechild to position the lantern, canted its bowl so that it yawned upward at the prongs of the *saisei* and at the naked white slope of the wall beyond. She pulled a ceramic plate from the lantern. A spreading beam of light shone forth from the bowl, projecting an im-

mense, druidic rune onto the wall. Y. The Pledgechild's face, touched by the passing beam, was that of
a gargoyle. As she continued to adjust the clips, her
hands and arms made shadow pictures on the wall.
Huspre moved the lantern mouth so that the rune on
Palija Dait disappeared.

"The wonder of this," Emahpre told Seth sotto voce,
"is that they continue to believe this hocus-pocus
means anything."

"What are they doing?" Seth whispered.

"Attempting to externalize, there on the wall, what
they persist in regarding as the deceased's 'final vision.' "

"The last thing Ifragsli saw?"

"Not the last physical thing, no," Emahpre replied,
leaning toward Seth discreetly. "That would be too
easy. The Sh'gaidu believe that during the deceased's
three days in the *kioba* she constructs in her eyes a
prophetic pattern that must be read and interpreted
by the Pledgechild. This pattern is her final vision, and
the community must share in it."

"The Sh'gaidu originated this practice?"

"Oh, indeed not. In the days before Seitaba
Mwezahbe, every nomadic gosfi band had its shaman,
who cast and then construed the altered crystalline
structure of the eyes of the dead. It's a wretched,
powermongering hocus-pocus designed to confer status
on the interpreter, and that's all it is."

"How do you know?" Seth asked. He looked from
the Deputy to the wall: Watery colors—ill-resolved
jades and melting blues—had begun to glide across its
face as Huspre fiddled with the lantern.

The Deputy gripped Seth's knee with hard, pincer-
like fingers. "Because Mwezahbe in his earliest
assaults on superstition demonstrated that the so-
called upheaval in the gosfi soul—which is supposed
to create the prophetic pattern—is nothing but a stabbing chemical change."

"But couldn't the chemical change be the means
of—"

"Are you purposely playing the fool?" Emahpre demanded, still urgently sotto voce. "The chemical change is a natural consequence of death. It shatters the molecular structure of the eyes, creating strange interthreadings and murky blooms that charlatans like that one"—he nodded crisply at the Pledgechild— "can pretend to read. Hocus-pocus, Kahl Latimer, disreputable hocus-pocus!"

"Enough, Deputy Emahpre," the Magistrate whispered. "Tonight we're in their house. Hold your tongue and watch."

No pattern had yet emerged from the colors swimming on the wall. Only fluid motion, a weird primeval sea roiled in the radiance refracted through the dead Sh'gaidu's eyes.

"Ifragsli!" the Pledgechild suddenly shouted.

Seth glanced to his left, past Pors and Douin and a host of silent, anonymous Sh'gaidu, to the place where Lijadu had disappeared.

"Ifragsli!"

Lijadu, rising from her place, answered in the same unfamiliar voice she had used earlier: *"Yes, Pledgechild."*

"Is this the state of your soul, Ifragsli? It's impossible to read a moving pattern. Tell us what swims in torment here."

"Chaos struggling toward a definition, Pledgechild."

"Is this, then, your final vision?"

"No, Pledgechild: That chaos has a shape."

"Reveal it, Ifragsli."

Lijadu began to sway in sympathy with the undulant patterns on the wall. *"I will. . . . I will. . . . But first return my fleshchild to herself, and consign me prayerfully into the keeping of our Holy One."*

"Very well. Depart, Ifragsli."

One of Lijadu's sisters rose and caught her—for at the Pledgechild's succinct command she had slumped back into herself, nearly collapsing to the floor. Ifragsli had departed her.

The Pledgechild, still crouching, slid her arms into

the incandescence of the lantern, turned the disembodied eyes in their clips. The colors on the wall revolved in great, slow wheels, melting into blue-green lava and languid ambiguity. A pattern began to take shape. Facet lines imposed a terrible geometry on the churning verdigris. Before the Sh'gaidu and their visitors a huge, organic mural grew. A pair of distorted arms reached out of the congealing emerald seas toward the ceiling. A thrown-back head lifted its agony to the night in a scream all too easily imagined.

These images froze on the wall, lingered upon it like a stain. Below them was the body of Lijadu's birth-parent, emptied, apparently, of her final watchtower fears.

Deputy Emahpre, a stranger in this gathering, rose to his feet. "Tell us what this vision means!" he challenged the Pledgechild. "Read it for us!"

Three hundred pairs of eyes revolved toward the Deputy, and Ulgraji Vrai sprang to his feet to rebuke the importunate deputy administrator. To Seth, it seemed a tiresome reenactment of the Deputy's outburst over the pregnancy of Tantai.

Huspre helped the old woman to her feet. Looking with obvious annoyance at Emahpre, the Pledgechild accepted from her attendant the cloth that had earlier covered the *saisei* and then dropped it over the mouth of the heartseed lantern. The projected image remained on the wall, however, slightly muted in color but just as starkly etched.

Shaking off the Magistrate's hand, the Deputy repeated, "Read it for us, harlot! Tell us its mystic meaning!"

The Magistrate, his mouth twisting, resorted to Tropish to rebuke his deputy. Seth was surprised to see how truly alien and unreal he looked in his anger.

"The *dascra'nol* is over," the Pledgechild said sternly in Vox, half lifting one thin arm to silence her visitors. "Ifragsli's final vision interprets itself. That which she dreamt in her soul is manifest."

"That?" Emahpre declared incredulously, gesturing

at the wall. "What can that hideous nonsense possibly mean?"

Gripping Emahpre by the shoulders, the Magistrate forcibly sat him down. Seth could feel his own face reddening, an unfocused embarrassment spreading through him. The Sh'gaidu, and their uncomprehending children, were watching; and Emahpre, in his singleminded allegiance to reason, had unreasonably insulted every one of them in their own house. By what standards of humanity, of gosfihood, was this intense little man sane?

Huspre bent and slipped a ceramic shutter into the heartseed lantern, and the grief-stricken figure on the wall disappeared. Then, letting her eyes roam over the faces of her bereaved but resolute people, the Pledgechild turned in a halting arc. Seth could tell by the involuntary nods of agreement or acquiescence of the Sh'gaidu that she was addressing them with cerebrations. A moment later they began to file out of the Sh'vaij, the children as solemn and orderly as their elders.

Soon only Lijadu, the Pledgechild, Huspre, and the Magistrate's party of five remained in the assembly building. Ifragsli, whose corpse still lay beneath the wall, no longer counted; her spirit had flown.

In much the way that she had approached him that morning in her reception cell, the Pledgechild approached Seth. He shrank back perceptibly, looking to the Kieri for moral support or even outright rescue. But Pors was in a state of repressed hysteria, evidenced by the way his hands gripped his tunic and his heavy jaw jutted, and Douin hung back as if afflicted with an attack of timidity or conscience.

"How do you interpret what you saw this evening, Kahl Latimer?" the Pledgechild asked.

"He doesn't pretend to be a shaman," Emahpre interrupted. The Magistrate, who had been hovering over him censoriously, gave up and sat down to stare disgustedly out the door at the night.

"I little care," the Pledgechild retorted, then turned

to the two Kieri. "Or you, Kahl Pors. Or you, Kahl Douin. How should I read what Ifragsli's altered eyes have vouchsafed the Sh'gaidu?"

"This is out of our province," Pors responded.

"You're not religious men?" the old woman asked. "I had thought you were religious men."

Pors and Douin stared at her blankly.

Lijadu approached from the left-hand side of Palija Dait. "How many days were you in transit from Gla Taus to Trope?" she asked.

Pors told her.

"Your departure from your home world coincides with the beginning of my birth-parent's illness, and your arrival here with the reading of her final vision."

The Magistrate looked up. "You don't contend the two sets of events have a casual relationship, do you?"

When no one replied, Pors said, "Is *this* the appropriate time to discuss our reasons for coming to you, Pledgechild? If so, Kahl Latimer's prepared to set out clearly and explicitly the terms our government has authorized him to convey. It's our belief that both Tropiards and Sh'gaidu will find—"

"This *isn't* an appropriate time," the Pledgechild said. "Nor do I see why Kahl Latimer must speak for the Kieri government."

Douin responded: "The *Dharmakaya*—the vessel by which we journeyed to Trope—belongs to the Ommundi Trade Company, which he represents."

"Then he's a go-between rather than a principal."

"Yes, Pledgechild, but he and his isohet have mercantile and mediatory experience which may well ensure a just arrangement for both sides."

"This one," said the Pledgechild, indicating Seth, "has very little experience of anything but her own heart—*his* own heart, I should say. But state governments don't ordinarily single out such persons for emissarial duties."

"If you'd talk with him," Douin urged, "you'd see that he's—"

"This isn't the appropriate time," the Pledgechild

reiterated with some annoyance. Huspre, having gathered up the paraphernalia that had revealed Ifragsli's final vision, was just now retreating into the rooms behind Palija Dait.

A silence descended. Without really grasping why, Seth felt caught out and exposed by this silence. He gestured toward the wall.

"What will you do with Ifragsli's body?"

Lijadu said, "She'll be cut into pieces and given to our crops."

"Of course," Emahpre said.

"Her dead self will nourish living beauty," Lijadu rejoined. "Is cremation a more reasonable method of laying the dead to rest?"

Seth recalled the Kieri myth of Jaud and Aisaut. Villages had sprung up from the severed fingers of Conscience, an entire civilization from his hands. But that civilization was seven light-years across the empty riddle of The Sublime. . . .

"And her eyes go into the Sh'gaidu familistery urn," the Pledgechild said.

Seth noticed how drained and frail the old woman looked. Her mottled head threatened to topple from her shoulders. If she refused to open talks, she refused because her weariness would permit her no more physical sacrifices. Huspre slipped behind the Pledgechild and put an arm about her waist.

"No more tonight," the old woman said. "We'll talk in the morning, here in the Sh'vaij. —What sleeping arrangements?"

"I'll take Kahl Latimer into the galleries with me," Lijadu said. "Huspre can escort the Magistrate's party to resting places here in the Sh'vaij after she's seen you to your own cot, Pledgechild."

The Magistrate said, "We'll return to our airship for the night." He stood. "Kahl Latimer will accompany us."

"This afternoon," Lijadu responded, "I showed him everything in Palija Kadi but the galleries. Let him come with me now. No harm will befall him."

"I don't *anticipate* any harm befalling him."

Almost slyly, it seemed to Seth, the Pledgechild asked, "Is there any reason why he must spend the night in your company?"

"He's a guest of the state," Magistrate Vrai replied.

"And for this evening you're all guests of the Sh'gaidu," the Pledgechild irrefutably pointed out. "Let Kahl Latimer decide for himself where he wishes to sleep."

Pors whispered something in Kieri to Douin, and Douin stepped forward to address the Magistrate: "We don't object to his going with the young Sh'gaidu, sir."

"Do *you* object?" the old woman asked the Magistrate.

Driven to intimacy before friends and foes alike, Vrai took Seth's wrist and pulled the baffled isohet aside. Even though his strength was at least that of the Tropiard's, Seth allowed himself to be pulled.

"We're bond-partners, Kahl Latimer," the Magistrate whispered, half embracing him. "I know you for a good man, and I don't command you anything. I don't forbid you anything. Yaji Tropei's an ancient protogosfi fastness with distasteful connotations for us. It represents what we were rather than what we are. Neither my deputy nor I wishes to cross back over a bridge that Mwezahbe directed us over a long time ago. Do as you wish. You can't betray me by being true to yourself."

"What's Kahl Latimer's decision?" the Pledgechild asked loudly.

Seth stepped away from the Magistrate and surveyed the faces of the "imperfect isohets" into whose daunting company he had fallen. In how many different ways he was the odd soul out . . .

"I'd like to go with Lijadu," he heard himself say.

Chapter Fourteen

Outside there were stars. One of them moved slowly across the sky, and Seth's first thought was that it was the *Dharmakaya*. He imagined Abel sitting in the light-tripper's library listening to Bach's *Selig ist der Mann* and working out a complicated hand of solitaire. Why hadn't Abel come, too?

Despite Lijadu and all the others, Seth regarded his human isolation on the surface of Trope as a variety of solitaire. You played the game out alone. If you cheated—that is, if you pretended you had a supportive apparatus of well-wishers and backers—well, odd as the notion might strike a skeptical intelligence, maybe that permitted you to beat the game. Gazing into Trope's pewter-on-ebony sky, Seth pretended that Abel was the focal point of just such an apparatus.

The cypresses around the Sh'vaij were lashing restlessly, sighing in the grit-casting wind. The crops in the fields murmured, too. They murmured and ticked as if each gust were a fusillade from the surveillance force bivouacked on the high perimeters of the basin.

Lijadu led Seth around the apron of the Sh'vaij toward the wide stone bridges climbing giddily to the eastern cliff. Torches burned at intervals along these rugged spans, but their flames were whipped and tattered by the wind. The scene had a fairy-tale grandeur, a fairy-tale insubstantiality and impermanence. But it was real, and Seth's understanding that Lijadu and he must mount and cross the convolute central bridge gave him cause to imagine their bodies sailing into oblivion at the nudging of a particularly violent gust.

"Kahl Latimer," Lijadu said, looking at him sidelong near the base of the central span. "Let me see something."

"What?" He gaped at the looming bridge, then turned to her.

She put her hands on his shoulders and peered into his face. "The tiny black eyes inside your outer eyes are widening. The blue's being eaten away from the inside out."

Seth laughed, a response which startled Lijadu away from him. He gained her back only by drumming his fingers on his chest to translate into gosfi terms the meaning of his laughter.

"Then you are not ill—your eyes aren't . . . misbehaving?"

"No. I'm well enough, I think."

They hiked together up the first long, swooping incline, barricades of dark red stone glinting beneath the buffeted torchlight, the warmth of the wind a benediction. The jagged, coral arc of another span passed over their heads, like a streamer of petrified dust. The roaring of the wind seemed inordinately loud.

Then Seth realized that a portion of this roaring was emanating from the galleries. He had heard this sound that afternoon in the *kioba,* and had taken it, if not altogether seriously, for the intransigent droning of machines.

Four pairs of eyes flashed in the darkness ahead of them, and a moment later four naked children came hurtling past Lijadu and Seth on a narrow span near the summit.

"When do they sleep?" Seth asked.

"When they weary of play. Or when the adults about them see that they're running on spent energies."

At the top—and the terminus—of the central bridge, Lijadu conducted Seth to the left along a gallery running north and south like a wide natural stratum in the rock. Here the roaring of Yaji Tropei was deafening. Heartseed lanterns placed about the honeycombed interior provided an almost phosphorescent illumination. By this light Seth could see wavering curtains of water pouring through the cliff, dividing it into rooms. How far back into the mountain these chambers went, Seth was unable to tell—but the silvery partitions falling continuously from ceiling crevices to narrow gutters in the floor, then cascading through deeper rock to irrigation conduits below the galleries, dazzled the eyes and drilled unrelentingly at the ear.

"Is it always like this?" Seth shouted.

Lijadu spoke to him mind to mind:—*There's a reservoir in the mountains north of Palija Kadi, and our irrigation system operates through the force of gravity. There are times when we let the waters fall.*

Having to shout while Lijadu simply eased her messages into his mind struck Seth as somewhat of an injustice, but a fascinating one. "You can turn it off, this system?" he cried.

—*Easily. The walls you see shimmering here exist only intermittently. The Sh'gaidu aren't altogether ignorant of engineering and technology.*

"The noise!" Seth shouted. "It . . . it hurts!"

—*It won't plague you much longer. We divert or shut off the flow at night—but in the evening, with the lantern glow playing on the curtains, isn't it beautiful, Kahl Latimer?*

"Indeed!" Seth looked inward from the gallery and saw Sh'gaidu shadows outlined against the veils. Yaji Tropei was full of shadow beings, some of whom emerged from behind their waterwalls to scrutinize him as intently as he scrutinized their fastness. Spray misted outward from the caverns.

"The protogosfi used this irrigation system?"

—*Oh, no,* Lijadu cerebrated. —*This was the result of nearly sixty years of labor, made possible by the many channels already present in the cliffs, the technical ingenuity of the Pledgechild herself, and much Sh'gaidu courage. Yaji Tropei claimed several lives toward the end, giving us to know that we had done all she would permit. The bones of our dead lie deep in her body, as sacrifices to her patience.*

At the northern end of the gallery, Lijadu took Seth into the cliff and halted him at a niche containing a large, slate-gray statue. Seated on an ottoman of rock, this naked figure had been worn smooth by constant contact with the people who passed by it on their way to and from the fields. Even now a young Sh'gaidu, only slightly older than Lijadu, had paused to drape her arm over the statue's shoulder in silent confession and prayer. The eye sockets of the statue contained no eyes. In the shadows beyond it, dozens of Sh'gaidu waited their turns to embrace or commune mind to mind with the stone figure.

—*This is Duagahvi Gaidu,* Lijadu cerebrated. —*We come to her with our prayers, our love, and our fears.*

"Who?" Seth made chiseling motions with his hands.

—*One of the first of the Palija Kadi communards made this image, working many days to achieve what you see. She spent her daylight hours laboring in the fields or crawling through Yaji Tropei to open irrigation conduits.*

Overcoming his reluctance to initiate contact with Lijadu, Seth drew her to him, then spoke directly into her ear: "What have they come for tonight? Are they praying, or confessing, or telling her their fears?"

"They're frightened, most of them." This time Lijadu also spoke aloud, using their closeness to make herself heard.

"Of what?"

"Of my birth-parent's final vision. The Pledgechild said that it interpreted itself, but no one here is certain of its meaning."

"I don't find the meaning of Ifragsli's vision in what I saw on the wall, Lijadu. In that, I suppose, I'm like Deputy Emahpre."

"And in very little else, thankfully. —But we may perhaps find its meaning in the Pledgechild's reticence."

"What meaning, then?"

"An evil, Kahl Latimer. The Pledgechild didn't

wish to interpret Ifragsli's vision for fear of frightening us."

"But she's frightened you by not interpreting it?"

"Yes."

"An error on her part."

"She's mortal, Kahl Latimer. Nor did she like to be prodded to her reading by Emahpre." Lijadu separated from Seth and strode purposefully past the curving file of Sh'gaidu waiting to commune with the statue. —*Come,* she cerebrated from beside a curtain of water. Then, astonishingly fleet, she leaped through it, and her image was but an evanescent pattern in the torrents of that swaying wall. Like a light-tripper skipping into The Sublime, she had more or less disappeared.

—*Come,* she beckoned him again, invisible.

The roaring of the waters and that of his blood virtually indistinguishable, Seth followed. Mist prickled his face and hands. When he leaped the wide gutter beneath the ever-falling veil of the wall, his heart leaped inside him, too; and the iciness of the water plunging down his back and running from his brow woke him immediately to the beauty of the farther chamber.

Taking his hand, Lijadu led him through a corridor whose left-hand wall was rock plaster and whose right-hand wall was water. An arabesque red and tan fresco dominated the plaster wall, depicting fish, gocodre, birdlike creatures, strange, four-legged landgoers, and an assortment of hominid, or protogosfid, figures arrayed in cryptic community together. The scene wasn't altogether idyllic. The farther along this fresco Seth went, the more vivid and disconcerting were the figures portrayed.

Gocodre ate gosfi, gosfi dismembered birds, and disembodied eyes, pressed into the plaster in pigments of metallic blue or green, surveyed the general carnage from lofty or well-hidden vantage points: cliff ledges or caves.

This fresco, a virtual mural, looked very old to Seth. Its surface was cracked in many places, or blistered, and portions of the underlying rock had long ago crumbled and broken away. The Sh'gaidu had probably spent a good deal of time and meticulous effort restoring the fresco, replastering, freshening the faded colors, maybe even improvising detail where the many indifferent millennia had wiped it out.

"How old?" Seth shouted.

—*We don't know. But older than any other paintings discovered on our world. Gosfi have lived here perhaps since the beginning.*

Sh'gaidu of every age passed them in the corridor. One adolescent, naked and amber-eyed, bore on her shoulder a silver-furred creature whose eyes almost exactly matched her own, both in size and color.

They continued inward, until—without warning— the roar of the falling water became a single stupendous crash, followed by a series of wet pistol shots echoing back and forth. Afterward, a thunderous whooshing and a pizzicato runneling away into the lower depths of Yaji Tropei. The waterwalls were gone. Even so, the ceilings continued to drip, and a blurry dampness hung in the air.

Now Seth could see other walls, rock walls—wide portals cut in their faces and earth-colored frescoes glistening in the lantern sheen. You could look from one chamber into the next, and so on, seemingly forever. Against the painted walls were sleeping pallets, urns, stone hampers, benches, woven baskets, and a variety of simple housekeeping items.

On many of the pallets, Sh'gaidu lay, either alone or paired, their eyes like brilliant signal fires. Although no one here wore slit-goggles, the community had not yet fallen apart because of the relentless provocation of so many uncovered eyes. No one here was property, Seth told himself; everyone here was a person. And, as several sh'gosfi muffled their lanterns and shadows began spilling through the connecting rooms, Seth walked and watched.

"Where are we going?" he asked Lijadu.

"To my sleeping place—only a little farther."

"Many portals, but no doors."

"Doors wouldn't make any sense among us," Lijadu said. "Palija Kadi and Palija Dait are the only doors we require."

At last they entered a cove in which a lantern was still fitfully burning. Lijadu pointed Seth to a ledge at the foot of the widest wall, upon which a fresco of erotic import blazed, and handed him two small bowls. One she filled with dark meal from a stone hamper, the other with water from a delicate urn. After serving herself, too, she climbed atop the hamper and began to eat. When Seth had finished the contents of his bowls, he handed them across to her and gestured for more. He had the distinct impression, as she replenished the bowls, that she regarded his appetite—his show of animal rapacity—as something extraordinary if not quite reprehensible. But he was hungry, almost famished, and he ate until the ache inside him had dwindled to a faint throb, which he understood to be the ebbing of his exhilaration and the resurgent pulse of his anxiety. What strange place had he come to?

"Are you finished?" Lijadu asked.

He nodded.

She removed her garment and used it to wipe the moisture from her limbs and flanks. Her dark body glistened, a configuration of planes, triangles, lines, and functional curves which implied health and vigor rather than any distinct sexual identity. Above Seth, the fresco. He leaned aside to look at it: two gosfi entwined about each other in an excruciating coital ballet. The eyes of both partners were visible, nearly twice life-size—at least in proportion to the figures themselves. Lijadu, meanwhile, dropped her abbreviated sari to the floor and crossed the chamber to douse the heartseed lantern.

"There's only one sleeping pallet," Seth said.

"Unless you object, we'll share it."

This frank invitation, so casually proffered, startled him. Still, he'd been expecting or at least hoping for it.

Paragenation. What intensified his confusion was the utter ambiguity of their relationship. Lijadu was the heir of the Pledgechild, ostensibly a female, and nothing in her behavior—if he were fair—had suggested anything more intimate about her intentions than the desire to be a good host. With the possible exception, perhaps, of her eagerness to bring him into Yaji Tropei . . .

"Share it?" he said.

"For comfort. For warmth. For sleep." A thin blue glow seeped into Lijadu's cove from another section of the Sh'gaidu hive, and her body was defined for Seth only by the highlights shifting on her limbs and the wan jade fires smoldering in her eyes. "I can get another pallet if you like."

Despite himself, Seth heard a Günter Latimer pragmatism surfacing through his bollixed ardor: "I don't know whether I'll be able to sleep."

"Then let me get another pallet." Lijadu turned as if to fetch it.

"We could *try* it this way."

"Very well." Lijadu came back and sank on her knees in front of him to smooth the pallet with her hands. Then she folded back the coverlet and arranged herself so that half the sleeping area remained for Seth. When he didn't move to join her, she asked, "You're not yet tired enough to sleep?"

"I'm taking off my boots." Seth took off his boots. He spent two minutes on each one, tenderly undoing every plastic catch. Then he aligned the boots on the ledge and wiped their toes clean with his sleeve.

"Remove your tunic, too," Lijadu said. "It's damp. You won't be comfortable wearing it to sleep in."

It wasn't cold in the galleries. The suggestion seemed sensible. Seth removed his tunic, rolled it into a bundle, and, damp or no, placed it at the head of his side of Lijadu's pallet for a pillow.

"And your leg coverings, Kahl Latimer, if your customs permit."

Seth looked disconsolately at the waistband of his

pants. "For sleeping? Yes, it's permissible. Besides, they're damp, too. And a little grimy from hiking through the basin today." He began, tentatively, to remove them. "I don't really like to sleep in my clothes, especially when they're grimy. Sometimes I do, of course, but not usually. It depends on the circumstances. In Master Douin's geffide—his house in Feln, that is—it was customary to wear a special sleeping garment. I didn't always conform, however." Lijadu was staring at him, and the words continued to spill out. "The term in Vox for such sleeping garments is pajamas. It's taken directly from an ancient language called Persian, I believe—an ancient *Earth* language, you see. My isohet Abel—my sibling, my brother—has a brown pair with yellow polka dots. Very gaudy. They're made of synthetic silk. But we don't consider pajamas a necessity. Some people never wear—"

"You're wearing a *dascra,*" Lijadu observed.

Naked but for the Magistrate's amulet, Seth hurried to lie at full length beside Lijadu, principally to take the greater part of his body out of the range of her vision. Gooseflesh stippled his arms, back, and thighs. Cued by his embarrassment, his penis maintained a decorous profile. He had never slept with an alien before. Douin and Pors, he told himself with belated gratitude, had kept to their own pallets last night.

"Whose *dascra gosfi'mija* do you have, Kahl Latimer?"

"Magistrate Vrai's."

"I saw in the Sh'vaij that he wasn't wearing one. Instead he had an additional pair of eye coverings."

"Those are mine," Seth admitted, still shivering. "I gave him the goggles in exchange for his amulet."

"He suggested the trade?"

"Yes, he did. Completely unbidden."

"Why?"

"I'm not sure. He seems to think we're . . . well, j'gosfi of one mind. He wants our mission to Palija Kadi to succeed."

Lijadu's breath was sweet, possessing the fragrance
of the pasty grain they had shared—but her eyes, so
close to his, seemed to belong to an intelligent, predatory insect: He was frightened by them. The dark had
dehumanized Lijadu. Her supple body might as well
have been made of chitin or calcium.

"What, exactly, is your mission?" she asked.

"We've come to offer the Sh'gaidu a territory on Gla
Taus richer even than your basin here on Trope. If
this offer pleases you, we'll transport your entire community there and free you from the persecution of the
state."

"And the state from the conscience-pricking of the
Sh'gaidu?"

"I shouldn't have spoken yet," Seth said, conscious
of having compromised the Kieri proposal by this
prematurity. "The Pledgechild said we'd negotiate in
the morning, and I ought to have said nothing to you."

"Have you heard of auxiliary births, Kahl Latimer?
We spoke of them briefly this afternoon, but do you
know what they are?"

"The Magistrate told me a little about them. They're
a means of promoting evolutionary diversity among
a long-lived but unprolific species."

"*Social* diversity, perhaps. Acquired characteristics
are no more inheritable on Trope than elsewhere,
Kahl Latimer."

"But the effects of gosfi society are the effects of a
much larger gene pool, aren't they? Isn't that why
Trope has outpaced the nations to the north?"

Lijadu, somewhat chillingly, put a hand on his flank.
"You're wearing the *dascra* of a j'gosfi who, for evolution's sake, has gone through perhaps five auxiliary
births. But from one rebirth to the next there's no
continuity. The old self dies, but the new self doesn't
even possess the soul of the old one. Everything
about the person is different."

"Better, the Magistrate says."

"*Different*, Kahl Latimer. Wearing the *dascra* of
a person who's not the person originally born out of

the birth-parent is an evil. The Magistrate, Deputy Emahpre—all Tropiards—have renounced their souls."

"Perhaps they have several souls in succession, one for each personality." Seth indulged this speculation for its outrageousness, knowing that Lijadu would despise it and resent his flippancy. He was tired, desperately tired. If none of his asinine erotic fantasies were going to come true, he wanted to table all discussion and sleep. Or at least try to.

"Among the Tropiards of the Thirty-three Cities the wearing of the *dascra* no longer has real meaning," Lijadu said. "You know that. And you know what the *dascra* contains, too, don't you?"

"*Jinalma.*"

"The eyes of our birth-parents. We treasure them for the final visions they give us before disintegrating. But the final visions of j'gosfi who've gone through a series of auxiliary births are nearly worthless."

"Why?"

"After so many different selves have succeeded one another, the final vision can belong only to the last one, and only partially to it. The j'gosfi loses part of himself each time he's altered."

Altered: Seth thought of the castration of domestic animals

"One must live her whole life with a unified consciousness, Kahl Latimer. She must change, but remember the changes. A person is a tower forever in the act of being built. The Mwezahbe Legacy destroys the tower by dividing it into segments, as if it were so many separate stools stacked one atop the other. Such a person never knows the soul."

"The Magistrate claims that the personality born from the Tropiard's final auxiliary birth is the best personality he may possess. It's a unified self: the *ultimate* unified self."

"It's a garment which hides the skin beneath. Tropiards bundle themselves in such garments, Kahl Latimer."

"Don't they remember anything of their past selves?"

"In Ebsu Ebsa I did the sort of work that permits them to 'remember.' Tropiards know their previous lives only through evo-step genealogies, which I reviewed and transcribed for the most influential among them. Still, if j'gosfi do have knowledge of their early selves, it's second-hand. They learn about these selves as if studying the biographies of dead historical personages."

"Maybe that's appropriate."

"Entirely. There's no sense of underlying union, however. There's distance from the essential self."

"Can't distance provide perspective?"

"In the context of the essential person, Kahl Latimer, distance is estrangement. Tropiards don't know who they are."

"Perhaps I don't know who *I* am," Seth said. "I'm j'gosfi by genetic dictate: a perfect replica of my dead isosire, whom I never understood, and a perfect twin of my isohet Abel, who has sent me to your Pledgechild when he might have come himself." As best he could, Seth explained the circumstances of his origins.

"Whose soul do I have?" he then demanded of Lijadu. "Or did Günter Latimer die with the only soul vouchsafed by the creative spirit to his personal DNA? If that's the case, Abel and I are as soulless as any of the poor, damned Tropiards you castigate for sacrificing themselves at their state-ordained auxiliary births! Abel and I are shadows of our isosire, and neither of us has a soul!" He had not shouted, but the pain of saying these things had pushed his voice toward the falsetto. Faint echoes came back to him from nearby caverns.

Lijadu touched his forehead and smoothed his hair back. —*You're a person,* she cerebrated. —*Persons have souls*.

"Unless they're Tropiards," Seth whispered, trying to emulate both the silence and the immediacy of the cerebration. "Then, in your eyes, they become nonpersons, forfeiters of their gosfihood."

"Not so," she, too, whispered.

"You've already said as much," he accused her fiercely.

"I've told you only that many Tropiards never truly know their souls—not that they're soulless. They dilute their essence by their auxiliary births, but they remain persons. To be j'gosfi on our world, Kahl Latimer, is to be self-estranged. I pity such self-estranged persons their lack of wholeness."

"Do you pity me, then?" Anger had purged him of his tentativeness; her touch seemed a deliberate goad. He thrust himself against Lijadu, putting a hand to the small of her back and finding in his willful erection a means of declaring his identity. It scraped the cleft between her legs and slid glancingly up the surface of her belly, lubricating its way like a macrocephalic snail.

—*Stop!* Lijadu cerebrated.

But the pain of this imperative was brief, if piercing, and Seth struggled to lower his hips in preparation for another angry thrust. She would know he had a soul even if he had to implant its seed in her as she had implanted her cerebrations in his brain.

Her body was a puzzle, though. It opened, then closed. And Lijadu, silently resolute, had begun to exert a willful counterforce against him. She was surprisingly strong. Before he could salvage any of the momentum of his initial assault, she was astraddle his buttocks. His left arm was bent across his back. So much leverage was deployed against it that he feared it would break. His identity, smothered beneath him, suddenly grew flaccid.

"Would you allow me to enter you without consent?" Lijadu asked.

Sweat stinging his eyes, he managed grimly, "You couldn't. You can't."

"I could. I could do so now. I won't, however. Such tactics are anathema even to Tropiards, Kahl Latimer. Such tactics, you should know, inhibit rather than induce *kemmai*."

Fear, anger, shame. Seth didn't know what she was talking about. He had run a gauntlet of unpleasant emotional states, and all he could do now was lie beneath Lijadu on his belly and hope for absolution. She had pinioned him as Abel had often pinioned him, and what usually came next was acceptable or degrading according to his frame of mind. The shame of a prodigal angel overwhelmed him. He had not consciously plotted his assault on Lijadu, and that he should find himself her captive, utterly at her mercy, had a justice about it that was also cruel and inequitable. Seth wept. He had no idea what she was talking about. He had little idea why he had tried to rape her. In heart and body, he hurt. The hurt intensified, and he muffled his weeping in the folds of his damp, wadded tunic.

"In *kemmai* we become lovers, Kahl Latimer, and only genuine affection and mutual longing create acceptable conditions. I'm sorry if it isn't also so with humans. Have I naively assumed the unassumable?"

"You invited me here," Seth said through his teeth, staring into blue darkness. "You bid me remove my clothes."

"I'm sorry." She didn't release him. "Among the Sh'gaidu—even among the general run of lowly, decent Tropiards of less than administrative rank—these things pass for simple hospitality. More may occur if guest and host modulate into *kemmai* together. Conscious orientations of life style—j'gosfi, sh'gosfi—mean nothing in such circumstances. Often I've passed in and out of both states during a single *kemmai,* altering with the alterations of my partner. Exchange and reciprocity are everything during such sweet arousal."

Seth heard her as if from several rooms away. His hurt—his shame—occupied the forefront of his attention: He was frenziedly conjuring ways to release and drain it off. "You've entered my mind unbidden," he said. "That's a trespass as violent as anything I've done. It's a rape and a trespass."

Letting go of his arm, Lijadu eased herself down to her place on the pallet. Seth turned to his left side, finding himself confronted again by the smoldering jade of the Sh'gaidu's eyes.

"You consider it a violation?" she asked.

"I do. Yes. We all do."

"You didn't object before. You're objecting now because I've rebuked you for your unseemly behavior?"

"Yes," Seth admitted.

"I won't do it again," Lijadu told him. "No more cerebrations, even if the roaring of the waterwalls prevents you from hearing my voice."

They lay in the dark, facing each other. The shame in Seth had not yet completely subsided. He had found these people's cerebrations more fascinating than obtrusive or painful, and yet he had just extracted from Lijadu a promise never to send such pleasant messages to him again. Was this a clever vengeance for his self-inflicted shame? Perhaps it was. A clever vengeance upon himself.

"Let's sleep," Lijadu said. "Let's hold each other and sleep." She draped an arm across his shoulder and with her other hand touched the amulet lying between them on the pallet: Magistrate Vrai's *dascra*.

Seth glanced down at it. "I don't know whether I can," he said. "I'm overwrought. You can hear my heart pounding."

Her hand went from the amulet to his chest, where it opened and spread out as it had that afternoon against Palija Kadi, the Great Wall. How long ago that seemed: a thousand transcended selves ago.

"If we hold each other, we'll sleep."

Lijadu and Seth held each other. Her beautiful, faceted eyes brushed his face, her body moved chastely against his body, and sleep came spiraling up to Seth's brain from the depths of a weariness he had tried to deny. Several portals away, a heartseed lantern bobbed in the blue darkness like a channel buoy. Seth's dreams ranged unceasingly up and down these waters.

Eventually his dreams began to trouble him. Nightmares of nitrogen narcosis, they were surreal and suffocating, and Seth awoke from them in self-defense.

Chapter Fifteen

Lijadu was gone. As soon as Seth realized that she had abandoned him, he sat up and cocked his head from side to side, trying to orient. It was still dark, perhaps darker than before.

"Lijadu!" he called. *"Lijadu!"* Then he rebuked himself for shouting: Did he wish to wake the children, the elderly, everyone?

His hand went to his naked chest. Where the Magistrate's *dascra* should have been, in the hollow between his breastplates, nothing! Nothing but himself. His hand moved in involuntary haste to his throat, groping about for the chain that had supported the amulet. That, too, was gone. Lijadu had betrayed him, and in permitting her to accomplish that betrayal, he had betrayed the Magistrate.

"Lijadu!" he shouted again, not believing in her treachery even though the evidence seemed far from circumstantial. *"Lijadu!"*

Instantly, Yaji Tropei was filled with the din of crashing waters. The caverns boomed with noise. A freshet of cool air swept through the chambers, a light spray circulating on its back. Seth rose on the twisted pallet, put his hands to his ears, and opened his mouth as if to scream. It was impossible—so misted over was his flesh—to know whether he'd been sweating in his sleep or the spray from the waterwalls had glazed him in a sudden burst. No matter. His blood ran hot. His heart was pumping fiery plasma through his veins.

"Lijadu!"

He could scarcely hear himself. He *couldn't* hear himself. Falling to his knees, Seth shook out his wadded overtunic. The Magistrate's amulet had not been concealed in it. Maybe, however, Lijadu had hidden the *dascra* somewhere close to hand. Seth pulled his damp tunic over his head, stepped into his pants, and, inefficiently, hopped about getting his feet into his boot linings. His boot catches still undone, he ransacked the urns, baskets, and stone basins arranged at seeming random about the open-ended cell. He found nothing but tools, trinkets, grain, cloth, and earthenware bowls. Finally, desperate, he even uncapped the heartseed lantern to peer into its ceramic bowl.

What would this theft mean to Magistrate Vrai? What did it mean to Lijadu and her people? Would she have taken the *dascra* if he hadn't revealed to her the gist of the Kieri proposal? Or if he had kept in check the indiscriminate stirrings of his own sexuality? Or if he had somehow induced *kemmai* in her by a gentle human chivalry? Or could he shed his guilt by attributing the theft to Ifragsli's haunting final vision?

Did the placing of blame finally matter? To Seth, it did. He had betrayed the Magistrate of Trope by permitting his own betrayal at the hands of a young woman—a sh'gosfi—whose loyalties were all to her persecuted people.

The amulet had to be recovered.

Seth stumbled out of Lijadu's cell into the adjoining one, which was vacant, and from that cell to a third chamber. Here, bending above a Sh'gaidu whose topaz eyes had lit his way inward, he shouted, *"Lijadu!"* The Sh'gaidu's eyes seemed to cloud, and he knew he would get nothing from this frightened person but an autistic silence, perfect and gemlike. He stumbled on, attempting to retrace the route by which Lijadu and he had first attained her cell.

Curtains of water danced where none had danced before, and every cell, every portal was like every other cell or portal. Frescoes might differ, their stylized figures killing, or cooking, or copulating in distinctive ways; even the waterwalls defining certain vast hollows in the rock might vary, swaying with movements and colors all their own—but the overall pattern of the hive was unreadable. Seth found himself breaking in upon the same groups of huddled Sh'gaidu over and over again, people who either spoke no Vox or had no desire to speak it to him.

"Show me the way out!" he pleaded. Maybe they simply couldn't hear him. He was an intruder, afflicted with the impenetrable *nuraj* of Tropiards. Instead of triggering their compassion, he terrified them. Or maybe Lijadu had warned them against aiding him. She had promised not to cerebrate to him again, and, even if these bewildered Sh'gaidu could cast their mental messages in Vox, none would do so. Their sole concession to his presence was the lighting of more heartseed lanterns—until all of Yaji Tropei flickered with radiance and the noise of the cascading walls seemed to build in increments with the light.

Suddenly Seth was in a room where dozens of gocodre stirred. Tiny dragons on ledges, stone benches, everywhere. Several waddled in a narrow sluiceway parallel to the chamber's rear wall. Omwhol, the child, sat up and stared groggily after Seth as he blundered into another room.

This room, wider and higher, sheltered a bevy of silver-furred animals like the one Seth had seen earlier that evening. They seemed to bear approximately the same relation to Trope's gosfi inhabitants as monkeys did to human beings. Resting on pallets, huddled in family groups, standing partially erect, they were more curious than frightened when Seth broke in upon them. All that Seth noted about the creatures was that the species very clearly possessed both males and females.

He retreated through the den of the gocodre, exited it by another portal, and found himself in an immense, open cavern where a solitary Sh'gaidu appeared to be waiting for him. Standing before a veil of water, she beckoned him toward her with her left arm: a brusque, raking motion. This person, Seth saw, was Huspre. He recognized her by her milky eyes and the odd misalignment of her facial features.

"Lijadu stole the Magistrate's *dascra!*" he shouted.

Huspre stared at him uncomprehendingly, with no desire to comprehend. Then she repeated the raking motion of her arm, turned, and strolled almost casually toward a farther portal. Seth followed. In less than five minutes she had led him along the mural near Yaji Tropei's entrance, past the nook in which resided the statue of Duagahvi Gaidu, and onto the balustraded balcony overlooking Palija Kadi, the basin.

"Friends below," Huspre said in stammering Vox, pointing to the Sh'vaij. Her words were just audible over the booming of the waters. Stars twinkled in the southern sky, but above the cliffs to the north reared several towering cancers of clouds, metastasizing in the darkness. The torches that had been alight along the bridges looping downward from Yaji Tropei were no longer burning, and the Sh'vaij was a circular smudge at the center of an indistinct abyss. Huspre set off undaunted toward that smudge.

Clefrabbes Douin was waiting for Seth on the assembly building's apron. His ministerial cap was missing, and his face was sallow and bloated-looking in the wan starlight. Huspre left them together.

"What're you doing here?" Seth demanded of the Kieri envoy.

"Lord Pors and I were given pallets in the Sh'vaij. Not long ago, the Pledgechild woke me and said I ought to come out here to intercept you on your return from the cliffs. That was all she would say."

"And Lord Pors?"

"I left him to his sleep. After the Magistrate and Deputy Emahpre returned to the airship, Lord Pors impulsively broached the major features of our proposal—not to negotiate them, he said, but to give the Pledgechild a chance to think about them before morning. That may have been a costly misjudgment, considering the old woman's negative state of mind."

"I told Lijadu, too," Seth admitted.

"What was her reaction?"

"I'm not sure, Master Douin. She seemed to think the removal of the Sh'gaidu to Gla Taus would be something of a coup for the state."

Douin uttered a mild Kieri curse. Abruptly, suspiciously, he looked up. "And what are *you* doing here?" he asked. "Why was I roused?"

"Lijadu stole the Magistrate's *dascra* from me as we —as I—slept. I awoke and went plunging through the galleries after her."

"To no avail?" Douin gripped Seth's shoulders and peered admonitorily into his face. The lashing of the cypresses was distracting, cold-blooded in its persistence. Seth could see the flailing of a nearby tree reflected in Douin's nearly human pupils.

"To no avail. Huspre rescued me. The Pledgechild knows of the theft, that's virtually certain. Perhaps she commanded it."

"What advantage do they hope to gain?"

"Our embarrassment, I think, yours and mine. They hope to discredit us with Magistrate Vrai and the entire Tropish state."

Douin shook his head. "If they didn't care for our proposal, they merely had to say so. This theft . . . it's . . . it's *senseless.*"

"Not to the Sh'gaidu, Master Douin. Not to them, obviously."

"Your carelessness has discredited us," the Kieri said. "How could you permit that child to deceive you?"

"She's not a child. She's nearly as old as I am. In some ways she's considerably older."

"Everything's falling apart," Douin lamented serenely. "I'm almost grateful.'

"You were never going to return the *Dharmakaya* to us, were you?"

"Certainly we were. I didn't mean to imply that I was grateful our failure would deprive you and Abel of your ship."

"Then for what are you grateful?" Seth cried, stepping away from the man in whose geffide he had lived for so long. "What's going on, Master Douin? Why am I here rather than Abel? What's supposed to become of these people?" He gestured grandiloquently, poignantly, at the basin.

"You'd better go down to the roadway and tell the Magistrate what's happened," Douin said. "I'll see to it that Lord Pors knows, and perhaps, with some cooperation from the Pledgechild, we can undertake a search for your Sh'gaidu sleeping partner."

Seth bridled. "Don't tell the Point Marcher," he said. As soon as the words were out, he regretted them.

"Young Seth, Master Seth, go to Magistrate Vrai. Tell him the truth. Don't attempt to wait until morning."

"Come with me, then. Help me."

But Douin pivoted and headed back into the Sh'vaij. The cypresses, meantime, had ceased to toss their manes, and the alien corn was making lonely ticking noises.

Only a few minutes later, approaching The Albatross on its makeshift landing terrace, Seth fixed his eyes on the pilot's bubble and scuffed his boot soles in the dust. No light shone in the craft.

Abel, he thought, why aren't you here in my place? Why can't I commune with you as isohets are supposed to be able to do?

His task set, he began pounding on the door of the

airship. A dull light came on in the pilot's bubble, like a filament in a coated bulb. Emahpre appeared behind this bronze coating, a player behind a transparent screen. He began motioning with his hands as if they were delicate, ivory-strutted fans. Be quiet, his gestures meant.

Seth stopped pounding. Then the side-panel slid back, and he climbed into The Albatross's narrow, confessional gloom. The Deputy helped him aboard. A small heartseed globe rested in one of the baskets suspended beneath the ship's skylight. Although a faint blue sheen encircled this globe, the surrounding dark was scarcely affected. The lamp appeared to draw rather than disperse illumination.

"Didn't your accommodations in the galleries suit you?" Emahpre whispered.

Seth's courage failed him. "Nightmares," he said.

Then the Magistrate let himself down from one of the bunks on the airship's opposite bulkhead. With a sleeping cape falling from his shoulders in voluted disarray, he stood in the shadows.

"You know you're welcome here, Kahl Latimer."

"Of course he is," Emahpre agreed. "But you'd best go back to sleep, Magistrate. The morning's still three or four hours away."

But Vrai said, "Now that you've seen these people, what do you think of them, Kahl Latimer?"

"I don't believe they're insane, stricken with *nuraj*." Seth glanced at the Deputy, who apparently believed they were.

"Do you think they're dangerous?"

Seth considered. If Lijadu had betrayed him, would the Pledgechild think to order some more devastating betrayal?

"I don't know, Magistrate."

"They're not in the least a peril to the state," Vrai said, moving aside a few steps and lowering himself into a swivel chair. He rotated it so that he was staring into The Albatross's aft section.

"Their existence undermines the authority of the Mwezahbe Legacy," Emahpre suddenly rejoined.

The Magistrate altogether ignored this. "One of the principal difficulties of my position, Kahl Latimer, is determining what constitutes reasonable action under extraordinary circumstances."

"It's reasonable to preserve those institutions which are predicated on reason," Emahpre said, "and to uproot those which are not." He pointed Seth to a chair and composed himself hurriedly in still another.

" 'Uproot'?" the Magistrate said, swiveling to face them. "That's an invidious euphemism, Deputy."

"A problem doesn't cease to exist simply because you cease to consider it a problem."

"Very often, Deputy Emahpre, it does."

Seth's hand went to his chest. Would informing the Magistrate of Lijadu's theft of the amulet alter him in his feelings toward the Sh'gaidu? Thus mocked and affronted, would Vrai, too, take an implacable stand against them? Seth glanced at the Deputy. He was startled to see that Emahpre had witnessed his involuntary fumbling at his chest and throat. Dear God, he'd discovered his secret to Emahpre even before breaking the news to the Magistrate. Now the Deputy was watching him with such rigid intentness that Seth feared to speak. His mouth opened. Emahpre, out of the seeing of Magistrate Vrai, shook his head in warning.

Didn't either of these rational Tropiards wish to know why he'd abandoned Yaji Tropei in the middle of the night? Emahpre had asked, of course, but Seth had offered up a lie—or, at best, a partial truth—and the Magistrate had subjected him to a pair of polite, if nonessential, questions. In truth, Vrai had been catechizing himself.

Obsessively, he continued: "My deputy thinks he's the only Tropiard who fully understands the Sh'gaidu. But I know something about them, too. You see—" He stuck, swiveled away, peered into the darkness aft. "You see," he resumed tentatively, "I'm capable of empathy even with rebels, pariahs, discards. I have to be. I'm the guilty conscience of my nation."

"These people are sh'gosfi by choice, Magistrate! They're harlots and mystagogues! By choice!"

But Vrai didn't respond to his deputy's outraged emendation. Instead he said, "Let's think again of sleep. Prepare a bunk for Kahl Latimer."

"Perhaps you'd better tell Kahl Latimer your decision. If he's at all like me, Magistrate, he may not be able to sleep."

"What decision?" Seth asked, spellbound by the conflict between the two Tropiards, and too intimidated by Emahpre to confess his sin.

Still facing aft, the Magistrate said, "Because we're bond-partners, I trust you'll understand my decision and accept it. It's not one that I've arrived at easily."

"It's one you arrived at quickly," Emahpre interjected.

"That's simply not so. My reasons have historical antecedents. What we saw in the Sh'vaij tonight played a part, of course, but really just to tip me toward the only possible decision among all my seeming options."

"Tell him, then," Emahpre urged.

The Magistrate swiveled toward Seth. Tropiards slept masked, apparently. Vrai's face was that of an aristocratic bandit.

"I've decided," he said, "that we must let the Sh'-gaidu be."

Seth lay in a berth opposite the Magistrate's. Deputy Emahpre slept, or pretended to sleep, in the bunk directly below his commander's. A half hour or more had passed. All that Seth knew for certain about this finite eternity of numbered moments was that the Deputy had spent them trying to gauge how soundly Magistrate Vrai was sleeping.

At last the little Tropiard eased himself out of his bunk, crossed the cabin, and tapped Seth on the forehead.

"Come into the pilot's bubble," he whispered.

Haggard and fearful, Seth swung his feet over the edge of his berth and dropped lightly to the floor. After ducking into the pilot's compartment, he slid into a frame chair before the instrument console.

"Where's the Magistrate's *dascra,* Latimer?"

Seth, noting that the Deputy had dispensed with the usual honorific, told Emahpre what had happened in the cliffs. His inquisitor stared through the dome of the pilot's bubble at the distorted stars and the thunderhead growing in the northern sky. As if silently commiserating with his superior, the Deputy fingered his own amulet, now and again rubbing the amber stone decorating its pouch. When Seth had finished his story, Emahpre was silent a long time.

"Latimer, you've given me a lever," he said at last.

"A lever?"

"Your crass negligence can be made to appear nothing but Sh'gaidu deceit."

Seth leaned toward the Deputy and hissed, "I had no reason to suspect this theft would happen!"

"The Magistrate warned you, I believe. Then you slept with the Pledgechild's heir without seeing to the safety of his *dascra.* If not negligence, what do you call such irresponsible flouting of a trust?"

Seth leaned back, averting his gaze. "It's past recall, Deputy Emahpre. Recriminations are pointless. We ought to see about recovering the amulet. And I'd better tell Magistrate Vrai what's happened."

"Let him sleep." The Deputy gripped Seth's wrist and held him in his chair. "My intention *is* to recover the amulet, Latimer. And I'll recover it by refusing to overlook this provocation."

"What are you going to do?"

The Administrative Deputy released Seth's wrist and touched the lighted console before him. The viridescent glow of the panel X-rayed his hand. Seth could see the bones of each finger strung together like elongated bamboo beads. Then the fingers played lightly across a series of communication keys, and

Emahpre's alien visage took on an almost ghoulish aspect as he bent forward to speak into The Albatross's batonlike mike. There then ensued a rapid, static-free exchange in Tropish with a disembodied voice that Seth had never heard before.

"What was that about?" he asked when Emahpre was finished.

"Using the Magistrate's personal code, I've just put through a call to Commander Swodi of the surveillance force. I informed him of the theft and ordered him to dispatch a convoy of evacuation vehicles to the roadway before sunrise. Support troops, too."

"That contravenes the Magistrate's decision," Seth said, dumbfounded.

"I'm seeing to it that you and the Kieri envoys return to Gla Taus with exactly what you came for."

"You've committed treason, Deputy."

When Seth attempted to climb out of his chair again, Emahpre's cerebration twisted through his brain like a fruit-corer: —*Sit down, Latimer*. Seth sat down. Aloud, the Deputy said, "The recovery of Magistrate Vrai's amulet hardly constitutes a treason."

"You've violated his personal code, deployed a portion of the surveillance force, and authorized an invasion of Palija Kadi. That's treasonous, Deputy Emahpre. At least in my eyes." Bracing himself against the inevitable, Seth rose from his chair and lurched sidelong to get free of it.

—*Sit down!*

The command seemed to paralyze him, then to direct his own animating will. Awkwardly he sat down again.

"Your eyes have nothing to do with this, Latimer. This is an internal state matter completely outside the province of you and your friends. Nevertheless, by acting in Trope's own best interest I'm going to help you fulfill your mission. All you need do is divorce yourself utterly from Tropish executive, political, and military concerns. Any other posture is illicit intervention. Even Interstel recognizes the truth of what I'm saying and forbids such meddlesome arrogance."

Seth whispered, "You're committing treason against Magistrate Vrai."

"*For* Magistrate Vrai, Latimer. I've enough love for both the Mwezahbe Legacy and Magistrate Vrai to commit such 'treasons' endlessly on their behalf."

Down the southern sky above The Albatross a meteor plummeted. It traced its path like a crisply burning fuse, fiery against the indigo of the night. Seth's heart plummeted with it. For a moment it seemed to him that the *Dharmakaya* had fallen from its orbit. Abel, he silently cried, save yourself. But the meteor was only a meteor, not a light-tripper skipping to its death; and Seth was hurled back into his unwilling complicity with Deputy Emahpre, who told him cheerily,

"It may please you, Latimer, how this works out. Why don't you withhold judgment until you see?"

After a time, exhausted, Seth slept where he sat.

BOOK FIVE

Chapter Sixteen

Dawn broke gray. Sixteen trucks descended out of the rocks to the west of Palija Kadi, floating down its dusty roadway in single file. They were clumsy-looking vehicles. Their high sideboards supporting rounded, plexiglass roofs, these trucks rolled on heavy rubber tires as tall as an adult Tropiard. The whine the trucks made seemed little more than the faint droning of an auroral breeze, and the helmeted Tropiards enclosed in their lofty cabs looked like mannequins or marionettes.

Emahpre saw the convoy coming and woke Seth up. "It's time to recover what you lost, Kahl Latimer. Come with me."

Seth rose groggily and followed the Deputy into the airship's passenger compartment. Rolled tightly in his sleeping cape, Magistrate Vrai resembled a creature undergoing an arcane metamorphosis. He was dead to the two intruders from the pilot's bubble, dead to the baleful susurrus of the morning.

"Go ahead," Emahpre said, scarcely bothering to whisper. "Wake him and confess your negligence."

It seemed both a pointless and a cruel suggestion. Seth glanced guiltily at the sleeping Tropiard and decided to let him lie. Perhaps Douin or Pors had found the missing amulet. Perhaps the Pledgechild, having recovered it from Lijadu, was even now awaiting his arrival in the Sh'vaij to restore it to him, and to explain the significance of the apparent theft. Perhaps Lijadu herself intended to hand it over. If any of these speculations approached the truth, why worry the

Magistrate with a premature and therefore needless confession?

Emahpre, drumming the fingers of one hand against his thigh, opened The Albatross's side-panel and gestured Seth through it ahead of him.

The trucks in the convoy had lined up sixteen abreast behind The Albatross, their noses pointing up-basin toward the Sh'vaij. At the driver's window of the only vehicle whose nose protruded a hood's length beyond all the others, Deputy Emahpre conferred intently with the officer in the cab. Seth took this opportunity to walk between two of the trucks, examining their construction and marveling at the indecipherable hieroglyphs painted on their flanks.

Behind the parked trucks, however, he came face to face with a group of Tropish soldiers who had spilled from the enclosed carriers into the light. They stared blankly at Seth, every one of them masked. They wore small chromium helmets, single-piece garments of white, and broad black belts from which several pieces of complicated metal equipment hung. Two or three of the soldiers held long, tubelike implements across their bodies; corrugated hoses ran from the tubes to gleaming, plastic canisters on their belts. Almost all of these warrior j'gosfi had laser rifles slung across their backs.

"Kahl Latimer!" the Deputy called.

Seth retreated, backpedaling away from the soldiers until he had at last turned about and confronted Emahpre. "What are *they* for?" he asked.

"Whatever's necessary." The Deputy gestured at the officer in the point truck. "Captain Yithuju will see to the comfort of the Magistrate. When he awakes, the captain will inform him of what's occurred and tell him where we've gone. I'm not abandoning the Magistrate, Latimer. My loyalty's still his."

"Why don't *we* tell him, then?"

"Go ahead. Follow your conscience. I'm to the Sh'vaij, however." He hurried up the path through the rich Sh'gaidu crops, his knees and elbows pumping, and Seth fell in behind him, demoralized by his grogginess and the weather.

The thunderheads which had formed above the basin during the night had toppled to the south, flattening out across all the visible sky. They had become something decidedly odd. Giving off a mother-of-pearl sheen, these clouds resembled clusters of depending human breasts. Palija Kadi was a shadow beneath their matriarchal heaviness. It was going to rain.

Almost as if he had been there all night, Douin was waiting for Seth and Deputy Emahpre on the assembly building's apron.

"Something's happening in there," he said, jabbing a hand toward the Sh'vaij. "The Pledgechild and several of the Sh'gaidu elders—"

"Midwives," Emahpre said. "They call their esteemed older communards by a title that translates 'midwives.' " The term plainly disgusted him.

"Very well, then. The Pledgechild and several . . . several midwives . . . have gathered in the old woman's cell," Douin said. "They know your trucks are on the roadway. The remainder of the Sh'gaidu are still in the galleries. The old woman says they'll remain there until this business is settled."

"Where's Lord Pors?" the Deputy asked.

"He went out a short while ago in search of Lijadu. He was convinced she'd abandoned the galleries for the fields. He said he wished to check each of the *kioba* in turn, beginning with the one where Lijadu's birth-parent kept her three-day vigil."

"You told him of the theft?" Seth asked Douin.

"Of course. Did you tell the Magistrate, Master Seth?"

"I encouraged him not to," Deputy Emahpre said, surprising Seth by the readiness with which he excused, before the Kieri, Seth's failure of will. "But I'd like to know if the Sh'gaidu allowed Lord Pors to traipse unmolested into the fields. Didn't they try to prevent him from going?"

"Indeed not," Douin replied. "Our freedom hasn't

been restricted in the least. Neither have the Sh'gaidu paid much attention to us this morning."

Inside the assembly building, Seth's party came upon the Pledgechild, Huspre, and three aged midwives kneeling at the tiny altar before Palija Dait. Ifragsli's corpse was gone, and only a single heartseed lantern burned. With assistance from Huspre and one of the midwives, the Pledgechild painfully stood to receive those who had interrupted her prayers or meditations.

"Where's your heir?" Emahpre demanded.

"I don't really wish to tell you," the old woman said.

"She stole from Kahl Latimer the Magistrate's *dascra*—last night, when she took him into the galleries."

"We don't deny that, Deputy. But Lijadu's reasons are her own."

"Her motives—her goals!—derive from you!"

The old woman said nothing. Seth shifted uneasily from foot to foot, while Douin kept his head bowed, as if to negate his existence among these argumentative people by self-effacing silence.

Deputy Emahpre slashed demonstratively with his hand. "The Sh'gaidu have been a carbuncle on the flank of the state for over two hundred years! What can't be healed must be cut away! Your heir has forced us—forced us at last—to perform that surgery!"

"And you are the knife?"

"I am the knife," the Deputy declared self-assuredly.

"Where's Ulgraji Vrai, Deputy?"

"This morning I act in his stead, Pledgechild. My hands are his."

"Then you're responsible for the trucks in the basin —also for the foolhardy soldiers scarring the face of Palija Kadi with their ropes."

Emahpre stalked away several paces. "The trucks, yes. The other, however, means nothing to me. Foolhardy soldiers? Ropes? If you're seeking to deflect me from the recovery of Magistrate Vrai's *dascra*, you'd—"

"Go outside!" the old woman cried, flipping her hand at the Deputy. "Go look at the Great Wall! See for yourself the *nuraj* you're perpetrating!"

After a brief hesitation, beckoning Douin and Seth to accompany him, the Deputy trotted toward the door. "I'll be back," he told the Pledgechild, over his shoulder. "Whatever you're talking about, I'll be back to conclude this business."

Seth and Douin bewilderedly dogging his heels, he exited the Sh'vaij. Then, outside, the three of them ran along the building's apron until they had reached a vantage from which the Great Wall was visible. Above the stair-step terraces ascending to Palija Kadi, upon the wall's awesome bone-white face, ten or twelve tiny figures were emulating the gravity-defying antics of ballooning spiders. They were rappelling down the wall on ropes no more substantial-seeming than threads of arachnoid silk.

"What're they doing?" Douin asked, nearly winded.

Emahpre's response was bitter: "I intend to find out."

With no other word the Deputy surged toward the ascending terraces, scrambling away from Seth and Douin like a puppet being lifted an entire body's length at a time. At the base of the terraces he halted, allowing his companions to catch up. Meanwhile, four or five of the rappelling soldiers had reached the bottom of the wall. Several more were beginning to drop themselves down its face from the summit. Seth saw that a couple of those already down were snapping pods off heartseed plants, scooping out the balls inside the fruits, and releasing the resultant spheres on the wind. A number of these were effervescing up the face of Palija Kadi like pale blue champagne bubbles. . . .

Emahpre swore in Tropish. In amplified counterpoint, thunder mumbled in the strange cloud cover.

The Deputy leaped away, bounded up the stair steps to the wall on a grim steeplechase.

Before Seth could pursue him, Douin intervened. "Don't, Master Seth. Even he doesn't know what he's going to do when he gets up there. Look to the east." He pointed toward the *kioba* in which Lijadu had told Seth of her sojourn in the Tropish city of Ebsu Ebsa. "Let's see if Lord Pors is there."

"We'll have to climb toward the wall," Seth told Douin, "and then cut across to the left from one of the terraces." If they tried to go directly to the lookout, uninterrupted stands of monarchleaf and silverbriar would impede their progress.

They climbed. More state soldiers dropped lightly down the wall, leaping out and sliding along their taut double ropes. Emahpre had disappeared on a higher terrace level, and neither Seth nor Douin attempted to spot him. They moved southward along a wide tier of slender bushes loaded with mottled, brown-and-yellow legumes.

"Look!" Douin cried. He nodded at the *kioba,* which was below them now. Two naked Sh'gaidu were digging in the loose earth beneath the tower's lookout. "What do you think they're doing?"

"Maybe they're burying a portion of Lijadu's birthparent."

Douin had no opportunity to debate this proposition with Seth because Lord Pors suddenly appeared in the lookout and hailed them with a wave and a shout.

"I've found the Pledgechild's heir!" he called. "Hurry, Master Douin! Hurry, Master Seth! She's here, the vicious strumpet!"

Startled, the two Sh'gaidu beneath the tower looked up. One of them rose from her crouch and began climbing the rope hanging from the platform. The other turned her topaz eyes on Seth and Douin.

"I've found her!" Pors shouted again, unaware of what was happening.

"Look to the rope beneath you!' Douin cried in

warning. "Look to the rope, Lord Pors!" A strange, anxious noise escaped his lungs, and he ran for the steps descending toward the *kioba.*

A low booming of thunder sounded.

An instant later, Lord Pors was screaming. His body was pulled away from the lookout's southern wall. The screaming grew more bloodcurdling, modulated into a banshee wail, then ceased. As Douin and Seth reached the stone-braced steps leading downward, Pors's body came hurtling out of the tower. It completed only half a somersault before striking the ground.

The Sh'gaidu who had knifed Pors came shinnying down one of the stilts of the tower—for she had pulled the rope onto the platform after her and purposely left it there. Her accomplice on the ground hurried to Pors's body and crouched beside it with her back to Seth and Douin.

Douin crumpled to his knees. Crucified with grief or incredulity, he threw out his arms and called out his compatriot's private Kieri name. Seth tried to pull him up. The Sh'gaidu, both of them, were huddled over Pors now, and a pair of wayward heartseed globes bobbed down the basin toward them. Rain drops began pattering among the leaves and pocking the dust.

"Master Douin, you can't stay here!" Seth cried. "It's going to pour! Enough to strangle us!"

As he hesitated over the grief-stricken Kieri, Pors's murderers rose from the body and scrambled away toward the Sh'vaij. At last Douin looked up. Seth, numbed by what he had witnessed, helped the other man to his feet. Then, the deluge threatening, they slowly descended the stone-braced steps together. Once down, Seth knelt over the corpse of the Kieri noble.

"Dear God," he said, "what have they done to him?"

Douin's reply was eerily calm: "They've cut out his eyes, Master Seth, as if he were Sh'gaidu."

"I'm sorry," Seth murmured, trying to compute the

degree of his own culpability in Pors's death and
mutilation. "Master Douin, I'm sorry."

"You'd better go up into the tower," Douin commanded him tonelessly. "He said he'd found the
Pledgechild's heir."

Seth stumbled away from the violated face of Lord
Pors, with its ragged, empty eye sockets and its
knocked-askew dentures. He began to climb hand-
over-hand up the *kioba*'s strut. The entire resilient
structure swayed in the wind. When Seth had reached
the underside of its platform, he had to lock his knees
about the strut, reach with both hands for the opening
in the floor, and swing out over the revolving ground.
He hung for a moment in free space, then exerted
himself and did a strenuous pushup into the tower.
His fingers had begun to bleed.

"Lijadu!"

She didn't respond. She appeared to be bound to
the lookout's central pole, as Ifragsli had been bound
there before her. But when Seth approached and
looked at Lijadu's hands, he found that she wasn't
bound at all. She was leaning against the pole as if in
empathy with her dismembered birth-parent. Angrily
Seth jerked her around and prepared to revile her for
her duplicitous treatment of him, for standing by so
complacently while Lord Pors was knifed, tossed
overboard, and mutilated.

But Lijadu's face was bruised and puffy, and her
eyes were shot through with crystalline clouds. She
was elsewhere, if anywhere. Was this a self-induced
spiritual trance or a protective catalepsy intended to
thwart his questioning of her?

Seth turned her face from side to side. "Lijadu,
Lijadu," he intoned. "What have you done with the
Magistrate's *dascra?*" Clearly she didn't have it. She
was naked this morning; no amulet hung from her
neck. Nor did it seem likely that she had hidden it in
the *kioba*. The only other artifact in the lookout was
the rope the Sh'gaidu assassin had pulled up after her.

Retrieving it from the corner, Seth considered what

to do. He had to get Lijadu down and back to the
Sh'vaij. He fashioned a harness, slipped it about her,
and eased her through the opening in the platform,
paying out more rope and bracing himself against her
weight. Douin received Lijadu and undid the makeshift harness.

"She doesn't have it," Seth called.

Glancing over his shoulder, he saw that the Great
Wall was streaked with blowing rain. The drops were
heavier now. Fewer soldiers rappelled down the wall,
and no one had thrown a new set of ropes over the
summit. Perhaps the Deputy had made his displea-
sure known. Several of the Tropiards were running
through the basin toward the Sh'vaij.

Seth tied his rope to the pole in the *kioba,* then slid
down it to the ground. Yesterday, he recalled, Lijadu
had braced it for him. . . .

Douin was waiting for Seth with Lord Pors thrown
over his shoulder like a sack. He nodded brusquely at
Lijadu, now lying on her side in the dust. The foliage
on the terraces above them crackled insanely in the
quickening rain.

"Pick up the Pledgechild's heir as I have Lord
Pors."

Seth knelt, struggled, hoisted Lijadu onto his shoulders. "She's been beaten," he said. "Lord Pors beat her,
Master Douin."

"For your sake," Douin said bitterly. "To recover
the *dascra.*"

"In that he failed miserably," Seth snapped.

Douin didn't reply, but trudged northward through
the lashing vegetation toward the Sh'vaij. Seth trudged
in his footsteps. Rain spilled in torrents, battering the
crops and running off underfoot in muddy floods.

Thirty or forty state soldiers—a few of whom may
have rappelled down Palija Kadi—stood huddled in
front of the assembly building. Drenched and dispirited, they made no attempt to enter. But as if they had
some vague notion who Seth and Douin were, they

backed away and cleared a narrow corridor to the door. The eaves of the Sh'vaij were the color of running blood.

"I'm not going in!" Douin shouted.

"Why not?"

"I'm going to take Lord Pors to the airship!"

"You'll wake the Magistrate!"

"If the rain hasn't already done that, Master Seth!" Lugging the dead Point Marcher, Douin set off down the muddy path to the roadway.

Seth looked briefly at the uniformed Tropiards huddled in the rain, then swung about, and carried Lijadu into the Sh'vaij. It was instantly quieter, but another noise—an internal noise—assaulted Seth, and he understood that the Sh'gaidu were keening together in their minds. A dissonant, angry, melancholy music. A choiring of cloistered but interwoven minds. He was "hearing" it. The sounds ran through his aching blood and pulsed in his very heart: cerebrations from Yaji Tropei, the galleries, and from the Sh'gaidu here in the assembly building.

In the short time since Seth, Douin, and Emahpre had rushed out of the Sh'vaij to check the unauthorized rappelling on the Great Wall, several more midwives had joined their sisters in front of Palija Dait. They sat in a semicircular prayer ring facing outward, each in a modified lotus position. Seth estimated fifteen elders altogether, all of them ritually naked, as if in protest of the state's heavy-handed maneuvers. In addition, a number of younger adults occupied the wooden benches about the circumference of the great room. The Pledgechild wasn't among these people, and it was she whom Seth most wanted to see.

On the verge of collapse he staggered into the open nave of the Sh'vaij. Two communards with muddy feet and ankles sprang from the shadowy perimeters of the room. They took Lijadu from his shoulders, as gracefully and quickly as if drawing a scarf from his tunic pocket, and he was surprised to find himself dripping but unburdened before the midwives. As

Lijadu's rescuers bore her into the left-hand chamber behind Palija Dait, their wet bodies and muddy feet registered in Seth's mind as telltale indictments and he pointed a shaking hand after them in accusation.

"They killed Lord Pors!" he cried. "Those two have just killed an official representative of Lady Turshebsel, Liege Mistress of Kier!"

This accusation impressed no one, although, echoing in the Sh'vaij, it reverberated upon Seth like his own feeble mind cry.

"I want to talk to the Pledgechild!" he insisted.

When no one responded, Seth started toward the door through which Pors's assassins had just disappeared.

"Latimer!"

He turned about and saw Deputy Emahpre coming into the Sh'vaij in the company of a tall, lean Tropiard in boots and siege helmet. Dripping rain water, they stamped their feet and picked fastidiously at their sodden clothes.

"This is Commander Swodi," the Deputy said, indicating the officer beside him. "It was he who thought the acrobatics on the Great Wall a fine method of getting his troops down from the basin's rim."

Swodi was plainly discomfited by Emahpre's remarks. He looked chastened and ill at ease. He undoubtedly had only a little Vox.

"An exercise in agility, adaptability, equipment use," the Deputy continued, berating the officer in a language which insulted him simply by being alien. "So realistic was the exercise, one rappeller fell and killed himself."

The Deputy gestured angrily, spoke a string of explosive syllables in his own tongue, and shouted out the crofthouse door at the men standing in the rain. A moment later four Tropish soldiers entered, carrying their rain-beaded laser rifles and glancing about the interior of the Sh'vaij as if it were the tomb of Seitabe Mwezahbe and they awestruck tourists.

Seth spoke up loudly: "Lord Pors is dead, too. Master Douin and I found Lijadu in the tower, but without the *dascra*."

Deputy Emahpre stalked across the nave, poised himself almost on tiptoe before Seth, and, his head draw back like that of a cobra preparing to strike upward at a hovering assailant, hissed, "Explain!"

As Seth was explaining, the two Sh'gaidu who had taken Lijadu from Seth reemerged from the Pledgechild's cells and moved along the wall to a bench. Their bodies were now dry, wiped clean of mud.

Emahpre interrupted Seth's story: "You permitted your friend to carry Lord Pors's body to our airship?"

"Was that wrong?"

"No, not wrong." The Deputy strutted about Seth in a jagged circle, muttering unintelligibly. Then he halted and said, "When the Magistrate learns what's happened here, when he sees the corpse of the Kieri envoy, he'll return to his senses. He'll see the need for harsh measures against these people."

"Lord Pors had beaten the Pledgechild's heir," Seth said. "He'd—"

"Would you recognize the murderers?" the Deputy overrode him.

"They're here in the Sh'vaij." Seth nodded toward the eastern wall. But at least a dozen Sh'gaidu sat on benches against this wall, three or four with topaz eyes, and Seth no longer had any notion who was who.

Emahpre whirled and spoke in Tropish to the soldiers who had just entered. The four of them strode purposefully to the eastern wall, yanked a pair of Sh'gaidu to their feet, and then bullied them across the nave and out into the rain. Four more Tropish dragoons entered to replace those who had left.

"You may have arrested the wrong ones," Seth protested.

"They'll do."

"Do for what? What's going to happen to them?" He was amazed that none of the midwives, none of the communards along the wall, had offered the soldiers any resistance. Their encephalic choiring had grown more baleful—he had a headache, a severe, melancholy migraine in his frontal lobes—but that was the extent of their opposition to the state's strong-arm tactics. Seth wasn't sure that the Tropiards were even *aware* of these people's dissonant mind cries.

Emahpre was speaking to the soldiers who had just come in. He gestured abruptly, raised his voice to a shout, and, when Commander Swodi said something in response, shook his head. Swodi, militarily rigid, pivoted and strolled into the rain.

The Deputy looked at Seth. "I told him to get outside with the other sufferers. What right does he have to stand beneath a roof after sending his troops over Palija Kadi, after precipitating a soldier's death?"

"Not all the sufferers in this basin are standing in the rain."

"Perhaps they should be," Emahpre countered.

Then the Pledgechild came through the tall niche to the left of Palija Dait, to halt near the ring of Sh'gaidu midwives. Her eyes glittered like those of a bird or a mouse: a small, brave creature in the clutches of something bigger than itself. She had shed her garment. In her shriveled nakedness she had the vulnerability of the newborn.

"Do you believe you've evened accounts, Deputy Emahpre?" she asked.

"Two of your people for the Kieri envoy?"

"A weighted ratio."

"Not when those two are the envoy's murderers, harlot. Not when your heir has stolen the treasure of my superior."

Seth stepped toward the old woman. "Pledgechild, you embraced me yesterday. I beg you to have Lijadu return the amulet, that I may give it to Magistrate Vrai before departing Trope."

"Please don't beg me to do what I can't, Kahl Latimer. It hurts me not to be able to accede to your wishes."

"Things have gone beyond the Magistrate's—or

perhaps even the Deputy's—control, Pledgechild. If you don't return the amulet, it's likely—"

"It's likely you'll suffer," the Deputy interjected.

The old woman's glittering eyes turned toward the little Tropiard. "It's what unites us, suffering," she said. "We come to unavoidable suffering—to your crass j'gosfi persecution—just as we came into our lives." She lifted her frail arms so that their loose skin hung like wattles. "Look upon this body, Deputy Emahpre, and tell me you don't recognize yourself in it."

He averted his eyes. "All I care to look upon, harlot, is Magistrate Vrai's *dascra*. Return it or suffer the consequences."

Hearing a commotion at the assembly building's entrance, Seth turned and saw a pair of apparitions gliding into the gloom from the rain: Clefrabbes Douin and Magistrate Vrai. The Magistrate had not removed his sleeping cape. So drenched was this garment that it clung to him like a sleek, black placenta. Douin led the bemused-looking Vrai toward the Pledgechild and her two anxious petitioners, Emahpre and Seth.

"Outside," the Magistrate said, speaking to his deputy but sweeping his arm at the door, "outside, a pair of Sh'gaidu lie garroted. Why?"

"They were Lord Pors's assassins, Magistrate."

"In truth they were not!" the Pledgechild said. "Your soldiers have indiscriminately escorted two of my people to a blind retribution!"

"This entire community must share in the guilt of the envoy's death," Emahpre rejoined. "Whether the two persons who've just died were actually the ones to kill him is irrelevant. We don't intend to sort and particularize the guilt."

The Magistrate, ignoring this exchange, approached Seth and put his hands on the young isohet's shoulders. "Master Douin says you allowed the young Sh'gaidu to steal my *dascra*. Then, last night, you failed to tell me."

"I wouldn't let him," Emahpre said. "You weren't

yet prepared to find your trust in these people shattered."

"Is learning of the theft along with Lord Pors's murder a revelation any less disruptive of my peace of mind?"

Emahpre, perhaps detecting some uncertainty in this rebuttal, pressed his own attack: "The treasure of your birth-parent, Magistrate Vrai, is the treasure of every Tropiard of the Thirty-three Cities. It must be recovered. We all owe allegiance to the final vision of your birth-parent because you're the embodiment of its dictates. Figuratively, Magistrate, your amulet contains the *jinalma* of Seitaba Mwezahbe."

"Figuratively," Vrai admitted. He glanced at the Pledgechild. His whole manner bespoke doubt and hesitancy.

"Magistrate," Emahpre persisted, "you've gone as far as anyone may go to credit the Sh'gaidu with generous, pacific souls. They've betrayed that magnanimity in you by stealing your *dascra* from Kahl Latimer and slaying a guest of the state simply for seeking to recover it."

"For brutally assaulting my heir," the old woman interjected.

Emahpre bore on: "Let me redeem their betrayal of Kahl Latimer's faith in them, Magistrate. Let me proceed with the recovery operations. Let me redeem their flouting of your generosity."

Vrai turned to the Pledgechild. "You know where my *dascra* is?"

Her eyes glittering fiercely, she said nothing.

"She knows!" Emahpre insisted.

"Return it to me, Pledgechild. You know I haven't deserved this. You know that since assuming this office my goal has been to achieve justice for the Sh'gaidu as well as for the Tropiards." Seth saw that Vrai had begun fumbling with the goggles he had given him.

"I'm unable to do what you ask," the Pledgechild said.

Besodden in his sleeping cape, the Magistrate stared bleakly at the old woman, then turned to his deputy.

"Do what you must," he commanded Emahpre. "Do what you must."

Chapter Seventeen

What followed was chaos. Given his head, Emahpre rigorously prosecuted the search for the *dascra*.

First, he asked Magistrate Vrai to examine the amulets of the midwives sitting before Palija Dait in their prayer ring. Vrai docilely fulfilled this task while a pair of rifle-carrying dragoons circled about inside the Sh'vaij collecting the amulets of the younger communards. When it was determined that none of these amulets belonged to the Magistrate, they were redistributed to their rightful owners. Seth helped with the redistribution. The Sh'gaidu seemed to know their own "treasure" as certain animals know their own cubs or fledglings, and the process took a good deal less time than Seth would have imagined. Afterward, the Pledgechild took up a position on the floor with the other midwives, and Magistrate Vrai, exhausted by this languid search and dispirited by its outcome, retired to the Pledgechild's rooms behind the Lesser Wall.

Seth and Douin accompanied the Magistrate to a nook where the two Kieri envoys had spent most of the previous night. On their way in, they saw Lijadu, either sleeping or unconscious, stretched out on a pallet in the Pledgechild's private cell. Seth wanted to halt beside her, ask her what was happening, plead with her to yield to him the secret of the amulet's where-abouts—but Douin gestured him on, and together he and the Kieri man-of-letters removed the Magistrate's sleeping cape and settled him comfortably onto a bench surrounded by shelves burdened with a dismaying variety of earthenware urns.

As soon as he was safely down, soldiers began marching back and forth through these rooms carrying clay vessels, wooden bowls, and ceramic amphorae, anything at all that might contain or conceal the Magistrate's *dascra*. The soldiers dripped rain water wherever they walked. When two paused beside the Magistrate's bench to indicate that they wished to search the pottery on the shelves around him, he sat up and shooed them away. His language rang with the intonations of disdain and invective.

"It probably ought to be searched," Seth pointed out, leaning over him.

"Master Douin will do that for me," Vrai said, easing himself back down to the bench. He moved as gingerly as if he had received a physical wound, and Seth wondered if the loss of the *dascra* had somehow actually deprived him of both courage and will. "You don't mind, do you, Master Douin?"

"No, Magistrate."

"What do you want me to do?" Seth asked.

"Watch my deputy. Go out there and see what he's doing. I can't empower you to intervene, but I want you to . . . to *watch* him."

"He's behaving like a tyrant."

"At my behest, Kahl Latimer, to accomplish what must be accomplished."

Seth gestured impotently at the ceiling, made a moue of bewilderment at Douin, and returned to the nave of the Sh'vaij, purposely not looking into Lijadu's cell as he passed it.

Deputy Emahpre was at the door, shouting orders into the rain. Seth joined him and saw that a unit of Tropish soldiers, armed with canisters and corrugated tubes, was disappearing around the eastern

corner of the Sh'vaij on its way to the bridges of Yaji
Tropei. Heedless of the rain, Seth dashed outside and
partially around the assembly building to watch the
soldiers depart.

They were a ragged lot. Close-order drill in a thun-
derstorm confounded them. One of them glanced
back toward Seth, revealing a mask atop his obligatory
Tropish goggles. This mask appeared to be made of
black plastic: It hooded the nostrils as well as the
eyes, giving its wearer the look of a serious, upright
raccoon. Seth had only a brief, unsettling glimpse of
the soldier's face. Then he ran back to the crofthouse
door.

"What are they going to do?" he shouted, pointing
after the soldiers.

"Whatever's necessary!" Emahpre replied. It was
almost comical the way he refused to leave the shel-
ter of the building. Seth ducked beneath the dripping
eaves and shook water on Emahpre like a spaniel
emerging from a lake. "Get back, Latimer! Watch
what you're doing!"

"That was a gas mask, wasn't it?"

"They're carrying gas masks, gas dispensers, laser
rifles, knock-out pistols, garrotes. They'll use whatever
they have to. If the Magistrate's amulet isn't returned
to us soon, we'll flush the Sh'gaidu from the cliffs."

"Is Commander Swodi in charge?"

"He's *with* them."

"And you think you can trust him to behave . . . ra-
tionally?"

The Deputy pivoted and crossed the assembly building to the Pledgechild and the ring of entranced midwives. Four dragoons, held back from Swodi's little
siege force, followed him at a respectful distance. Seth
watched from the door, weary of trekking back and
forth and no longer eager to place himself so directly
in the old woman's field of vision. Both she and Magistrate Vrai seemed to be afflicted with complementary
varieties of *nuraj*. . . .

The mental choiring of the Sh'gaidu continued, in

a bleak minor key that made the incessant rain seem, by contrast, joyous and invigorating.

Pacing and gesticulating, Emahpre raged at the Pledgechild in their own tongue. She made either curt, quiet responses or no response at all. After a time, the Deputy urged a pair of dragoons forward and directed them to lift one of the midwives to her feet. She rose unsteadily, still elsewhere. The soldiers patiently escorted her past Seth into the basin.

As Seth looked on in disbelief from the door, one of the Tropiards removed a self-constricting metal garrote from his belt, fitted it about the midwife's neck, and let it strangle her on her feet. This done, the executioner and his companion dragged the Sh'gaidu's body into the stalks of monarchleaf west of the path to the roadway. Seth could see another stray pair of feet sticking out into the path from the field a little farther down: one of Lord Pors's "assassins." Where was the other?

When the soldiers, drenched but uncomplaining, reentered the Sh'vaij, the whole episode dissolved in Seth's imagination as if it were a nightmare from which he had escaped by an exit marked Objective Reality. Except that he hadn't escaped. The episode instantly reconstituted itself in his mind, and he knew that he had seen the real.

"Deputy Emahpre!" Seth cried. "You can't do this!"

Gesticulating, pacing, the Deputy had no time for Seth's offworlder's scruples. He harangued the Pledgechild and the remaining Sh'gaidu elders, ordered a second pair of dragoons to lay hands on a midwife, and stepped aside so that they could goose her through the Sh'vaij and into the rain. This victim was Huspre, and she was going as docilely to her doom as had the other three Sh'gaidu. Even the Pledgechild raised no protest on her behalf.

Without thinking Seth interposed himself between the door and the dragoons. "Deputy!" he shouted. "Three deaths are enough! These people are going to resist you passively until none of them remains! You won't recover the *dascra* like this!"

"Get out of their way, Latimer!"

"Emahpre, be reasonable!"

"You can't confront irrationality with reason, Latimer! Get out of their way! If the Sh'gaidu wish us to exterminate them, so be it!"

Seth levered a kick at the soldier to Huspre's left, striking him squarely in the genital region. This sent the Tropiard sprawling backward on the stony floor, eerily screaming his pain and his surprise. His laser rifle bounced free, and the tools on his equipment belt jingled and sang like temple bells. In retaliation, the other dragoon plunged the butt of his rifle toward Seth's belly. Seth easily sidestepped the blow, took a relieved breath, and then shouted his dismay when the follow-through caught him beneath the chin and knocked him into the wall.

Huspre, formerly as tractable as if she'd been drugged, used the occasion to dart into the rain.

The dragoon who had struck Seth shouted a command and swung his rifle about to laser the fleeing midwife. Dazed, Seth watched Huspre go zigzagging down the path toward the roadway; he watched a pencil of light burst from the muzzle of the soldier's rifle, shooting out like a filament of ruby and sizzling through the rain in vengeful pursuit.

Huspre evaded it. She leaped into one of the battered stands of monarchleaf and disappeared. As the dragoon was preparing to fire again, Seth kicked the rifle out of his hands, simultaneously clubbing him on the back of his head with his left arm. The Tropiard pitched out the door onto his weapon, and Seth jumped over his sprawled body to see if Huspre had survived and where exactly she was going.

But even the Deputy appeared to recognize the idiocy of standing on legalities now. Screaming brusque orders at his fallen dragoons, he ran through the Sh'vaij and reached its door before the first man whom Seth had laid out could get back on his feet. This time the Deputy didn't hesitate to brave the rain. His head tick-tocking from side to side as he scanned the blurred landscape, he darted past Seth to the top of the pathway. Huspre was still nowhere in sight.

"Where is she, Latimer?" the Deputy demanded. "Did she head for the galleries?"

"Why would she do that? They're filling up with state soldiers."

Somewhat recovered but holding no apparent grudge against Seth, the two dragoons stumbled forward from the Sh'vaij with their belts straightened and their rifles canted across their chests. Seth was nevertheless leery of them. As Emahpre signaled them to begin the search for Huspre, Magistrate Vrai's *dascra* momentarily forgotten, Seth sidled away along the outer wall of the assembly building.

"Come with us, Latimer!" Emahpre cried.

Reluctantly Seth obeyed. The Deputy, understanding that Seth didn't intend to tell him anything about Huspre's likely whereabouts, asked Seth no questions but kept him beside him like a dog at heel. Meanwhile, the dragoons separated to east and west and began moving down-basin through the crops. Occasionally one or the other would throw a laser bolt into a sodden thicket just to see if anything jumped. Seth was glad to see that nothing did. For nearly twenty minutes they combed the entire area north of the Sh'vaij . . . without result.

"Futile! Useless!" Emahpre exclaimed, angrily indicting Seth for their failure. "Back to the assembly building!"

He called to the dragoons and swung about on the flooding pathway. When his feet slipped out from under him in the mud, he loftily permitted Seth to save him. Seth, for his part, had to resist the temptation to throw Emahpre back down, rip his slit-goggles from his eyes, and hold his face in the muck until he choked on it. All that prevented Seth was his knowledge that he would be shot down instantly and left to rot on a world that he had never made and had no desire to belong to. Trope was worse than Gla Taus, and the Gla Tausians—the Kieri—had martyred his isosire in a way that still haunted him, that ate at poor Abel's dreams like a chronic and ultimately fatal disease. Here, however, genocide.

And Earth?

Earth was an unfulfilled promise. Interstel determined its policies, but Ommundi owned its soul. . . .

One of the dragoons shouted something from the depths of his lungs. His counterpart then took up the cry, and when Emahpre and Seth looked around to discover the source of the soldiers' excitement, they saw The Albatross—the state airship in which the Magistrate's party had flown from Huru J'beij—lifting off the roadway. Rising above a stand of monarchleaf on the basin's northern perimeter, it hovered in the thinning rain like the ghost of its real self. Its bronze pilot's bubble was a grotesque eye. It seemed, briefly, that The Albatross would falter and plunge back to the ground—but it steadied, tilted heavily, and swept toward the Sh'vaij with rapidly increasing speed.

As The Albatross passed overhead, Emahpre, Seth, and the two soldiers involuntarily ducked. Seth feared that Huspre—assuredly it was she at the controls—intended to perform a spectacular kamikaze maneuver into the Sh'vaij. If her people were going to die, she must be reasoning, let at least the midwives die in a symbolic blaze together. . . .

But The Albatross lifted, as if on an updraft, and floated erratically toward the Great Wall. Although Huspre had probably never flown before, she had somehow managed to get the craft airborne and now she was goading it upward through the rain to higher and higher altitudes. Emahpre, Seth, and the soldiers pursued The Albatross as far as they were able, sprinting along the western margin of the Sh'vaij, past the disheveled cypresses, to the building's southern end. Here—winded, soaked through, and incredulous—they halted.

Because she had not suicided into the Sh'vaij, Seth

had expected to see Huspre sailing off over the wall
to some ill-defined utòpia of self-fulfillment and freedom. What Emahpre and the soldiers had expected
was unknown to Seth, but what they all saw was appall-
ing.

The Albatross collided with the Great Wall about
three quarters of the way from the summit. Although
the machine made a doomed effort to keep going, it
was suddenly a shell. Scattering odd pieces of equipment, it slid down the wall in a slow-motion parody
of disaster, impacted against the highest terrace level,
and toppled sidelong down the next several tiers before coming to rest amid a bank of clotted vegetation.

"Lord Por's body is in the wreckage!" Seth shouted.

The Deputy resorted to his own language.

"What?"

"Unrequited *kemmai* to Lord Pors!"

This makeshift curse was so awkward in the Deputy's mouth that Seth laughed mirthlessly. "Very good!"
he said. "But you've a duty to recover his body. And
to see if Huspre's still alive."

Pointedly ignoring Seth, Emahpre dispatched one
of the dragoons up the terrace levels to the fallen airship, and another to Yaji Tropei to recruit reinforce-
ments for the search through its wreckage. This second
soldier would also bring a pair of his fellows back to
the Sh'vaij so that Emahpre could continue his vivid
harassment of the Sh'gaidu midwives. These plans,
along with a warning that he would brook no more
interference, the Deputy spelled out for Seth on their
way back to the assembly building.

"The loss of the airship is as much your doing as
was the loss of the Magistrate's *dascra*," Emahpre said.
"I won't let this go on."

"Pledgechild, this is the familistery urn of the
Sh'gaidu," the Deputy said a few minutes later, hold-
ing up the huge black vessel for all those seated before
Palija Dait to see. "Is that not correct?"

Seth stood to one side, helpless before Emahpre's

demonic singlemindedness. A soldier had found the urn in the Pledgechild's private rooms and had given it into the Deputy's hands as soon as Seth and he had returned from pursuing Huspre. Several other soldiers were lined up behind Emahpre as he confronted the Pledgechild.

"This *is* your familistery urn, isn't it?" he asked again.

The Pledgechild looked at him contemptuously. "Why would I admit such a thing to you if it were?"

"Then I'll assume that it is indeed the familistery urn."

"Or why would I correct you if you were wrong?"

Emahpre looked at Seth, hefted the urn as if for his benefit, then turned back to the Pledgechild and the midwives. "Unless you return the Magistrate's *dascra,* this urn becomes the property of the state."

"Even if you take it, Deputy, you won't truly own it."

"And neither do you truly own the *dascra* of the Magistrate of all of Trope, even though you've stolen it!"

"It belongs to us as well as to the people of the Thirty-three Cities."

"You've long since forfeited your interest in it, Pledgechild."

"Our interest in it is greater now than at any time since our Holy One departed Palija Kadi."

"Return it, harlot!"

"No, not even to save ourselves—for we wouldn't be saved thereby. Do what you think you must, j'gosfi pervert. Whatever you do, you'll do through the combined wills of Seitaba Mwezahbe and Duagahvi Gaidu."

"The combined wills!" Emahpre exclaimed. "What Sh'gaidu vomit are you attempting to set before us now?"

But the Pledgechild spat out two crisp syllables— *"Smai donj!"*—and folded her hands in her lap.

Outraged, Emahpre lifted the urn to shoulder

height, thrust it out before him, and dropped it. The vessel shattered, kicking out a cloud of glittering, greenish dust. Shards whirled savagely across the floor in every direction.

"*Smai donj!*" the Pledgechild repeated more vehemently.

But Emahpre was playing to Seth. "For so long as Magistrate Vrai continues to suffer the absence of his birthright, we will periodically escort one of your midwives into the rain. Do you understand?"

"*Smai donj!*"

"It's time for one to go now, Pledgechild." Emahpre gestured to a pair of soldiers, who approached the prayer ring and lifted to her feet an old woman to the Pledgechild's far right. Swinging their chosen victim about, the dragoons walked her past Seth almost tauntingly.

Seth saw no opportunity to intervene. An anonymous martyrdom here on Trope would mean nothing to any of these people. He could die for himself, he supposed, for the sake of his own integrity—but right now that seemed both an overheroic and a downright fatuous course. It was premature. He made an angry, impotent wave at the Deputy, lowered his head, and stalked toward the rooms behind Palija Dait.

"Where are you going, Latimer?"

"To join the Magistrate and Master Douin behind the wall. I'm not going to watch this."

"You've my personal invitation to remain."

"*Smai donj!*" Seth told him. But he was disdainful of his own bravado. On the edge of fury, he watched the frail, passive midwife stagger into the rain between her executioners.

As Emahpre, mock-scandalized by Seth's Tropish curse, drummed the fingers of both hands against his breast bone, Seth marched into the first tiny room behind Palija Dait. Here, leaning against the wall, he expelled a long, tense breath. His heart thudded. But something inside him was different. With a start he realized that the telepathic choiring of the Sh'gaidu in the galleries had ceased. What remained was the feeble droning of the midwives and those few adult Sh'gaidu who occupied the benches in the nave. A sensation like music drifting into audibility from a long way off.

When Seth looked up, Lijadu was standing before him. She had come into the room as soundlessly as snow.

"They're killing my sisters, Kahl Latimer."

"Your people killed Lord Pors."

They stared at each other. Facing her, trying to brave the accusation of her bruises and her pitiless eyes, Seth wrestled with his torment. Lijadu had wronged him by her theft of the *dascra,* which act, willy-nilly, had precipitated the chaotic events of last night and this morning. Wasn't she at least as responsible as he for everything that had happened? The whole, crazy tapestry of provocation, reprisal, counter-reprisal, and systematic slaughter was senseless. It got crazier and more tangled as it unraveled, and Seth couldn't see the point. Not of any of it.

"Damn it, Lijadu, why did you do it?"

"They've gassed the Sh'gaidu in the galleries. They've put them out of their minds on their feet."

"Why did you do it?" he hissed at her.

"I took what was ours, Kahl Latimer. Nothing more."

"It's only symbolically yours, Lijadu! Surely you don't claim sole ownership of the birth treasure of the Tropish Magistrate. Surely you must have known Emahpre would use the theft to justify what he's doing now."

"They're killing my people."

"Exactly. Of course they are. It's maddening, Lijadu. Everything about this is maddening."

"Get the Magistrate, Kahl Latimer. Have him stop it." Like a wraith, she vanished beyond him into the Sh'vaij: Emahpre's slaughterhouse.

When Seth arrived in the tiny room where the Magistrate had sequestered himself, he found Clefrabbes Douin slumped in a chair asleep and the ruler of all Trope staring at the ceiling with uncovered eyes. His goggles hung limply from his left hand, which dangled off the side of the bench like a dead man's. His eyes were pale diamonds.

"Magistrate," Seth said.

Douin awoke, and the Magistrate tilted his head back to see who had spoken. Then, slowly, he sat up, making no effort to cover his eyes.

"Have you abdicated to Emahpre entirely?" Seth challenged him.

"You see me naked, Kahl Latimer. This is who I am. I'm helpless to be anything but what I am."

"Despite all the vested authority of the state? Despite a half dozen auxiliary births? I thought you could be anything you wished."

"The Pledgechild's heir has stolen my identity."

"Emahpre is *killing* people, Magistrate."

Douin, who had found his ministerial cap somewhere in his clothes, put this on his head, picked up an effects kit that Seth recognized as Lord Pors's, and struggled to his feet. Clutching the kit under his arm, he went to the Magistrate and raised him from the bench as if lifting a statue to an unsteady pedestal. It amazed Seth how debilitated and tractable Vrai had become. Maybe Lijadu had in fact stolen his identity— in some gut-deep, psychological sense which defied mere human understanding.

"We're going out there," Douin said. "This is very much our fault, Lord Pors's and my own, and we must stop the killing."

"I'm bereft of power," Vrai protested—but, with Seth's assistance, Douin headed the Magistrate out the door and through the jumbled suite of cells toward the Sh'vaij. At every step the Tropiard reiterated his powerlessness, his absence of identity. This lament took on something of the nature of a chant.

As soon as they had entered the nave of the build-

ing, they saw Lijadu against the left-hand wall, just
ahead of them, staring into a pair of laser rifles. The
dragoons who had drawn down on her were several
meters away, near Deputy Emahpre, who had sent
another midwife into the rain since Seth's departure
and who was now conducting every aspect of this impromptu pogrom like a maestro on fire with self-
importance.

"She's just confessed that she has the amulet,"
the Deputy said. "See—it's in her hand."

Lijadu turned toward Seth. She held the *dascra*
aloft in her right hand, the *dascra* for which her people
had already suffered several deaths and the ignominy
of gassing in Yaji Tropei.

"She insists she'll scatter its *jinalma* if we approach
her," Emahpre went on, affecting a calm he obviously
didn't feel. Then he caught sight of Vrai's naked
face. "Magistrate—!"

Vrai shrugged off both Douin's and Seth's supporting arms and approached Lijadu, his hand extended.
"That's mine," he said. "Give it to me, and you have
my word that no representative of the state—no j'gosfi
—will ever set foot in Palija Kadi again. Do you understand?"

Although the Magistrate's naked gaze seemed at
first to mesmerize Lijadu, she shook off this paralysis,
stepped lightly toward the semicircle of Sh'gaidu midwives, and with a graceful, underhand motion pitched
the amulet to the Pledgechild. It landed in the old
woman's lap. In response, every set of eyes and every
rifle barrel in the Sh'vaij swiveled toward the Pledgechild. She lifted the *dascra* in cupped hands, cher-
ishing its weight and feel. The Magistrate moved
uncertainly toward her, interposing himself between
the prayer ring and the armed dragoons of the state.

"I'm too old to be transported to another world,"
the Pledgechild said, glancing sidelong at Douin and
Seth. "But perhaps the Sh'gaidu who are younger than
I will find the Holy One there, in her spirit if not her
flesh. Perhaps we were foolish to attempt to recover

what we could of her in this world, particularly since
we are few and our strength is in our souls rather
than in our arms."

"Pledgechild—" the Magistrate said.

Emahpre shouted something in Tropish, something
curt and high-pitched.

"I've been too long without the solace of my birth-
parent's eyes," the Pledgechild declared. With that,
she broke the Magistrate's amulet against her chest.
Then she pulled the pouch along the inside of her
left arm, switched hands, and pulled it along the
slack flesh of her right arm, grinding *jinalma* into her
body and bringing out the plush crimson of her blood.
Crimson.

*We are all imperfect isohets of the same perfect
progenitor. . . .*

"I'm both the reader and the reading of Ifragsli's
final vision," the old woman said. The empty amulet
had fallen into her lap. She lifted her arms to the ceiling and let the blood flow down.

Horrified, unable to move, the Deputy, the Magistrate, and all the state's soldiers watched. Lijadu,
meanwhile, crossed to the Pledgechild, knelt before
her, and laid her head on one of the bleeding woman's
gnarled knees.

"I here appoint Lijadu as my successor, Kahl
Latimer," the Pledgechild said. "In the islands of
our exile she'll lead the Sh'gaidu to communion with
our Holy One and so redeem us even on a strange
world."

Lijadu expostulated briefly with the Pledgechild in
the Sh'gaidu dialect. Otherwise, she appeared to be in
complete control of herself, as if she'd foreseen everything that had happened since her return to the nave
of the Sh'vaij.

Recovering somewhat, Vrai stumbled forward and
went down on his knees beside Lijadu. Seth and Douin
hurried to his aid. Attempting to lift him to his feet,
they murmured words of consolation. He was having
none of it. He shook himself free of their ministrations

and put his face directly before the dying old woman's. Lijadu was trying to support the Pledgechild now, but the Pledgechild's mottled head was lolling toward one shoulder as if broken at the neck.

The Magistrate whispered, "Pledgechild, you've deprived both of us of our heritage. My amulet contained the *jinalma* of your Holy One."

"I know," the Pledgechild managed, wheezing the words, her eyes sparkling incongruously. "Therefore the theft. Therefore my dying here in Palija Kadi. Home. Home, Ulgraji Vrai. . . ."

"How could you know?" the Magistrate protested. "How?"

The midwives around the old woman cleared a space and Lijadu eased her dying benefactor to the floor. As the Magistrate, Seth, and Douin helplessly looked on, Emahpre directed his soldiers to escort the midwives to the trucks waiting to evacuate them and their sisters out of the basin.

"No more deaths!" Seth shouted at the Deputy.

"Of course not. You don't want damaged goods, do you, Latimer? You don't want your capital depleted."

"Emahpre—"

"No worry of that now. Our search is over. The responsibility for the debacle lies at your feet." The Deputy, too, exited the Sh'vaij, apparently to assist with truck assignments and loading.

The rain was at last beginning to abate, but the gloom in the building gave no sign of departing with it. Seth felt isolated and defeated.

"Our Holy One has come home," the prostrate Pledgechild said, the fire going out of her eyes. "She's come home. . . ."

It took her a while to die, but Seth knew the exact moment of her death because at that instant the last faint droning of the Sh'gaidu mind cries ceased and there was a terrible stillness in the world.

Later, a pair of dragoons carried the Pledgechild's body to one of the waiting trucks and placed it in a preservation cylinder so that it might be transported to Ebsu Ebsa, the nearest of the Thirty-three Cities, and eventually off-planet with her people. Neither Seth nor Clefrabbes Douin had anything to do with this business, for they had gone into the fields to join Deputy Emahpre and several other soldiers in sifting through the wreckage of The Albatross for the corpses of Huspre and Lord Pors.

In the steady, remorseless drizzle that had supplanted the rain, this party worked for over an hour and a half without success. Huspre's crumpled body was extracted from the caved-in pilot's bubble, but no one could find any sign that Porchaddos Pors had also been aboard until a puzzled dragoon turned up the Point Marcher's surrogates—his false teeth—on the topmost terrace level.

But what had happened to the body itself? Had it been thrown into another dimension? Or diced into so many pieces that no one would ever be able to find them all? What? This was a great mystery. Perhaps Huspre had done something sinister to Lord Pors's corpse before taking The Albatross aloft. . . .

"I'm going to have to return to Feln with only a name for the body," Douin said despairingly. "The Point Marcher is lost."

Emahpre assured Douin that his soldiers would continue the search. Then he explained that since Huspre had destroyed their transportation back to the tablerock, they would have to ride to Ebsu Ebsa in a truck, just like the Sh'gaidu evacuees, transferring from there to an airship suitable for the return trip to Ardaja Huru. This would be an inconvenience, but perhaps not an unabidable discomfort. Later, the state would see to it that the Sh'gaidu were lifted into orbit aboard a series of shuttles. The *Dharmakaya* would receive the evacuees and convey them through The Sublime to their promised land on the southern coast of Kier.

"They don't want to go," Seth said.

"At this point their wishes are immaterial," the Deputy replied. "Even the Pledgechild, before she killed herself, saw fit to annoint her heir with the burden of leadership on Gla Taus. That, Latimer, was because she knew the Sh'gaidu would be leaving Trope."

Sick of Emahpre, of the drizzle, of his own complicity in this affair, Seth was about to protest when Douin said:

"Did you hear the Magistrate tell the Pledgechild that his amulet had contained the *jinalma* of Gaidu?"

"I heard." But the Deputy's tone indicated he didn't like the subject. He wiped his wet forehead with a wet sleeve and continued hiking down-basin with the angry jauntiness that typified him.

"Why would he tell her that?" Douin persisted. "Was it to intensify the Pledgechild's problematical guilt for ordering the *dascra* stolen?"

Emahpre halted and faced Douin. "What the Magistrate said was nonsense, a forgivable lapse. He couldn't accept that his birth treasure was lost to him forever. He attempted to project the loss onto the Pledgechild. It was all a fabrication, Master Douin, a fabrication he was helpless to avoid."

"And the Pledgechild trumped him with a fabrication of her own?" Douin asked. "Is that it?"

"I suppose so. When Gaidu disappeared, the Magistrate—who was not then Ulgraji Vrai but a j'gosfi named Ulvri in his fifth lifetime—carried the *dascra* of his natural birth-parent. That's one aspect of a Tropiard's life that doesn't alter through all the various watersheds of his personal evolution." Emahpre set off again, forcing Seth and Douin to keep pace, his knees and elbows jabbing the air.

Breathlessly Seth asked, "Was the *dascra* really the Magistrate's? Could Lijadu have substituted another for it?"

"If it wasn't the Magistrate's," Emahpre said, halting again, "the damage is nevertheless done. We'll never recover the real one."

"Indeed not," Douin interjected pointedly. "It's much smaller than a man's body."

"We'd better get to the trucks," the Deputy replied.

When they reached the northern apron of the Sh'vaij, Seth saw several dragoons bracketing a group of Sh'gaidu children. The children's bodies were coated with a substance dreadfully similar to mucus, an exudation summoned in self-protective response to the gas that the Tropiards had used in the galleries. With rifle butts and the tubes of their gas dispensers the soldiers were jostling their young captives down the roadway to the trucks. Groggy and docile, they slipped and staggered in the mud but neither cried out nor made any attempt to escape. They would recover quite soon, Emahpre assured his guests; the effects of the gas were purposely short-lived.

On the roadway itself Seth caught sight of Lijadu between a pair of dragoons several trucks away. Her eyes seemed almost to stream in the unremittant drizzle; they were beaded and mutated-looking, like melting chrysoberyl. Before Seth could hail her, however, she was shoved out of sight—on her way to a truck carrier apparently reserved for children and other latecomers.

Chapter Eighteen

"This one's ours," Emahpre said. "Let's board."

The driver, Seth saw, was Captain Yithuju, who had led the trucks down into the basin early that morning. Emahpre took a moment to rebuke the captain for failing to secure The Albatross and for permitting Huspre to sneak aboard, take its controls, and lift the airship off the roadway right in front of his nose.

The dressing-down was animated but brief, and Emahpre returned to Seth and Douin in a viler mood than any he had displayed since coming back from the wreckage.

His eyes still uncovered, Magistrate Vrai was already in the truck carrier, sitting with his back against the port sideboard. As a concession to the eminence of this group of evacuees, Yithuju had covered the truckbed itself with a clean, white, spongy mat. As Seth, Douin, and Emahpre climbed aboard, pausing to clean their boots on a scraper near the tailgate, the Magistrate turned his head toward them but said nothing. It was Seth's private opinion that he was still replaying the Pledgechild's death and mourning the loss of his invaluable birth treasure.

Although Seth had expected the convoy to get moving at any moment, none of the trucks on the roadway budged. This delay—as Tropish soldiers scoured the honeycombs of the galleries for stragglers and those few wretched Sh'gaidu holding out against the inevitable—lengthened toward twilight. It was dark before Yithuju fired their truck's engine to life and urged the groaning vehicle up the muddy gradient out of Palija Kadi. Theirs was the lead truck, however, and Seth stood at its tailgate to watch the basin drop away and the headlights of all the trailing vehicles bob fuzzily in the mist. He by no means regretted leaving this place —but he would have been happier if he had never come at all.

After a time, having noted that his companions all appeared to be sleeping, Seth lay down, too. Despite the jouncing of the truck, the sluthering of the monstrous tires, he fell asleep, exhausted by everything that had happened and vaguely conscious of his hunger. His sleep was almost a delirium. Abel came whistling across his mind like something made of blown glass, its surfaces reflecting countless distorted images of Günter Latimer. When this Abelesque bauble had shattered against the transparent wall of Seth's dreaming, there arose from the shards a dust of glittering fireflies, as thick and mobile as gnats. Seth tried to brush them away.

—*Kahl Latimer, wake up.*

He awoke to find the Magistrate sitting beside him in the dark, his hard naked eyes like match flames.

"It's time to conclude our bond-sharing, Kahl Latimer."

Seth neither moved nor spoke. The Magistrate dangled something over his chest, then dropped it. Automatically Seth's hand crept up his body to claim what Vrai had dropped: a pair of goggles.

"I'm returning them," the Magistrate whispered, "because we've concluded this enterprise. But the bond between us will never really be severed. Had I another amulet to give into your keeping, I would readily do so. One failure doesn't disgrace you in my eyes, Kahl Latimer. I would bond with you again."

"Even if your *dascra* contained the eyes of Gaidu?"

The Magistrate didn't flinch. "Especially then," he said.

"What would Ulvri, a simple j'gosfi in his fifth lifetime, be doing with the eyes of the Sh'gaidu Holy One?"

This time Magistrate Vrai drew back from Seth a little. At last, however, he admitted, "I'm still Ulvri, Kahl Latimer. Even today."

"How?"

"I've undergone only four auxiliary births, you see. Since long before the disappearance of Gaidu I've been one continuous personality, a Tropiard defying the Mwezahbe Legacy even as I struggled to uphold it."

"Were you once a Sh'gaidu?" Seth asked, unable to make sense of what the Magistrate was telling him.

"No, no. You jump ahead of me."

"Then why should you have ever possessed the *jinalma* of Gaidu?"

"Before I was Ulvri, Kahl Latimer, when I was in my first incarnation, I repudiated the vision of my birth-parent and cast his *jinalma* into the winds screaming across the prairie Chaelu Sro."

"But why?"

"Because on a journey between Ebsu Ebsa and Ardaja Huru my birth-parent betrayed the Mwezahbe Legacy by taking up with a small group of nomads— sh'gosfi, perverts, thieves—people at odds with the progressive policies of the state. These outlanders have always been with us, Kahl Latimer, traveling together in the vacancies among the great cities, usually in groups of from four to twelve people. Gaidu drew on some of these pariahs for her first converts. My birth-parent lived too long ago to become one of her followers. Instead he allied himself with a small but active band known for chicanery and violence, and so abstracted himself from my life. I never saw him again."

"But you acquired his *jinalma* when he died?"

"The private records say that I was preparing for my first auxiliary birth when the *dascra* was delivered to me. My birth-parent had entrusted it to a fellow pariah, who risked capture and rehabilitation to enter the dormitory suite of my horticultural workers' brotherhood in Ardaja Huru. I woke up to find the amulet about my neck and a long, discursive letter atop a work console near my door. I tore up the letter immediately after reading it, then delayed my auxiliary birth long enough to go out into the wastelands of Chaelu Sro to repudiate my birthright. The records say I cast away the dust of my birth-parent's eyes."

"And you wore no amulet at all into your second lifetime?"

"I did as all Tropiards who have lost their treasure do, Kahl Latimer. I wore an amulet filled with sand."

"Until you acquired the eyes of Gaidu?"

The Magistrate leaned close to Seth in the truckbed and told the strange story of his meeting with the sh'gosfi messiah, the self-proclaimed redeemer of all Tropiards, dead now for 172 years:

I was a soldier with the previous magistrate, Orisu Sfol, whom I came to know very well indeed. He instituted a pogrom against the Sh'gaidu. I wasn't a common soldier, you understand, but a troop controller with a vehicle of my own and a compelling responsibility.

On a night I have never been able to forget, from a vantage high on the western rim of Palija Kadi, Ulvri—the self I haven't yet shed—directed an operation designed to harass and frighten the people of the unlawful sisterhood. It resembled what happened today in the basin except that it was deadlier. The mission of Orisu Sfol's dragoons that night was to slaughter at least three quarters of Palija Kadi's inhabitants, including Gaidu herself if that were possible.

The Fifth Magistrate understood true intimidation. Those dissidents who remained alive would give up their fanaticism and return to the state; potential converts to Gaidu in the Thirty-three Cities would be dissuaded from falling from grace. And to some extent Magistrate Sfol's ruthless variety of intimidation had results: Fear of reprisal, along with the Holy One's disappearance, worked to chill the fervor of the original Sh'gaidu and to discourage the defection of impressionable Tropiards.

Ulvri, from his communications vehicle, directed one portion of the state's assault on the basin. He relayed an order to a lieutenant on the northern roadway, then watched a single line of three hundred dragoons fanned out across the basin floor firing their laser weapons and running the fleeing sh'gosfi to ground. There was nothing subtle or surreptitious about this assault. The state meant business, and it carried out its objectives with the utmost efficiency.

His own role in the slaughter fulfilled early, Ulvri left his van and climbed to the edge of the western wall to watch the final sweep of the dragoons. Crop fires and intermittent laser bursts illuminated Palija Kadi. Although Ulvri could not see the dead, already he could smell them: an acrid stench rising through his nostrils and seeming to sear even his eyes. The operation had been a success. The rumor of this cruelty would perhaps avert the necessity for a follow-up.

As he stood on the basin rim, his feet straddling a crevice that deepened below him, Ulvri heard the sound of small stones snicking and sliding away in deceitful avalanche—deceitful because the sound betrayed someone climbing up from the basin's floor through the narrow crevice. Ulvri was fascinated. As if amplified by the natural funnel of rock, the sound of the sliding stones muted the roaring of the crop fires into mere background noise.

The fugitive's ascent deserved admiration. Having wedged herself into the crevice, she used the pressure of her hands and arms to lever herself slowly upward through the funnel. When she finally reached a slope where she could crawl, she scrambled on her hands and knees, dislodging pebbles behind her but advancing steadily nonetheless.

Ulvri stepped back to wait. At last the fugitive emerged, and her nakedness identified her as a Sh'gaidu. Wearing only a greatcoat of shadows, she crept forward a few tentative steps and then stood upright as if the starless darkness would protect her from discovery. Ulvri leaped out at her and beat her cruelly before she could either plead for mercy or raise an arm to fend off the assault. Then Ulvri bent the fugitive's body over an angular slab of rock and turned her head from side to side to see what she looked like.

The biting, sky-blue eyes were enough to tell the troop controller who she was: Duagahvi Gaidu herself. And Ulvri realized that duty dictated his course of action: He must kill her.

"What will you do with my eyes after you've killed me?"

Ulvri reared back, startled. "Cast them into the planet's deepest gorge and lose them forever," he finally said.

"A senseless waste of power."

"Don't attempt to bribe me from my purpose."

"I lead no thinking being from its duty—but once I'm dead, my eyes are yours. Don't waste them on the wind."

"How are they mine?"

"You have no *dascra*. As a consequence, you reside in neither the past nor the future, but exclusively in the now. Since you must kill me, I beg you to take my eyes and wear them."

Ulvri had no answer. He was dumbfounded that this should be happening. To wear Gaidu's eyes, however, would be an unspeakable offense against the Legacy of Seitaba Mwezahbe.

"Tell me your name," the Holy One asked, still bent beneath his hands, and he told her. "Ulvri, if you become my heir, if you accept my eyes, one day you will be more. You will become the benefactor of all Tropiards, of the docile and the dissident alike, and you will rule the Thirty-three Cities."

"*Nuraju!*" Ulvri cursed her. To end her life, there beneath the starless sky, all he need do was tighten his fingers about her neck and squeeze until she could neither speak nor cerebrate.

"Yes, kill me," she urged him. "But keep my eyes and submit to no more auxiliary births. When Magistrate Sfol comes to die, tell him of your deed so that you may be preferred. Give him the proof of my *jinalma*, of my bones—but tell him that he may not announce my death in the Thirty-three Cities. If he should announce it, the Sh'gaidu will claim my resurrection and evangelism will begin again. Let everyone think me abroad in the world, and my people will wait—

wait patiently—growing in their power and in their dependency on one another."

"If I wore your *dascra,* I would be Sh'gaidu myself."

"No, Ulvri. You must be Tropiard. It's fitting that I should have a j'gosfi heir, hostile in his appointed position but sympathetic in his inmost self. In this way the Sh'gaidu, who will always be few, may come to fulfill themselves on Trope."

"And I will become Magistrate after Orisu Sfol?"

"For having killed me. For having preserved the secret of my death. For being who you are."

"One isn't preferred to the magistracy of all Trope for a single deed, even that of slaying Duagahvi Gaidu!"

"In the years that follow this one, you'll grow in wisdom, compassion, purpose. Your elevation to the magistracy will have its basis in a body of achievement completely apart from the murder you're about to commit. Only you and Orisu Sfol will know of this murder."

"How can you possibly guarantee this?" Ulvri cried.

"I'll work for you in death, as will my people, infusing you with wisdom, compassion, purpose. . . . "

"Enough!" Terrified by these speculations, Ulvri tightened his hands about Gaidu's neck, slammed a knee into her abdomen, and bent her body backward over the rock. Crimson spilled from her nostrils, and the Holy One, still youthful in her appearance, lay dead.

Ulvri considered what to do. Deeply agitated, he went to his van, found a small, flat-bladed knife in a compartment beneath the driver's seat, and returned to the body to cut away its eyes. Although his hands were trembling, he removed the eyes cleanly, emptied the sand from his *dascra,* and replaced the sand with the two eerily perfect eyes of the Holy One. Lost in the lofty dark, he felt like a vivisectionist as well as a murderer. The person he had killed was in some ineffable, threatening way still alive. He had started back toward his van when a faint cerebral tingling halted him between steps.

—*My body, Ulvri. Don't leave my naked body the prey of your soldiers.*

Ulvri, willing each step, went back to the body, lifted it to his shoulders, and carried it along the edge of the basin rim. When he had found a funnel in the cliff similar to the one Gaidu had climbed, he dropped her body into the shaft and nearly toppled headlong after it as it plunged invisibly in the dark.

Who would find the corpse in this place? Only Ulvri, no one else. One day he would secretly reveal the site to Orisu Sfol and would be believed. He would bring the bones up, and the bones would be analyzed by Tropiards ignorant of what they studied, and eventually he would be formally preferred both for killing the Holy One and for wisely withholding from the world the fact of her death. In the years between the murder and the secret revelation he would grow in moral stature just as Gaidu had predicted, developing a character commensurate with the needs of the position he would one day assume. He would be deserving.

Eventually everything would happen just as the Holy One had said.

Ulvri became Ulgraji Vrai, Sixth Magistrate of Trope, without renouncing his former self or the understanding of that self acquired after the Holy One's death. He didn't completely understand the process by which he had reached this pinnacle, but he hoped that one day he could bring about a spiritual reconciliation of his people similar to the private one that had taken place in his own heart. When he became magistrate, he discon-

tinued the persecution of the Sh'gaidu pursued so
vindictively by Orisu Sfol, a well-meaning butch-
erer, and waited. Although he feared that because
of the Mwezahbe Legacy few thoroughgoing
Tropiards would agree to accommodate themselves to the "illogical," he hoped that a more
rigorous and humane logic would eventually pre-
vail.

Officers and advisors—Ehte Emahpre among
them—pressed for a policy of watchfulness,
along with discreet applications of force. Vrai
accepted surveillance as reasonable, but the latter
he resisted with all his strength for as long as he
was able. The power of the magistracy is not
unlimited, he had learned, and under intense,
unremittant pressure even moral force is subject
to erosion. He began to fear that he was no
longer strong enough for the task that Gaidu, a
dreamer and a magician, had said he would carry
out with skill and honor. Sometimes it seemed to
him that compassion and tolerance were pro-
grams incompatible with the priorities of his office, and that he must either abdicate or enforce a
minority tyranny that would ultimately drive him
from power.

Then came overtures from Kieri officials
aboard an Ommundi ship in orbit about Gla
Taus, and Vrai began to believe that if reconciliation were impossible, perhaps the voluntary
removal of the Sh'gaidu to another world contained the prospect of a lasting solution. He re-
joiced. Upon learning that two men from Earth
had agreed to intercede, his hopes soared. There
was something fatefully compelling about aid
from so distant a source, particularly since for
decades Trope had permitted itself only limited
contact with representatives of Interstel.

As the *Dharmakaya* traversed The Sublime,
Vrai cultivated the conviction that the human
being destined to speak for the Kieri must be

someone with goals and motivations like his own. After all, a native of neither Gla Taus nor Trope, he would be inclined to view the situations on both planets with a keen and impartial eye. The Magistrate's first interview with this person confirmed him in his initial opinion. By a rare but fortunate concatenation of events, Seth Latimer had arrived on Trope, and a new era had arrived with him.

The Magistrate fell silent. A less fortunate concatenation of events had destroyed his belief in this apocryphal "new era," and even if the Sh'gaidu ended up seven light-years away, Trope would go on as hidebound and as enmired as before—in the name of Mwezahbe, Reason, and Holy Technocracy, the sacred trinity by which it had lived for over nine hundred years.

Seth whispered, "Magistrate, you can reverse what happened today. You can send the Sh'gaidu back to the basin."

"Emahpre had Palija Kadi destroyed the moment this convoy was safely clear of the cliffs."

"Destroyed?"

"The reservoir above the basin was undammed, explosives were planted in Yaji Tropei, and what wasn't blown apart, Kahl Latimer, lies under at least fifty meters of water. Tonight Palija Kadi is a lake."

"Then relocate the Sh'gaidu somewhere else!"

"Yes, Kahl Latimer. On Gla Taus. They deserve the benefit of what you propose, and I'm bequeathing the Pledgechild's people into your care. Do you understand me? They're your responsibility and your charge."

"Magistrate—"

"The Pledgechild knew for years that Gaidu was dead, you see—but she continued to have visions presaging the Holy One's mysterious return. I think, Kahl Latimer, that you are Gaidu, returned from death at this crucial time."

"That's nonsense!" Seth exclaimed, trying to keep his voice low. "Abel and I undertook this mission in order to regain our ship."

"Your eyes, although different in structure, have the same biting blue as did the Holy One's."

Seth shook his head and tried to speak.

"None of us knows exactly who we are, Kahl Latimer. That's as true for Sh'gaidu as for Tropiards, and as true for you as it is for me."

"You're talking like the Pledgechild or Lijadu."

"In my own way I'm one of them. Tonight, in fact, I declare myself sh'gosfi. I repudiate both my office and the state."

"Declare yourself sh'gosfi?"

But the Magistrate rose from the mat, stumbled across it past Seth to the tailgate, and stared out into the darkness. Seth followed. They were still in mountainous country, not yet having descended to the vast prairie known as Chaelu Sro, and the vehicle trailing theirs had fallen almost a quarter of a kilometer behind. They could see its headlights, along with those of two or three other trucks, burning fiercely in a rugged declivity far below them. The remaining vehicles in the convoy were eclipsed by the rocky terrain through which the switchbacking road twisted and climbed. Despite the low whine of the truck's engine and the continual jouncing, Emahpre and Douin slept on.

"Farewell," Magistrate Vrai said. She embraced Seth, parted from him, and eased herself over the tailgate so that she was standing on the truck's steplike rear bumper. Her eyes coruscated almost merrily.

"What're you doing?" Seth asked her, stunned.

"Defecting to the outlanders. What the Sh'gaidu represented must be kept alive here. Although they go to a better place with you, I intend to range about this nation like their righteous, walking ghost."

"Then be their ghost from a position of power!"

"That's impossible, Kahl Latimer. I was too hemmed in by the magistracy's restrictions and limitations, and today I disgraced myself by a spiritual failure. Nothing like that will ever happen to me again. Tonight I'm free."

Seth pointed at the sleeping deputy. "What must I tell him? How am I going to explain your absence?"

"Pretend to be asleep. Explain nothing."

At the top of a steep grade the Tropiard called Ulvri leaped free of the truck. Seth watched her roll several meters down the slope, a tumbling shadow in the vast blackness. Then, in stark silhouette, limned by the trailing headlights, she struggled to a crouch and scrambled into an outcropping of rocks at roadside. When the lead truck crested this grade and headed down the opposite slope, toward Chaelu Sro, Seth felt that a portion of his life had departed with that unexpected sh'gosfi convert. He would never see her again.

Much later, with dawn seeping up from the east and the sixteen-vehicle convoy strung out single-file across the prodigious tabula rasa of the prairie, Seth was still standing at the tailgate. Deputy Emahpre awoke, stirred, looked about, abruptly sprang to his feet. Bracing himself with one hand against the truck's wall, he made his way to Seth.

"Where's Magistrate Vrai?" he said in his most piercing falsetto. "Where's the Magistrate?"

"Gone," Seth said. "She's long gone, Emahpre."

That evening Clefrabbes Douin and Seth shared the dormitory room on Huru J'beij where they had slept only a single night past. This time there were only two gravelike indentations for pallets in the carpeted platform comprising the room's floor, and the smell of fehtes tobacco—simultaneously acrid and sweet—was only a memory.

They had arrived by airship from Ebsu Ebsa late that afternoon, and already a Tropish shuttlecraft containing a quarter of the Sh'gaidu dissidents had been dispatched from the tablerock toward the orbiting *Dharmakaya*. Another shuttle would depart in the

morning, and by tomorrow evening two more shuttles
would complete the transfer of Lijadu's people from
Trope to the Ommundi light-tripper. Once all the
Sh'gaidu were safely aboard, Deputy Emahpre—in
his capacity as interim magistrate—would permit Seth
and Douin to pilot their transcraft back to the light-
tripper's underslung hangar; and the history of the
Sh'gaidu community on Trope would be a chronicle
written entirely in the past tense.

Douin was sitting in the same chair from which he
had directed his last game of naugced against
Porchaddos Pors. Barefoot and shirtless, Seth paced
the perimeter of the arbitrarily delimited room, anxious to be off-planet and on his way home. The ache
under his breast bone derived from the utter impos-
sibility of his second desire: Magistrate Vrai, before
leaping into the dark, had given him a charge to fulfill.

"I must confess something to you," Douin said. His
words fell into the silence like pebbles disturbing the
surface of a pond.

Seth kept pacing.

"Lady Turshebsel and the Kieri government—
meaning, specifically, Lord Pors and I—were re-
luctant to engage the Magistrate in face-to-face
negotiations."

At this, Seth halted and stared at Douin.

"We needed an innocent, Master Seth, someone
who could present our case with conviction because he
believed in it implicitly and therefore felt no need
for subterfuge or dissembling."

"What are you talking about?"

"We lied to you, Master Seth. The Sh'gaidu won't
be given a fertile piece of property in the Feht
Evashsted. This was a lie we also foisted upon
Narthaimnar Chappouib—since we knew the aisaut-
seb would disapprove of the plan upon which Lady
Turshebsel, Lord Pors, and I had secretly agreed."

"Where, then, will the Sh'gaidu go?" A tattered indignation began fluttering in Seth—as if his con-

science, a tiny homunculus somewhere near his heart, were trying to blow up a ruptured balloon.

"An arid group of islands in the Evashsteddan called the Fire Chain, where they'll labor under Ommundi supervision to exploit those islands' animal and plant resources for the pioneers in the Obsidian Wastes and incidentally for themselves. Much of the Feht Evashsted, you see, is wasteland. Its volcanic topsoil is tainted by a chemical indigenous to the subterranean geology there, and we've no cheap way to remove it. Even Chappouib doesn't know this. You see, then, why we couldn't tell either Chappouib or the Magistrate our true plans. Chappouib would have objected for religious reasons stemming from antiquated superstition, the Magistrate for reasons of conscience."

"Are reasons of conscience antiquated, too, Master Douin?"

Douin stared out the window at the massive red-brown J'beij, far across the tablerock. "From the beginning, Master Seth, I've believed that we would be doing the Sh'gaidu a service by getting them off Trope."

"Then why in God's name did you need someone to lie for you?"

"To make it work. Nonetheless, I'm ashamed that it's worked out as it has, that we deceived you in order to effect a larger deception."

Seth approached Douin, halted in front of him. "Did Abel know about this, too?"

Douin scarcely hesitated. "From the beginning," he said.

Turning, Seth hurled the sunfruit in his hand through one of the paper partitions dividing their room from the empty darkness of the dormitory beyond. The fruit thudded away and was lost.

"My own isohet! The flesh to which I'm twin!"

Douin said, "He wished to regain the *Dharmakaya* and take you home, Master Seth. He saw no other way. Neither did we, for our purposes."

Seth resumed pacing, dazed by the terrible quantities of disillusionment and outrage he ought to be mining from his hurt. It was somewhere beyond him, this vein of disillusionment and outrage, but he ached too badly to break through to it. Besides, its coal-black gleam daunted and mystified him.

He looked at Douin. "There's an aisautseb aboard our light-tripper. How are you going to transfer three hundred Sh'gaidu to the Fire Chain without his knowing and reporting the fact to Chappouib?"

"One of the taussanaur aboard will help him have an accident before we reach Gla Taus. Chappouib will simply be told that our mission failed."

"I would never have believed that you would sanction murder, Master Douin."

"The tyranny of the aisautseb moves me to it. For too long their ritual obfuscation of simple truths and their bloodthirsty commitment to bogus mysteries have betrayed the Kieri into superstition and needless dread. Lady Turshebsel is a beacon out of that darkness, Master Seth, and my belief in her leads me to otherwise uncharacteristic deeds. I make no apologies."

"Except to me," Seth corrected him.

"Except to you, Master Seth, for implicating you in a scheme that has gone awry. The Sh'gaidu are victims twice over, and so perhaps are you."

"Ulvri—Magistrate Vrai—bequeathed the Sh'gaidu into my care, Master Douin. Spare us all further victimization. Let me fulfill this charge."

"And remain on Gla Taus?"

Seth waved one hand distractedly. "For a time," he said. "For a time, at least. I swear, Master Douin, it seems I'm under a painful obligation. . . . "

We are all imperfect isohets of the same perfect progenitor.

Lying awake in the dark, half encoffined by his pallet, Seth silently cursed Abel for betraying him: an inventive litany of malediction. He wished Abel in Hell, he commanded his testicles enshrined in hardened clay, he envisioned him strapped to an immense rotating spit and flayed alive by beautiful Kieri women wielding strigils, he consigned him to suffocating vacuum. None of these horrors conveyed either the vehemence or the confusion of his hate, however, and at last Seth inflicted upon Abel the ultimate curse at his disposal:

He wished for Abel a death like Günter Latimer's.

—*Seth, don't do this to me!*

The words sounded in his consciousness as clearly as if they'd been spoken. They came accompanied by a corollary of Abel's emotional pain and a vague sensation which seemed to Seth an analogue of his isohet's rising nausea. For the first time in their lives, even though separated by a great distance, Abel and he were connected through the manifold links of their common biological heritage. It had finally happened: They were attuned.

—Abel, you used me like a whore.

—*We needed someone free of any motivational taint,* Abel replied faintly, still recoiling from the vision Seth had sent him. —*Someone who believed in the righteousness of what he was doing.*

—Taint! Seth cerebrated. —Then you see the taint in your own soul? You know your own guilt?

—*We've no world of our own, Seth. Not where we are now. I wanted to get us home. . . .*

—You knew the Sh'gaidu were to be transshipped not to the coast of Kier but to a group of islands in the Evashsteddan?

—*I knew.*

—Then picture the Kieri Obelisk in Feln again, Abel, and see yourself going up its side like a trussed pig!

—*Seth, have pity. . . .*

A wave of undiluted hysteria—pain, bewilderment, nausea—swept through Seth, a comber of such crushing emotional flotsam that in order to divert its course he had to scatter his thoughts. He negated Abel in his mind, said No to his isohet's image, and broke contact.

Suddenly Seth was back in his dormitory room on the tablerock of an alien world. Bathed in clammy sweat, he got up and paced barefoot about the sleeping chamber until Anja was a pale hemisphere of blue light on the cold, northwestern horizon of Trope.

Epilogue

At a point ostensibly equidistant between Trope and Gla Taus, where the nearest suns were mere points of fire, Seth Latimer and Clefrabbes Douin pushed away from a maintenance airlock on the *Dharmakaya*'s conning module, fired their back-pack rockets, and floated out into the awesome vac-uum of interstellar space. Between them they hoisted a spacesuit exactly like the ones they were wearing—except for the fact that it was empty.

This unscheduled stop, which had required the *Dharmakaya* to emerge from The Sublime fourteen E-days after its departure from Trope, was Seth's do-ing. The empty suit between Douin and the younger isohet represented the dead Porchaddos Pors. Seth had insisted that the murdered Kieri noble be given an impromptu but decorous "burial" in space, a funeral ceremony to commemorate his efforts to bridge the light-years between two distinctive and dissimilar worlds. Nothing anyone aboard the *Dharmakaya* could say to Seth—whether to cite the astrogational problems such a stop would cause, or to argue that Pors would have angrily rejected a funeral in space, or to castigate Seth for trying to salve his own conscience in the matter of Pors's death—*nothing* would dissuade him from carrying out this ritual. It was as if only the lineaments of ritual had the power to exorcise for Seth the trauma of what had happened on Trope. Consequently, no one held out against him too insistently or forcibly, for no one wanted an avenging madman loose in the corridors of their light-tripper the last fourteen days of their voyage.

Looking "down" at the elevated conning module and the stark, trailing superstructure from which hung the passenger and cargo nacelles of the ship, Seth felt isolated and lost. Much had happened since departing Trope, and most of it had either enraged or perplexed him. The beadlike lights winking along the skeleton of the *Dharmakaya* seemed to him more illusory than the flashes of clairvoyant doubt which had come to plague his sleep. Even aboard the great ship, he was isolated and lost.

Two days out from Trope the young aisautseb accompanying their expedition had been found dead in the lavalet of his cabin, his head plunged forward into the hopper of the chemtoilet. The cause of death was prolonged inhalation of the chemical solvents designed to decompose and deodorize waste matter. Although Seth knew that one of the taussanaur had murdered the proud young priest, he found it hard to credit that Douin had truly sanctioned the act. The Kieri, with whom Seth had lived and worked, was an exemplar of good behavior, a writer of books, the head of an enviable geffide. How could he have demonstrated his loyalty to Lady Turshebsel by authorizing one of the orbital guards to hold the face of the unfortunate aisautseb in a chemtoilet? Now the priest's body lay in a preservation cylinder in an aft cargo module.

This same module also contained the corpses of the Pledgechild and the thirteen Sh'gaidu dissidents who had died from the aftereffects of gassing, close confinement, and peremptory transshipments into orbit from Huru J'beij.

As far as Seth was concerned, the empty spacesuit

between Douin and him represented all these unfortunate people, too: priest, Sh'gaidu, and Lord Pors alike.
They all deserved commemoration. Once, briefly, their
lives had meant something to others, and that they
should all go to the spectral territories beyond death
without eulogy or remembrance struck him as insup-
portable. The truth, as Seth himself understood, was
that this funeral for Lord Pors, the aisautseb, and the
fourteen Sh'baidu was also a funeral for a portion of
himself. That was why he had insisted so vocally on
what still seemed to both Abel and Douin a ridiculous
and time-consuming ceremony.

Seth and Douin fired their backpack rockets again.
By unresisting arms they pulled their tenantless companion along, out into the tenantless wilderness of
night. Amazing, the silence and the ebony cold . . .

No longer did Seth share a cabin with Abel. He had
taken up the farthest aft compartment in the same passenger nacelle where Douin lived and where the Kieri
priest had met his mocking little death. This change of
quarters, considered objectively, had done almost nothing to separate Seth from his isohet, for the ability to
commune with Abel on both the psychic and the
physiological planes had come from Trope to the
Dharmakaya with Seth. He could tap in on his isohet's
emotional and mental condition whenever he wished;
and Abel, although less adept than he at initiating such
contact, was suddenly possessed of a similar skill. They
had intimacy without proximity. What they no longer
had, however, was sexual intimacy. In that context,
Abel had always been the tender aggressor, and for
Seth it had meant a submergence of himself in the
grander image of his isohet's desire. No more. That
was over. He was never going to discover the whole of
his identity in Abel; and, if nothing else, the fiasco of
their expedition to Trope had given him the freedom
to discover the boundaries of his own autonomy as a
moral agent. Perplexedly, he was still trying to stake
these boundaries out. They were, he had found, far

more nebulous and far less arbitrary than those of death.

In the meantime, he had forgiven Abel his trespasses.

Douin was becoming alarmed at the distance between them and the dreamily floating bulk of the lighttripper. Infinitesimal specks in the obsidian fishbowl of the universe, they were nearly half a kilometer from the *Dharmakaya*.

"Master Seth," Douin said, and his voice was hollow-sounding in the earphones of Seth's helmet, "Master Seth, let's conclude this."

"Let me take Lord Pors a little farther out," Seth replied, peering critically through two sets of faceplates at Douin's shadowy features. "Far enough out to send him to this death privately—to commit him to the stars, the infinite suns." He had come out here expressly to put distance between himself and the hovering Ommundi ship, and he couldn't understand Douin's reluctance to proceed.

"Lord Pors was my kinsman," the Kieri said. "I'll take him out, Master Seth. It's for me to do."

The empty helmet of the empty suit gaped at Douin, who, before Seth could protest or interfere, fired his backpack rockets and whirled the suit away with him in a slow-motion waltz. Tilting his cumbersome helmet back, Seth watched the two figures dwindle "above" him, moving faceplate to faceplate like lovers in a ballroom of translucent black marble.

Meanwhile, he was left hanging in the middle of nowhere, suspended in a dream. In one direction, the *Dharmakaya* maintained a surreal and gaudy hauteur; in another direction, Douin and the empty spacesuit climbed into the dizzy-making recesses of the night. Elsewhere, only the star-dusted void.

"Master Douin," Seth said. "Master Douin." But a dead light on the inside of his helmet, just below the faceplate, indicated that Douin had switched his suit radio off, at least insofar as contact with Seth went. He undoubtedly continued to maintain at least listening contact with the light-tripper's conning module, but Seth's umbilical to him Douin had cruelly and deliberately severed. Why? Did they intend to murder *him*, too? Abel and Douin, conspirators together?

Alone, Seth recalled boarding the *Dharmakaya* fourteen days ago to find that the Sh'gaidu were cramped together in one aft cargo nacelle with only minimal life-support facilities: four chemtoilets for 274 people, water from a condensation tray slung beneath the ceiling of the nacelle, once-a-day food calls at the twelve automatic dispensers in the port bulkhead, and a pathetically inadequate supply of bedding. About all you could say for the accommodations was that the air was good and that no one harassed or intruded upon the Sh'gaidu.

Indeed, after looking in on them on that first evening back aboard ship, Seth had conscientiously refrained from setting foot in their squalid, metallic barracoon. Ulvri—Magistrate Vrai—had bequeathed the Sh'gaidu into his keeping, yes, but he would begin to exert himself on their behalf once they had made planetfall and established a permanent colony in that cindery little group of islands called the Fire Chain. For the time being, however, he had to come to terms with the custodial duties awaiting him and the peculiar chain of events that had dropped these duties in his lap. Earth was Paradise Lost. In the hardship of honor he had given himself to Gla Taus, and, dear God, he deserved at least a brief reprieve from the onerousness of that commitment. Reasoning thus, he stayed away from the compartment where the Sh'gaidu were housed.

Lijadu had been somewhere in the crowd on the first and only occasion that Seth had gone back there. He hadn't seen her. Or, if he *had* seen her, he had not recognized her among the naked and gem-eyed scores confined in the nacelle. They had stared at him as if he were Ehte Emahpre, Seth had thought, or some other tight-assed, unyielding representative of the Tropish state, and he had hurried away without trying to locate the one pair of crystalline, tiger-green eyes that would have unfailingly identified their owner as Lijadu. What would he have said to her?

Seth had no idea.

Abel and Douin had seen to the most pressing needs of the imprisoned Sh'gaidu, without ever suggesting that any of them come forward into the main passenger compartments. The only change of accommodations they had supervised was the shifting of the thirteen dead Sh'gaidu to the compartment where the Pledgechild and the murdered Kieri priest lay. Later, they had permitted one of the midwives to visit this compartment in order to cut away the eyes of the corpses, in accordance with Tropish custom. Abel had also provided medical treatment on a regular basis ever since the first death, but the *Dharmakaya* was not equipped to handle so many living passengers in the cargo sections, and Seth felt sure that three or four more Sh'gaidu would die before they reached Gla Taus. He grimaced inside his helmet and opened his eyes on the painful indifference of space.

"Seth, how are you doing?"

The voice was Abel's, coming to him from the conning module through a faint rush of static. It surprised and disoriented Seth.

"Fine," he responded fuzzily.

"What're you doing? Are you about finished?"

"Douin's waltzing the empty suit away from me. They're almost as far from me as I am from the ship. I seem to be something for Douin to mark distances by. Yes, we're almost finished."

"Would you like me to pipe you some music?"

"Abel," Seth said wearily. "I don't care."

"All right. Hang on, then. I will."

There was a scratching in Seth's earphones, a withdrawal, and a moment later the "Ode to Joy" from Beethoven's *Ninth Symphony* was spilling into his helmet from the light-tripper's conning module. Although Seth spoke Abel's name admonitorily, the music overrode him, climbing on strains of exultation and praise.

Looking about, Seth suddenly realized that he could no longer find Douin or the empty spacesuit; that, in fact, he had somehow managed to lose even his fix on the *Dharmakaya*. All that remained as reality supports were Beethoven's music and the illimitable night.

"Abel!"

In an attempt to glide out of his vertigo Seth fired his backpack rockets. He moved, but he still seemed to be moving in a drowning pool of nimbused stars. What were Abel and Douin trying to do to him?

Then he spotted Douin. The Kieri envoy was alone, hanging motionless some distance away. Seth headed for him, and as the pale flames of his rockets propelled him ineluctably toward Douin's suited figure, the music in Seth's earphones died. He shot a quick glance "downward," but instead of the *Dharmakaya* he saw only the depthful obsidian of space. His only orienting focal point was the motionless Douin, who hung "above" him like some nameless god's pathetic trophy. Why didn't he move? Why didn't he fire his own rockets and approach Seth?

If Seth had thought for a moment, he would have known. But in striving to reach the one thing in all the cosmos that seemed in any way familiar, Seth didn't think; he glided desperately toward solace and companionship. No voices spoke to him to set him right. He had only his own imperfect knowledge for guidance.

The result was that Seth came face to face with the tenantless suit which Douin had waltzed into this place and then solemnly deserted. Bemused, Seth stared into the vacant helmet. He saw himself reflected in the warp of the faceplate, a hundred colors dancing in the glass. Then he saw something else: He had forgotten to screw the suit's heavy, corrugated gloves into its sleeves. As a consequence, he could look into one of the spacesuit's bent arms, right into the blackness of its nonexistent occupant. Inside his own suit, Seth recoiled and shuddered.

As if dredging through some prehistoric era of his

own consciousness, he remembered the myth about the jongleur-thief Jaud that he had read in Master Douin's geffide, from one of Master Douin's books, and he remembered how Jaud had confronted his own handless image in the final wall of the Obsidian Wastes. Somehow, Seth knew, this was the same thing, this confrontation. He couldn't move. He couldn't draw away from the empty suit's aura of accusation and reproach, not even when voices at last began to call to him in his earphones. At any moment, Seth feared, the creature confronting him would throw out its empty arms and embrace him as the aged Pledgechild had embraced him in her reception cell in Palija Kadi.

Not until the real Clefrabbes Douin came from out of nowhere, touched his sleeve, and pulled him away from the vacant suit did Seth begin to grasp what had happened. Then his perspective returned. He found the fragile lights of their ship blinking in the dark, and he acquiesced as Douin, who had sanctioned murder, guided him safely through the directionless void to the haven that was the *Dharmakaya*.

Through the ritual of a mock-funeral he had contrived to make himself whole, and if no one else understood either the mystery or the mechanics of such a feat, Seth no longer cared. Let them ridicule him.

Later that "evening," Seth recommended that many of the Sh'gaidu be allowed to take up quarters in the forward passenger compartments. There were forty-two unoccupied cabins in the two adjacent passenger nacelles, and if they put three dissident sisters in each available cabin, they could almost halve the number of Sh'gaidu crowded together now in the bay of the aft cargo nacelle.

It was contemptible, even criminal, that they had not already effected such an arrangement, and if Abel and Douin chose to resist his suggestion, Seth vowed to delay their reentry into The Sublime by plying K/R Caranicas with dodecaphonic messages of moral outrage that would seduce the triune to mutiny against them, too. Caranicas would strand them all in normal space until they submitted to Seth's superior humanitarian view. To prove that he meant what he said, Seth took up the microphone from the astrogational console and regaled Caranicas with the particulars of his plan. The computer translated his words into a weird electronic toodling; and a moment later, after the triune had spun about on its gyroscopic track to face Douin, Abel, and Seth, a response was coded through the communications unit:

"We'll remain here until the transfer is complete."

Seth headed for the aft cargo section. When he presented himself to the clustered occupants of the nacelle, which stank now with the natural effluvia of living bodies pent together for long, uninterrupted stretches, he strolled through their ranks until he found Lijadu caring for an elderly sister near the starboard bulkhead, not far from a segment of the transparent condensation tray cutting across the ceiling.

Lijadu looked up at him without accusation. He explained why he had come, what they could do, and how the change of quarters might best be carried out. He would leave it to Lijadu and the Sh'gaidu themselves who would come forward and who would remain in the aft section. No matter who went forward and who stayed behind, Seth said, they would do their best—Abel, Master Douin, and the taussanaur—to clean up and refit the cargo nacelle.

"Tantai is one of those who should have a forward cabin," Lijadu said. She stood up, hailed a sister across a group of onlooking Sh'gaidu, and waited until Tantai had threaded her way through the others.

Seth remembered the woman. Along with Huspre, she had waited on Magistrate Vrai's party in the Sh'vaij. Emahpre had indignantly run her off.

"*Gosfithuri,*" Seth said.

"*Gosfithuri,*" Tantai and Lijadu both agreed. Even the midwife lying on a soiled blanket beneath the condensation tray drummed her fingers on her breast bone, and the word went around the cargo nacelle like the refrain of a carol.

Three hours later, the transfer of passengers had been completed, and the *Dharmakaya* was once again effortlessly treading The Sublime.